STABLE OF TOUTS

By

Bill Gillis

A necessary evil for a crime-fighting detective who
sometimes bends the rules to get the right result.

Published by Gallus Press

Gallus Press is an Imprint of Olida Publishing
established January 2013
www.olidapublishing.com

First printing: January 2013

Printed in the United Kingdom and the U.S.A.

Cover Design: Scott Wallace
ISBN: 978-1-907354-39-7

I recognised that Bill Gillis was a dedicated officer who was keen to engage with the local community, in a truly professional way, in order to make neighbourhoods safer places. During his time, he was able to build strong partnerships with local people and his expertise was used at every opportunity as he developed his career, eventually leading to him becoming Head of C.I.D. Those years provided Bill with many challenges, and there can be no doubt that his professionalism in leading a dedicated team, resulted in many dangerous criminals being taken off the streets of our rural towns and villages, as well as preventing some of these same individuals being able to carry out activities which could have had a seriously detrimental impact on the lives of many decent people. I am delighted that Bill is taking the opportunity to share his writing skills with a wider audience"

Russell Brown. *MP for Dumfries & Galloway*

Although Stable of Touts is a fictional account of a detective's life, it does portray the pressures that some detectives actually experience both at home and at work, on a daily basis. As a detective for 20 out of my 30 years police service I well appreciate the demands this can place on family life. I could never have coped with these demands without the support of my wife, family and faith. Indeed, it was my wife Jane who encouraged me to put my detective experiences and vivid imagination into words when my police career ended. Accordingly, I dedicate this book to my wife and family.

I would also like to dedicate the book to Allan Sneddon for showing belief in my efforts at being an author and to Doug Archibald journalist with the Galloway News for his advice and support.

Bill Gillis. *B.A.(Hons) M.A.*

PREFACE

Jimmy McBurnie was the product of a hard, working- class background that was common in mining villages in the central belt of Scotland in the 1950s and 60s. In this environment his childhood and adolescence, like many others, was shaped by miners' beliefs, values and their unwritten but collective social code of equality and honesty. Within this environment poverty was common and, although hardship was a shared experience, the sense of community was strong. Here respect had to be earned and this could only be gained by standing up for yourself.

Jimmy's grandfather was a miner all his working life and had been exposed to the constraints of the class system and knowing, but in his case, not accepting his place in life's pecking order. His rebellious nature, and frustration at the inequality created by those who defined class, reached boiling point about once a month. This being when he could afford a few pints, which subsequently loosened his tongue and sometimes ended with him on the wrong side of the law.

Jimmy's father, too, was a miner and his mother was a miner's daughter. Although his father did not express views as fervently as his grandfather, he did share a hatred of the propertied classes. Subsequently, between them though in particular his grandfather they instilled in Jimmy the belief that he should never feel he had any 'betters' and indeed should regard all men as equal. They reinforced in Jimmy from a very young age a belief that he should never be subservient to the upper classes or what they saw as *their* police. There was however the provision that whatever he did in life he should always be honest.

It was no surprise then that Jimmy, like many other working class youths in Scotland, left school at fifteen without any qualifications and at the behest of his family, who knew that mining in Scotland was finished, got a trade. Neither he nor his parents had any aspirations of further education, believing it to be under the control of the upper crust, which to a certain extent at that time was true. Anyway, hard work with your hands proved you were a man, gave you a wage to live independently and endowed due respect for your labours. With this in mind, in 1966 Jimmy undertook a five-year apprenticeship as a blacksmith in one of the Clydeside shipyards.

He was not to know then the life-building experiences he would have in this testing work and social environment. In this urban setting there wasn't the same sense of community as in his mining village and, for some of those he would come into contact with, honesty appeared to be an alien term. At work and while socialising, he regularly met and associated with likeable rogues, out-and -out crooks and even violent criminals. Nevertheless, he remained honest. However, he couldn't have foreseen at this time that the experience of his teenage years would later provide him with skills to use in another world and the know how to assess both individuals and situations quickly would be integral to his career. This skill of being worldly wise and armed with a listening ear'would also come in useful.

During his apprenticeship years he flirted with the hated law enforcers, got involved in a few fights, drank too much, and, like many of his peers, chased girls, but he always remained honest. Like many of the working-class, his method of escaping the constraints of social and work environments was gambling, especially horse racing, which was his passion. He had admiration for these thoroughbred animals who gave their all in every race and a certain degree of envy for the trainers who got their animals to peak condition.

Subsequently, when he wasn't drinking or after women he spent many hours scrutinising the form and the potential of horses, stables and trainers. As we all know, gamblers experience highs and lows, winning a great deal and losing everything. Jimmy was no different.

The more he gambled the more he became addicted to horse racing. His daily research meant that he knew the form of horses inside out and this enabled him to identify his favourite trainers, both in flat racing and over jumps. He spent hours studying the horses before placing substantial bets, using his nom de plume, at different meetings, always with a belief that the next big winner was just round the corner. Sometimes this was the case and he had quite a few winning streaks, especially in the early days. Nevertheless, he was under no illusion that trainers always twisted or bent the rules a bit to ensure which horse won, and as a result he monitored his trainers' actions closely.

On one such winning streak he had a 'Yankee' bet on four horses which, in betting parlance meant six doubles, four trebles and an accumulator. His bets were mostly placed in the local village betting shop, and at this time no TV coverage of racing was allowed in the bookmakers so customers had to rely on 'the blower', which only provided commentary. The local bookmaker only accepted reasonable wagers and if they were above his limit he 'hedged' them to larger bookmaking businesses.

Jimmy's bets were always on the limit.

On the day of this Yankee bet his first three horses all

won at odds of 8/1, 5/1 and 4/1, and his last horse was sitting at 8/1. On this occasion the bookmaker had not hedged the bet and all the punters, including Jimmy, knew that if his last horse won, then the bookie would be out of business. None of the punters would feel sorry for the bookie as he had in the past taken their hard-earned wages from them.

As the race started everybody in the betting shop was rooting for Jimmy's fourth horse. That is, everybody except the bookie who was in a cold sweat as the commentary began. It was a hurdle race over three miles. For the first two miles Jimmy's horse was last, but as they approached the third last fence, his horse moved up to fourth in the field of fifteen runners.

At the second last fence the commentator stated that his horse was not only third but making strong progress.

The whole betting shop, again with the exception of the bookie, was cheering and Jimmy's actions became that of a jockey riding a horse. As they went over the last fence his horse was second and only half a length behind the leader and, according to the commentator, still making strong progress.

On the long run-in it hit the front, and the bookie held his head in his hands while his punters went berserk, none more so than Jimmy who now stood to win close to £2000, which was a good deal of money in 1968.

As they approached the finishing line the second horse caught up, and the commentator stated that both horses had crossed the line together in a photo-finish.

The suspension of waiting for the result hung in the air and the bookie almost collapsed when it was announced that Jimmy's horse had been beaten by a short head. Jimmy was annoyed, but still walked away with £350 – a fair amount of money. He became every punter's pal when he asked them next door to the pub and bought each of them a drink.

However, sometimes his nose for a good thing could not always be trusted and he could have as many losing streaks as winning ones. This meant he was always chasing the money and the more he chased the more he lost.

As a result, on occasions when the bookmaker had taken all his cash and he had a date with a girl he'd promised to take to the cinema or for a meal, he wouldn't turn up. At other times he was flush with money and would be treating her to meals, drinks and expensive gifts.

Ultimately, his finances and, to some extent, his life seemed to be increasingly controlled by horse racing and trainers. That said, he could never have foreseen that he too was destined to have a future as a trainer...though not of horses, but of humans.

THE NOVICE

As Jimmy progressed into adulthood he continued to enjoy a social life of drinking, womanising and gambling, provided of course that the horses he picked ran favourably. Having these vices, you might wonder why he gave religion any consideration, and even he could not provide an explanation as to why he started attending his local church, other than that he had respect for the minister, who was an ex miner. This minister had a reputation among his miner parishioners for 'sorting out' some of his parish who had been the worse for drink and who, on occasion, had been abusing their wives. He knew miners' ways, and as well as showing miscreants the error of their ways he provided both a place of refuge in times of trouble and sound advice, which Jimmy, like many of his peers, had needed.

Stupidly, he didn't always heed this good clergyman's advice and was still falling head first into the goldfish bowl of central Scotland's working-class life. Here, opportunities to break out and better yourself were few and far between, even in the liberal 1960s. Consequently, the longer he was in it the more he felt trapped by it. This era had seen many changes in society for the better; class barriers were outwardly being removed but in reality they were just being re-categorised. With some sections of British society flourishing, the bourgeoisie had grown, but the proletariat and the lumpen proletariat remained dependent on them for work, wage and handout. The capitalist system was robust and it ensured this growing, wealthy elite and their cohorts retained control of society, while those reliant on waged labour or welfare remained subservient.

In the 1970s Scotland's manufacturing base was shrinking, particularly shipbuilding and engineering, with many Clydeside shipyards closing. Jimmy's employment was no different and the writing was on the wall for him and many of the workers: namely, get out and get into something else and quick.

The change was even more pressing as he had just got married, like his father, to a miner's daughter named Doris whom he had known since primary school. She accepted what she perceived as her future role: that of working-class mother, and she also accepted Jimmy despite his gambling and drinking. She had no aspirations of social grandeur nor of breaking away from her roots.

Now their first child was on the way, and Jimmy wasn't slow to realise he had to break away from the chains of disadvantage that had bound his parents, even if that meant compromising his principles. Nobody now wanted blacksmiths and what could he do without qualifications or education?

There was one option open to him but that would mean swallowing his pride and entering into conflict with his family.

When he was on the fringe of trouble as a teenager a local cop, PC Agnew, who had a well-deserved reputation as a 'hard man' had taken him behind the pub, given him a good punch in the mouth and told him to behave. He could have arrested Jimmy for his drink-fuelled rowdy conduct but he didn't and the corporal punishment meted out meant this was the end of the matter.

In hindsight and with clear thinking, Jimmy could see

this course of action by Agnew was worthy of his respect as it helped him avoid a criminal record and consequently a better chance of getting a job. He could easily recall other disturbances caused by excessive consumption of alcohol, common in mining villages, where he had seen PC Agnew enforce the law in a similar manner. Strangely, nobody ever raised a complaint against this police officer, perhaps because of his reputation, though more likely due to the grudging respect they had for him because he played by their rules.

All the locals, including Jimmy, knew that when Agnew was first stationed in their village it had been common for the two local pubs to allow drinking after closing time. With no police around at last orders, probably because they feared for their personal safety, and the licence holders being fearful of their clients, the locals felt they had a right to drink as long as they wanted. Often this was until their money ran out and even then the scared publicans would give them drink 'on tick'. They were a rough and lawless community who sorted out their own problems and who had no time for the police.

The situation changed when Agnew came.

Jimmy remembered Agnew's first late shift weekend. This cop entered one of the pubs at shutting time and told the licensee to close the bar and the locals to drink up and get out. This was met with abuse and he was told to "fuck off" by some of the patrons. One in particular who had a reputation as a bit of a fighter told Agnew to "get to fuck out of the pub" or he would get a beating like some of his predecessors. On hearing this Agnew removed his Police helmet and to the astonishment of the patrons placed it on the end of the bar and head-butted and punched this local, knocking him to the floor, bleeding, and with his ego deflated. As you can imagine, the remaining locals were shocked but they now held a grudging admiration for their new cop. This was reinforced when Agnew asked if there were any more "fucking heroes" willing to try their luck? Not surprisingly all the locals left and then Agnew instructed the bar man to supply him with a double whisky as 'payment' for him keeping the peace. This request was met with promptly.

Part of the miners' social code was that you didn't 'shop' or 'grass up' anyone and as the cop was now playing by their rules this code extended to him. Accordingly, never were complaints registered against PC.Agnew. Through his actions he had set new ground rules for the village inhabitants who now feared him.

Closing time for the regulars in the two local pubs thereafter was always on time, except that is for P.C. Agnew who visited at the appointed hour but always stayed behind to get his 'reward' for ensuring licensing regulations and peace were maintained.

The more Jimmy thought about PC Agnew the more he liked this cop.

One particular memory still vivid in his mind was when trouble had erupted at a dance he was at in the local miners' hall. This was a common occurrence when young men from one mining community entered the territory of the next, looking to steal their women. As usual a fight developed in the hall and spilled outside with all the dancers going out to view the aggravation.

However, this time someone had called the police. PC Agnew arrived on his own and proceeded to take on the three main protagonists single-handedly. After inflicting some corporal punishment, rattling their heads off the police van door, he put the three in the van,placed them under arrest for Breach of the Peace and transferred them to the small local police station, incarcerating them in the one cell there.

Following their release the next morning after being

issued with a summons to appear at court at a later date, Jimmy spoke to them and they recounted their treatment by Agnew. They told Jimmy when they had been put in the cell they began shouting and singing. This obviously annoyed the constable and, as they were singing 'gaoler bring me water', Agnew duly obliged by throwing a bucket of water over them and telling them to "fucking shut up!", which they did.

This story got round the village but still no complaint was made against the cop. In fact, nearly everyone, including the three arrested men, saw the humour in it and this again raised Agnew's status with them.

Jimmy now reflected on how crime had gone down in the area shortly after Agnew's arrival.

With hindsight he recalled that this cop nearly always knew where to go to get the culprits as soon as the crimes were committed. But how could he when nobody grassed or shopped in his community? It was, however, no surprise that when they were detained by him, bearing in mind his reputation, they usually admitted responsibility.

How did PC Agnew do it?

In reminiscing about the actions and the reputation of Agnew, Jimmy started thinking that perhaps here was a role model for a new career; maybe Jimmy could join the police and go one better than Agnew and eventually become a detective?

Accordingly, after some serious thought and bracing himself, Jimmy approached, firstly, his wife Doris and asked what she thought of his joining the Police? She said it was up to him and that she would go wherever he went. He then spoke to his grandfather and father and as expected he was accused of betraying his community by working for the 'agents of the state' who were controlled by the upper class. He had a number of fall-outs with them after this but nevertheless he told them he was going to try and join because he had a wife and child to support. Trades in Scotland were dead, and anyway what options did he have?

He duly applied to join, though did not choose his local force, instead opting for the neighbouring region which had a population of 250,000. Here, Jimmy could make a fresh start, was an unknown and would be unlikely to come across anyone he knew.

A NEW CAREER

To his surprise he passed the entrance exam and the fitness test, and was called up for an interview at Police Headquarters in Newholm, the largest town in the region. Before attending he had to get his shoulder-length hair cut short, shave off his sideburns and wear a suit. This was a first for Jimmy and he had to borrow one from a friend.

The interview gave him his first taste of police discipline.

On being shown into a very austere room with a large photograph of the Queen on the wall, he saw Deputy Chief Constable McDonald, who was due to retire soon, seated at his leather-bound desk below the photograph of the Sovereign. He was reading some papers he had in front of him and did not acknowledge Jimmy's presence in the room. After ten minutes of silence, as cocky as ever and frustrated by the man's ignorance, Jimmy grabbed a seat and told the Deputy he would sit down.

This resulted in a verbal outburst from this senior police officer, who told him that he would say when to sit and more importantly when to speak.

The interview lasted nearly an hour and Jimmy was grilled savagely by McDonald, who came from a high-ranking military family and had himself been an Army Officer. Most questions were about Jimmy's background, his attitude towards his betters, his response to discipline and, lastly, his reasons for wanting to join the Police. Sometimes during his interview Jimmy felt like calling this cop an 'ignorant old bastard' but thought better of it.

As he left McDonald's office Jimmy could hear his father's and grandfather's advice thundering in his ears.

Unknown to him, his responses during the interview must have struck a chord with the Deputy: in particular, when he reinforced his working-class work ethic, sense of community, and life experiences in an environment where crime and criminality were commonplace.

These experiences and apparent acceptance of his working-class status appealed to the Deputy, who felt they would equip him with the tools to be a good constable. However, Jimmy thought McDonald had been unimpressed with the interview and, when he left the room, he was thinking there was no chance of him being accepted into this Police Force.

To Jimmy's surprise, four weeks later he received a letter from the Police confirming his acceptance, giving him a start date and allocating him a 'tied' Police house in a scheme of police-occupied dwellings. Some of his earthy responses at the interview must have made a good impression after all.

He was informed that he would now be stationed in Newholm which had both a rural and industrial environment and a population of eighty thousand, comprising many social classes and with many social problems.

With his wife Doris and one-year-old son Derek, they moved into what was another close- knit community, though this time one where not everyone shared socialist values or the miners' sense of unity. Here, all his neighbours were Police Officers and their families. The cops were of different ranks and experiences and it wasn't long before Jimmy felt confined. Consequently, he made a vow to himself that he would avoid mixing socially with Police officers, especially when, as in this case, your actions would be under constant scrutiny twenty-fours hours a day.

As Constable Jimmy McBurnie, life was now different and, as he had expected, he had to comply with a code of conduct both on and off duty. To add insult to injury, the wages were much poorer than that he had been used to in the shipyard and he struggled to make ends meet. Nevertheless, he was at least in a job and could provide some security for his family.

If he thought the discipline of the interview was bad then there was a shock in store at the Police Training College, where he found that new recruits had to salute everybody, call them 'Sir' and carry out nonsensical duties like repeatedly marching around a parade square or directing imaginary traffic. Even some of the Scots Law he had to learn, as his grandfather and father had told him, was designed to protect the propertied and land-owning classes. For example, some statutes like the Burgh Police Scotland Act, enacted in 1892, gave the police powers of arrest and 'stop and search' to deal with those who they deemed as having criminal intent, such as threatening property or possessions. This statute was still being enforced in the 1970s. Constables were still defining and arresting those individuals they classed as loiterers, those they deemed to be vagrants and those involved in poaching fish, deer etc. Jimmy felt these, together with many other statutes, were not being enacted for the benefit of the whole of society and were, in fact, tools of social control protecting the wealthy.

He now questioned whether he had done the right thing. Had his father and grandfather been right all along? Was he now an agent of the ruling classes, acting at their behest and within legislation structured to protect their assets and maintain their position of power?

His social conscience was being tested and he became

further exasperated at the Police College with the regular inspections of uniform and dormitory. It felt like he had joined the army, not the police. Here he was in a manufactured quasi-military environment controlled by extreme discipline and social class; privilege and rank were all too prevalent. He was now in his mid-twenties with a wife, child and a number of life experiences behind him, while some of his fellow recruits were only eighteen and still wet behind the ears.

Some recruits, like him, were poorly educated, others had a good education and were well connected in police circles, while yet others were sons and daughters of senior police officers. The latter category had been told what to expect at the Police College and warned not to let their families down. Accordingly, they followed their instructor's orders to the letter and never questioned them or the regime.

For Jimmy, his grandfather's words about having no betters rang in his ears again and he worried that this new career was almost a step too far.

He did consider packing it in but believed that 'the man above' must have decided he was sticking it out. This came about after a visit to his father who had reluctantly accepted that his son was now a police officer, but stressed that with his background he would never go beyond the rank of constable. Jimmy took this opportunity to look up his old minister and seek his words of wisdom. The minister told him he was wise to have taken on this new job especially when he had a wife and child to support and, with due diligence, he could prove his father wrong about promotion. He also advised him not to let the snide comments and dirty looks of his former friends and colleagues upset him, as they were not supporting his family, Jimmy was. Before he left, the minister said that God had a plan for Jimmy and he should put his trust and faith in him.

Consequently, by biting his tongue and keeping his feelings to himself he successfully completed his two-year probationary period which included another long stint at the Police Training College.

His training periods in the force and away from the Police College had been spent as a beat cop, sometimes accompanied by an experienced cop. When he had the older cop with him they dealt with minor misdemeanours and exerted the social-control powers bestowed upon them as Constables. As his time in the police progressed, it became ever more obvious to Jimmy that the class system was still prevalent even though few of his colleagues mentioned it. At ground level he had met some good guys and there was a bond with most of the ones he worked shifts with, especially those containing officers from working-class backgrounds.

Having said this, the subservient attitudes to the upper class, especially by some bosses, continued to madden him.

On one occasion, he and one of his colleagues were sent to keep watch on a wealthy landowner's property - which housed many valuable possessions - during the landowner's daughter's wedding. Jimmy nearly lost the place; this is not what he joined the Police to do. Had it not been for his shift sergeant, who had been a bricklayer in a previous life, telling him to watch what he said and keep his thoughts to himself, then Jimmy would have fallen foul of the system and found himself out of a job.

He could control his words but not his thoughts, and he wondered what the general public would think if they knew about this nonsense because ultimately they were footing the bill. He knew his grandfather was right all along about the class system and here it was in police circles.

A senior officer had sanctioned this guard duty, and

Jimmy was sickened as he watched other officers trying to climb the promotion ladder by placing themselves at the beck and call of the wealthy. These officers knew that if they were noticed by their betters then a word could be whispered in the right ear and promotion wouldn't be far off. The result was that some senior cops had achieved their high positions without any front-line or ground level police experience or even any court appearances as a witness. They in turn reared the next generation of senior officers.

Not surprisingly, this upper-class group had little respect for the working-class cops on the ground, and certainly none for the bad boys of the Criminal Investigation Department (CID) whom Jimmy admired.

Jimmy's grandfather's words were always in the forefront of his mind, and the novelty of wearing a uniform had long worn off. However, he had found, just as he had anticipated, that he loved investigating crime and criminals. Surely this was what the public expected of their police officers? Not cops who were promoted under the umbrella terms of 'Personnel' and 'Administration' without ever seeing an angry man.

Accordingly, he became increasingly envious of the CID cops, who, unlike him, didn't wear a uniform and didn't seem to be subject to the same militaristic and archaic discipline.

He had seen detectives on the late shift going into pubs and dances and coming out half-cut. They got away with it because they were mixing with the criminal fraternity, getting information from, and recruiting, informants, commonly known in police terminology as 'Touts'.

This was for him...

He knew through his previous life and work experiences and from some of the people whom he had come across who were classed as being 'on the other side of the fence', that he could relate to criminals, or 'neds' as the police called them.

He was proud of this background and experiences and even in uniform he found that he could build a rapport with these people.

During his first two years of police service he had occasionally turned a blind eye to a minor misdemeanour if the culprit supplied him with information about other crimes he was investigating. Adopting this tactic he had achieved some success, and he regularly received good 'info'. However, he had to conceal his actions from some of his bosses who felt that negotiating with criminals and cultivating 'touts' was a dirty business and shouldn't be considered by any respectable police officers, let alone inexperienced ones. However, Jimmy had gained some respect from the criminal fraternity as being a cop you could deal with and he began, in keeping with his interest in horse racing and trainers, to recruit 'touts' to his informants stable.

His ability to solve crimes, albeit minor ones, and to cultivate informants, caught the attention of some experienced detectives in the CID These guys, Jimmy felt, were not as short-sighted or blinkered as some uniform colleagues and it was no surprise he was now being earmarked as a potential detective.

APPRENTICE TOUT TRAINER

The CID in Newholm comprised six Detective Constables (DC), two Detective Sergeants (DS), two Detective Inspectors (DI) and one Detective Chief Inspector (DCI) who was the Head of the Department.

Between them they had significant experience and one of the DSs, Sgt Martin, Jimmy knew was feared by the local criminals. Some of them said that if Martin couldn't get them by fair means then he would resort to whatever tactics were required to convict them.

Three years after his probationary period, Constable McBurnie, who now had a stable of twenty low-level touts in his 'yard', was summoned by the new Deputy Chief Constable, Mr Cobble, who had replaced McDonald and had a background in the CID. He told Jimmy that he would be joining the CID. and would be part of DS Martin's shift.

Jimmy was delighted as he would now be Detective Constable Jimmy McBurnie, and the icing on the cake was that he would be working under DS Martin for whom he had the utmost respect. Many of the neds that Jimmy knew had told him Martin was always putting pressure on them to 'grass up' (inform against) some of their criminal friends and relatives. Nor, allegedly, was the infamous DS slow at giving them a belt around the ear or locking them up when he had only minimal evidence.

Jimmy, reflecting on what these neds had said, made a vow then to follow only what he saw as the good points of Martin's approach.

In his first week in the department he worked the late shift (6pm to 2am) and as he was the new boy, albeit he was approaching 30 years of age, he was the driver for his colleagues. He took them to different pubs in the town and waited as they went into pubs and clubs in an effort to identify new criminal associations, meet informants, and gather information about crimes being investigated in Newholm.

Anyway, this was supposed to be their purpose, but Jimmy soon discovered some of his colleagues had other more insidious intentions. Accordingly, by the end of the shift many of them were the worse for wear through drink. In addition, a few of them, he had learned, had got too close to the girlfriends and wives of known criminals in an attempt to gain information. Some even became involved with them sexually and this crossed Jimmy's boundaries of morality. He was wide enough to see that this behaviour left his colleagues open to blackmail, threat and violence and he made it a rule not to cross this line.

He intended to keep a safe distance from women, not to drink during working hours and to stick to business. He had found that, while in uniform, the best way to recruit touts and gather information was by negotiating with the neds and, on occasion, by rewarding them, though certainly never sleeping with their partners. With his newly-formed 'stable' he knew that he would remain the trainer, not the trained, and he would dictate the terms his charges operated under. In horse racing parlance he would, metaphorically speaking, blinker them and neuter them as required.

He had learned that nearly all neds, including those with

known reputations, hated being locked up, and they would willingly trade information to escape a night in custody. Furthermore, the CID ran a 'tout fund', which allowed detectives to pay out money for reliable information that would clear crimes as well as covering expenses when recruiting a tout. In CID parlance, those informants who provided information for money were classed as those who took the 'King's Shilling'.

The other bonus from this two-pronged approach to cultivation and training was that once a ned had exchanged information with him, whether for release from custody or for money or indeed any other motive, then they became lifelong members of his stable and under the control of the trainer. He vowed his situation would never end up like some of his colleagues who he felt were becoming increasingly under the control of the neds they were supposed to be handling. Jimmy decided this would be the time to be a trainer of purely 'flat' runners without the obstacles or hurdles that would arise if he became too close to these neds.

COURSE AND DISTANCE WORK

In his first few weeks as a detective Jimmy was constantly reminded by the bosses, DCI Chambers and DIs McLaren and Stewart, to be careful when dealing with touts. They viewed them as a necessity but always a dangerous and volatile commodity, which at best could supply quality information and at worst lose a cop his job or put him in court. The dock, not the witness box! Further, his bosses weren't slow to warn that he would get no support or backing from the force if he crossed the line, and he would be on his own. This advice was not missed by Jimmy, and the experiences of these senior officers who relayed some personal difficulties they had with touts, reinforced the wisdom.

They highlighted how devious and troublesome some touts had been, who attended pre-arranged meetings complete with hidden recording devices. During the subsequent conversations they had tried to elicit comment from the detectives, which implied they were being encouraged to commit criminal acts. In other instances they tried to get cops to say they would give them immunity from prosecution for crimes they had committed.

It was clear to Jimmy's bosses that if these neds had gained this information they would retain it and hand it to their solicitor. Thereafter, it would be used as a bargaining tool to ensure criminal proceedings against them were dropped, or to ensure no serious investigation was mounted against them. The only losers would be the cops, who could lose both their jobs and their liberty.

In these situations the trained became the trainer...

The advice was certainly timely, as one local detective had recently been under internal investigation. This had been instigated by a female he had been having a relationship with in an attempt to infiltrate a large drug-dealing network. She was a junkie and a good-looking girl but also the long-term girlfriend of one of the main local drug dealers. She had secretly recorded the detective while they were in bed together discussing local drug dealing. Her boyfriend was on remand in prison at this time, awaiting trial on drug-dealing charges, and when she gave the recording to his solicitor he forwarded it to the Crown Prosecuting authorities. As a result, they abandoned the case against the dealer and ordered an investigation into the actions of the detective.

The detective had been suspended for a year, and both his nerves and career were shot through. He nearly ended up in court after being charged with perverting the course of justice, before eventually being cleared of any criminality when the junkie withdrew her statement after her boyfriend died of an overdose.

Jimmy was now taking on board all the advice he was given, and thinking long and hard about what he had said to any of his touts during previous meetings. However, DS Martin, Jimmy's shift sergeant, didn't seem to either heed or need this advice and he was classed both within the job and the criminal fraternity as a law unto himself. He wrongly thought that as long as he was locking up the bad people he would have the full support of the force bosses, some of whom were riding on the back of his success. Unlike some of Martin's colleagues, women were not a problem for him and he wouldn't become involved with any ned's woman.

On most day shifts Martin came to work with a hangover. He was a heavy drinker and it took about three cups of coffee in the morning before he rallied round and was able to face the world. Once he recovered he was like a drug user who had taken a stimulant and had bags of energy. In Martin's case this 'high' was accompanied by a wicked laugh and a sense of humour that only he understood. For him, crime in his community was a personal matter and one which he would not tolerate. He would frequently refer to the fact there was a 'war on', which he would win and from which he would take no prisoners.

In Jimmy's first week at work with DS Martin he had been left in the office on a late shift to develop photographs of crime scenes. This was one of the jobs of a rural detective as there were no Scenes of Crime officers appointed by the force at this time. Subsequently, all crime scenes were the remit of detectives armed with their own kit containing cameras, fingerprint powder, brushes, lifting tape, plaster of Paris and other necessary items.

While working in the photographic developing room in the CID office Jimmy heard a knock at the door. When he opened it he found DS Martin in an agitated state. Martin had been dealing with a break-in at a local businessman's house where a large quantity of gold jewellery and Royal Doulton figures had been stolen. He told Jimmy that a tout had named gypsies responsible for the break-in. Consequently, he had made contact with the head of the gypsies locally and bluffed him over how much evidence he held against his clan.

The upshot was that the head gypsy, whom Martin respected, had invited him to a meeting that night but stated that he should attend on his own.

Martin told Jimmy where the meeting was and left him a number to contact him if he was not back by 11 pm. He also instructed Jimmy not to tell any of the other officers where he was. Jimmy would not have gone to this meeting on his own, but Martin was fearless and didn't consider that he could be walking into a trap or a set-up. He was of the opinion that his no-nonsense reputation amongst the neds would ensure his safety.

At 11.30 pm. that night Jimmy was still in the office on the first floor of Newholm Police Station. He had tried without success to contact his DS and was becoming increasingly worried when he heard a clatter in the corridor. He went to investigate and saw a cardboard box lying on the floor with its contents of Royal Doulton figures and gold chains strewn around. Behind the cardboard box DS Martin was lying in a heap on the floor, laughing maniacally to himself and totally drunk.

Jimmy got his boss to his feet, escorted him to his desk and seated him there before retrieving the contents of the box, which thankfully had not smashed. When he asked Martin how he managed to get the stolen property back his question was met by another manic laugh. Eventually, and after a lot of black coffee, DS Martin told Jimmy that his bluff with the gypsies had worked. He had got them believing he had enough evidence to lock them all up and they accepted that this was the case, even though the only evidence he had was the word of a tout.

Being true negotiators, the gypsies then offered him a deal that if the stolen property was returned and there were no charges against any of them they would forever be in his debt. Unknown to them, they never spoke truer words. Martin was sure to hold them to their promise and regularly call in the debt which would be paid by supplying information about crimes he was investigating.

To seal the deal in true gypsy manner they slapped hands and had a drink.

They were obviously trying to get him to declare what evidence he had by supplying him with more drinks. However, they were not aware of his capacity for alcohol and even when he was drunk he only said 'goodnight' and reiterated how much they were in his debt before instructing them to get the stolen property and arrange his lift back to the police station.

As was normal for Martin when he was relaying his 'war stories' it ended in bouts of manic laughter. After this particular one Jimmy helped him home to his understanding wife.

The next morning they were back on day shift and Martin was suffering with a huge hangover which wouldn't abate, even after his third cup of coffee. Uniform Chief Inspector Sharkey was in charge of general policing in Newholm Division. He was aware of the victim of this crime that Martin had cleared, and the influence this individual carried both in the local community and with the police executive. He came to congratulate Martin on reclaiming the stolen property back and foolishly asked the DS how he managed it. If he got this information, then he thought he would be better placed to explain to the victim how good his officers had been while acting under his direction.

He was informed by D.S. Martin that this information was on a 'need to know' basis and he didn't need to know.

This Chief Inspector had been a constable at the same time as Martin and knew only too well his no-nonsense reputation, both within and outwith with the job. Consequently, it was no surprise on this occasion when he left without pulling up Martin about his insolence or failure to disclose any information about the recovery of the stolen property.

Jimmy had already witnessed DS Martin's lack of discipline and respect for those who did not deserve it, and privately he applauded it. Martin was, in some ways, his hero but there was no way Jimmy intended to be as cavalier as him.

Not long after this incident, he was assisting Martin in investigating a robbery where two wealthy old farmers had been tied up and beaten by three intruders who had forced their way into the old mens' home and demanded money. Once they had found what was a substantial amount of cash in a wardrobe, the robbers sneered and laughed at the old men before slashing one of them on the cheek.

When the alarm was raised, DS Martin drove to the scene, arranged for a scene of crime examination to be carried out, got the police surgeon to attend to the old men and arranged to brief his troops. Martin was many things but, in his own mind, he had no difficulty in deciding what was right and wrong and what was trivial enough to be classified as 'acceptable' crime. This crime, like ninety-nine per cent of other crimes he investigated didn't fit the latter category, and he declared to all the detectives in the CID office at the afternoon briefing that they were going to get these bastards and give them their dues.

If you view police investigations as a hard slog of interviewing and searching for witnesses to gain evidence and supplement it with painstaking forensic examination then on most occasions you would be right. This is normally how investigations are undertaken and successful completion of them takes a lot of dedication, time, manpower and expense.

However, both Martin and now Jimmy knew that one way of shortening the process is to utilise a good tout. If they are well-enough informed or positioned they can usually point the investigators in the right direction at an early stage and sometimes even disclose the identity of all the culprits. In 'management speak' this strand of investigative strategy usually provided value for money (VFM) not that this was ever a consideration of DS Martin.

Using well-informed touts did provide VFM but most police managers who used the term didn't want to dirty their hands with criminals. All they wanted, as far as Martin and Jimmy could see, were good news stories to relay back to the media to increase their standing locally and their chances of promotion.

Jimmy felt as bad about this crime as DS Martin and was delighted when he was informed that he would be his number two, or corroborating officer, in this investigation. His chest puffed up and he now felt accepted as a real detective.

He vowed to himself that between them they would get these animals.

DS Martin's first port of call was the home of an informant who lived in the roughest housing scheme in Newholm. This tout was well-known locally for stealing scrap metal and petty fraud. He lived with his girlfriend, whose family and herself had had many dealings with the DS. In fact nearly all of them had been locked up at one time or another by him, sometimes with little evidence… as a result she hated him.

Jimmy had never met DS Martin's tout and didn't know anything about this woman's family dealings with his boss. You can imagine his surprise then when Martin knocked on the back door of the tout's house. Immediately upon seeing Martin she said, "you fuck off ya bastard, I hate you!" Martin's response was to ask if she was putting the kettle on for tea for him and Jimmy. She curtly replied, "tea ya bastard I'll throw it over your head, now fuck off." This time Martin told her not to forget the chocolate biscuits. She was now irate, and the tout, hearing the commotion, came to the door, summoned Martin and Jimmy in and told her to go into the living room. She eventually left the kitchen but cursed and swore the entire time.

The tout made tea and, during coded conversations, Martin got the names of the three culprits and where they spent some of the money stolen from the old farmers. To deflect attention from himself as the informant, the tout provided the names of others who knew about the crime. This tout was known by the DS to take the 'King's Shilling' and was duly well-rewarded at a later date.

DS Martin now had a real lead and he didn't hang about. He recruited some of the office DCs to his 'snatch team' and, a short time later, they had the three suspects in the police station for interview along with all the others who knew about the crime.

As was normal for Martin, he always insisted on speaking with the suspects first. All the detectives knew to stay out of the way at these times. After he had spoken to them he came into the main detective's office and announced that he felt they would admit responsibility for this nasty crime and were probably sorry they had committed such a foul offence. He then instructed pairs of detectives to carry out interviews with the three suspects, and others to interview those individuals who knew about the crime. This blanket approach would protect the identity of the tout.

Jimmy wasn't allowed to interview any of them but he did later speak to the interviewing officers and they indicated that the suspects had all admitted responsibility for the crime, just as Martin had said they would, and in fact couldn't wait to tell their version of events. In the process they 'shopped' each other, while some other detainees who had knowledge of the crime provided witness statements. The police ended up having more than sufficient evidence to convict all three, and the identity of Martin's tout remained secret.

At the end of this successful day the DS summoned Jimmy and his interviewing officers to a nearby pub to celebrate. Under no circumstances could you refuse, and after four hours in the bar everybody, including Jimmy, was 'smashed'. The licensee was well-known to Martin and had been on his radar for a while so said nothing when he started goading his other punters, (most of whom had criminal records), and began his manic laughter.

By the time Jimmy got home to Doris he had a lot of explaining to do, and she told him that if this is what CID. life was about then he should think seriously about getting a transfer.

He woke up the next day with a thumping head like the rest of his peers who had been celebrating the previous night. Martin was no better and when Jimmy got to work he was drinking coffee as if it were going out of fashion. By now, most mornings Martin would have the 'shakes' and it took a while for him to get himself together.

The next few months saw Jimmy follow in Martin's wake, investigating serious crime and on many occasions the CID. office was heard to resound with maniacal laughter.

This place was a madhouse...

Jimmy loved it but he could see that those higher up were becoming increasingly concerned by what they were hearing about the tactics of DS Martin and the potential risks he posed, not just to the reputation of the force, but also, indirectly, to their careers.

Previously his success in detecting crimes had given him some immunity from their attentions and they could ride on the back of his efforts, spreading good news stories to those who could aid their advancement. In addition, crime statistics produced by Martin and his team at the end of the year always made good reading, especially the detection rate for serious crime.

Now, however, they were keeping a watching brief on him to ensure that if he fell foul of the system, which was becoming extremely likely through his investigative tactics and drinking, that none of the flak ended up at their door.

Life carried on for the CID but those who worked closely with him knew that Martin's drinking was getting out of hand. For example, when he was under the weather he was forever decrying the growth of the Community Involvement Branch and telling community cops and their bosses what he thought of them.

Martin's philosophy, which he tried to instil in his detectives, was that the removal of criminals from the street was crime prevention at its best. This view was not shared by many of the politically correct cops who preferred a softly, softly approach to criminals.

They felt that opportunities to commit crime could be reduced by adding security measures to the design of buildings. This could be supplemented by providing advice on personal security to potential crime victims. For them, the police needed to be more involved in the community and take the lead in diversionary schemes and projects, like restorative justice, as well as providing other routes away from crime for recidivists.

This was too much for a hard-nosed detective like Martin and he often told Jimmy that these cops, their bosses and their 'goody goody' approach was a waste of time and they would be better employed as social workers. Jimmy concurred but did not voice his view publicly like his boss. Most detectives, however, did agree that community cops were the 'tea and scone brigade', who sat on community groups and came up with hare-brained 'namby pamby' schemes. In other words, nothing that would truly detect crime or, ultimately, help the community.

To hold such views was not surprising, especially when detectives heard many of the neds they dealt with laughing about how little punishment they were receiving, and the help police were giving them to avoid prosecution or imprisonment.

As far as Martin was concerned and what he tried to instil in his officers was that the detective's' core role was to detect and lock up criminals. He was in no doubt that crime should equal punishment and, metaphorically speaking, no prisoners should be taken in what he classed as ' the 'war'. If community cops were a walk-over for the neds then the CID were not. However, Jimmy knew it was becoming increasingly difficult to maintain this position in the politically correct world of policing.

War, as we all know, is a grim reality which relies on humour to alleviate the hardship it causes and relieve some of the tension felt by those involved in the conflict. With Martin this humour often came at the most unexpected times.

One such moment, which brought a smile to Jimmy's face, was during the investigation into a break-in at a garage which sold high performance cars. These premises had been the subject of many break-ins in the past but the culprits were seldom caught.

The owners of the garage were fed up with all the attention they were getting from the crooks and the damage it was doing, both to the garage's reputation and its finances. Subsequently, after being prompted by the community police and their insurance company, they installed CCTV and fitted internal alarm systems. At each of the previous break-ins, entry had been gained through various locations on the workshop's high sloping roof, which could only be reached by scaling a drainage pipe. To supplement their CCTV and alarm systems, the owners, again on police advice, had covered the drainage pipe in 'anti-thief' non-removable paint.

On a Saturday morning, Jimmy went to work at 7am as usual, made strong coffee for DS Martin and read through the last twenty four hours' reports. Included in one of these reports were details of another break-in at the garage where both the CCTV and alarm systems had been disabled. The crooks had entered the premises through a Velux window in the roof and then forced open a floor-safe containing a substantial amount of money.

Martin, at the subsequent briefing, informed his officers that the security equipment had been little deterrent and reiterated his view that the cops who gave the garage the security advice must think the neds were daft or stupid. As usual they had soon learned to overcome it and he was left to clear up the mess.

Jimmy didn't fully agree so said nothing

However, he suspected he knew who the culprits were and made a phone call to one of his stable. This tout was able to confirm his suspicion and stated that the main culprit, with a reputation as a 'climber', had just returned in the early hours of the morning to the address of his girlfriend, who lived close by. Along with a weary DS Martin, Jimmy managed to get a Justice of the Peace (JP) search warrant for the address of the ground floor one bedroom flat. When they arrived at the front door it was lying open so they walked in. No-one was in the living room so they opened the bedroom door and found that the occupier, a well-worn 30-year-old blonde and the suspected culprit were in bed together, apparently asleep. Martin knew both well and roused the girlfriend, who peered above the covers, to ask where her boyfriend had been during the previous night. She said in bed with her...

He told the male suspect to come out from under the covers. It was then that Jimmy and Martin noticed paint on the suspect' hands, identical to the security paint that had been smeared on the drain pipe. At this point Martin then let out his manic laugh.

This ned's girlfriend didn't see the humour, jumped out of bed naked and asked Martin if he wanted to see her "fucking hands as well". Martin was by now in raptures as he looked in her direction to see her whole body covered in hand prints left by her amorous lover. By now he was uncontrollable and Jimmy had to tell the culprit and his girlfriend they were being detained.

During the journey to the police station, Martin cracked jokes at the culprit and his girlfriend's expense. Jimmy was sure they were both delighted when they were later locked up as it meant they were away from Martin and his wicked sense of humour.

Eventually, all the culprits for this crime were arrested and some of the money from the safe was recovered. DS Martin now had another war story to add to his list but this time even he had to concede that security measures in the form of anti-climb paint had helped.

During preparation for the trial Jimmy was left with a dilemma of how to produce the girlfriend of the crook, who had been covered in his hand prints, as a 'Production' (exhibit) for court purposes.

The writing seemed on the wall for Martin.

REMOVED FROM THE WAR ZONE

The DS was now becoming too hot for the bosses to handle and his drinking was out of control. There were also now criminals who were prepared to make complaints against him and he was increasingly becoming the subject of internal investigation.

The last straw came when he was investigating a sequence of break-ins in Newholm where property and large amounts of money had been stolen from eight commercial premises during one night. They included a pub where fruit machines had been forced open and their contents stolen, and a shoe shop where forty-five pairs of new, branded shoes had been taken.

On this occasion, one of Jimmy's stable, who took the 'King's Shilling', came up trumps. He named two half-brothers as responsible for this series of crimes and mentioned the address of their sister, where he said some of the shoes and monies from the fruit machines were hidden.

Immediately after passing the names of the culprits to Martin, he told Jimmy and a young DC to get a car and a warrant for the house in question. This they did and when they arrived DS Martin ran to the door and began banging it.

After a couple of minutes a local petty thief who didn't normally live at this address opened the door. Martin asked him where the woman of the house was and he said he didn't know. DS Martin was not used to non-compliance and he let the man know it. He told him to clear the way as the house was being searched under the terms of the warrant he had with him. He then pushed the man aside, and he, Jimmy, and the female officer entered the house.

In the kitchen was the woman they had been looking for, named by Jimmy's tout. She was preparing the tea for her two small children and boyfriend. She ignored Martin as he was telling her about the warrant. This made him go completely mad and he shouted at her that he was there on official business, not for his tea. She continued to ignore him which made matters even worse. Martin, after he calmed down, told Jimmy and his colleague to search the house and it was in a bedroom that Martin recovered five bags of change.

In a cupboard in the hall Jimmy and his colleague recovered over forty pairs of new shoes. The game was now up and all the adult occupants of the house, including the woman's half-brothers who had arrived after a phone call from their sister, were detained and taken to the police station in Newholm.

By now DS Martin was hyper and, on arrival at the station, quickly instructed pairs of detectives to commence interviewing the house occupants he had detained. Martin himself had left them in little doubt about the seriousness of their position, and warned them that they must inform him about who brought the stolen property to the home.

Potential witnesses, all of whom were close associates of the culprits, were rounded up and also spoken to by Martin. One decided he wanted to punch the DS and a fight ensued in the CID office. By this stage Martin was out of control and Jimmy and other colleagues had to physically remove him from the office. He had been seen by both police and civilian staff fighting with this ned and he was going to pay the penalty for it.

The two half-brothers interviewed were singing like canaries. They had been responsible for twelve break-ins at commercial premises in the town that week and they admitted their involvement, provided their sister was not charged with anything. Through Jimmy, Martin agreed and she was released without charge. Her half-brothers were kept in custody and they eventually received twelve-month prison sentences after pleading guilty at their first court appearance.

This case for Martin confirmed that the 'war' against crime and criminals was still on. Martin however, was not to know that he was soon to be a casualty of war…

One of the civilian staff who had witnessed him fighting with the witness in the CID. office, complained to her line manager. This resulted in an internal enquiry, but the 'victim' refused to make a complaint against Martin. He knew he had tried to assault the DS first and he didn't want to remain a marked man if Martin lost his job.

Nonetheless, those above deemed that the DS would now be moving to uniform duties and away from front line crime fighting. This action would limit any detrimental effect he could have on on both the force and their careers.

They might as well have executed him and it was a sad day for the detectives when Martin left the CID office and donned a sergeant's uniform in the smaller neighbouring town of Culweather. The local neds were certainly not unhappy. They couldn't believe their luck, and the fact that DS Martin was not around meant the door was open for them to commit crime without his attentions.

Jimmy didn't intend to let the honeymoon period last long.

THE WAR GOES ON

Jimmy felt the loss of his boss more so than any of his CID colleagues, but it again served as a warning to him about what happens when you cross the line. By now Jimmy was expanding his stable of touts. The fact he didn't wear a uniform gave him both credibility with the neds and opportunities to meet his charges covertly.

Being in the CID and working so closely with DS Martin had allowed him to come into contact with criminals involved in serious and serial crimes. They knew the score and most played the percentage game where supplying information meant escaping custody, gaining revenge on other neds or getting a financial reward. Being the good cop in the good cop /bad cop interviewing team with Martin, Jimmy had managed to gain the trust of some of these neds. As a result he was starting to get phone calls, out of hours, telling him about jobs some local criminals were planning.

His stable was now being filled with what he classed as potential 'thoroughbred' touts.

After two years as a detective Jimmy had truly learned the ground rules. He'd overcome the 'hurdles' that some of his peers had come across and identified when his charges needed to be 'pulled up'. He was now very much his own trainer with a growing stable of touts.

He still had a lot of time for now ex DS Martin, and he kept in contact with him on a regular basis, being sure to tell him the war was still being fought. In the meantime, Martin's new bosses at Culweather were astounded at the rise in their crime detection figures and reduction in crime since his arrival. Their patch was now the scene of a new battlefield for the ex D.S.

With Martin's absence, Jimmy's success as a thief catcher grew, and some fellow detectives became envious, on occasions, vindictive. The situation came to a head when one of his touts was locked up for a minor offence. He asked the custody officer in charge of the cells to contact Jimmy and let him know he had been arrested. The custody officer contacted the CID office but Jimmy wasn't on duty, so the officer was told by the detective taking his call that he would contact Jimmy. However, this didn't happen. The detective receiving the call visited the cells and spoke to Jimmy's tout who obviously refused to discuss anything with him. This detective threatened this ned that if he didn't supply him with information then he would make it known to the local criminal fraternity that he was a 'grass'. The ned supplied some low-grade info and was released.

The next day he contacted Jimmy by telephone and told him he would no longer be supplying information, nor helping the police in any way after the threat he had received from the detective.

As you can appreciate, 'trainers' don't like to have their best charges 'tapped' and keeping a good tout is similar to keeping a good racehorse: give them the best of treatment, training and care and you should get results.

Accordingly, after receiving this news, Jimmy located the detective who had threatened to expose his tout and told him he had found some photographs in the darkroom that this detective had been working on. As they entered the darkroom Jimmy pulled the draw-string light, punched his colleague on the head and swept his feet from beneath him.

Unlike DS Martin's explosive approach, Jimmy's action was in private. The detective was left deflated, and in no doubt that Jimmy's touts were his alone. Further, if he tried to shop him to his bosses for this 'reprimand' he would disclose his underhand tactics, which threatened the whole ethos and integrity of the CID.

Needless to say, the detective said nothing and when asked the following day where he got the bruises on his forehead and cheek, he said he slipped in the darkroom. After this incident Jimmy had a quiet word with DI McLaren, whom he respected and trusted. He told him what had happened and how the detective in question was worth watching. McLaren confirmed that he would ensure this guy's future duties and career would be well-monitored.

The longer Jimmy worked within the CID the more he was exposed to criminals Martin had dealt with. Some of them used to relay stories about how he had outfoxed them and as a result they admitted crimes they had committed. Many alleged he had threatened them and used further unorthodox means to nab them. Remarkably, none of them held a grudge against him, in fact they stated that they mostly got what they deserved and even had a grudging respect for the ex DS.

Jimmy listened intently to these stories, some of which he found unbelievable.

For example, one ned told him that he and his his pal were brought in by Martin for a robbery they had committed where the victim was a woman collecting money from her catalogue clients. They had carried out surveillance so knew her route, the significant amount of money she collected, her means of transport and time schedule. They eventually attacked her, though left her unharmed and stole the money she had with her. The jungle grapevine must have been buzzing because the next night they were detained by Martin and, as they were being transported to the police station, they made a vow with each other that neither would talk.

The ned relaying the story told Jimmy that someone must have talked because when they were being interviewed DS Martin seemed to know quite a bit about their methods in committing this crime. When this ned was interviewed, Martin pointed to a red and white light on the wall in the room. The DS allegedly told him it was a new form of lie detector which the police had been supplied with. Anyway, this ned did lie in response to some of Martin's questions and to his amazement each time he lied the red light came on.

The end result of this particular technique meant that he and his co-accused, who later said that he had gone through the same process with Martin, admitted their involvement and eventually received two years each in prison. This ned said that before he appeared in court he told his lawyer that the police in Scotland were now using a lie detector and that was how he had been found out. The lawyer said this was nonsense and although the ned kept repeating his claim his lawyer, told him it was too preposterous to bring before a judge. He told his client he must have been under the influence of drugs during the interview.

This lawyer did, however, informally speak to the DS questioning him about his client's claims. This resulted in a manic laugh from Martin and his telling the lawyer not to be so stupid as to believe anything his client told him. Interestingly, the other culprit relayed the same information to his lawyer, but he too thought it was nonsense and guilty pleas were duly tendered.

After Jimmy heard this story he spoke to Martin and relayed what the ned had told him. This again resulted in his maniacal laugh and Martin telling Jimmy not to so stupid as believe anything a ned said. This puzzled Jimmy but he knew better than to bring it up again.

If he had learned anything from his ex DS it was the benefit of good touts. The quality information they could supply meant enquiries were focused, costs were reduced and the neds were taken off the street more quickly. This was true crime prevention.

Accordingly, Jimmy set about recruiting more touts always hoping to find a 'classic' winner among them.

STABLE NAMES

All racehorses are given a name for the track as well as a stable name. Similarly, touts are provided with a 'nom de plume' to protect their identity. Jimmy, who as a gambler betting on horse racing used a nom de plume and, in keeping with his earlier passion for racehorses, chose to retain this analogy with his touts. He supplied his new breed of what he classed as 'thoroughbred' informants with names known only to him that would not be out of place in racing circles.

'WISE ARCHIE'

Archie was a very active criminal in Newholm and part of a criminal family where not just his two brothers, but his mother and sister were also involved in criminality.

When Jimmy first came across Archie he had been locked up on a charge of assault after a disturbance in a local pub. This was not unsurprising for him as he was 28 years old with a physique like a wrestler and a wicked temper to boot. He was feared locally because of his temper and the fact that if he couldn't win fights with his fists, feet, or head, he would resort to using weapons or anything at hand.

In a previous case he had been charged with attempted murder after his involvement in a fracas at a local bar. His opponent was an amateur boxer and Archie was struggling to overcome him until he lifted a pool cue and smashed it across the boxer's throat, leaving him breathless on the floor. Everybody in the pub could see the boxer was defeated but that was not enough for Archie who started kicking him on the head, stamping on his face and throwing beer over his now unconscious rival.

The boxer had been rushed to hospital and en route had stopped breathing before being revived by ambulance staff. In hospital he lapsed into a coma and nearly died. He did later recover but suffered a broken jaw, two fractured cheeks, a broken nose and bruising to his throat. His boxing days were through. Archie was arrested and charged with attempted murder after friends of the boxer, who had been in the pub at the time, gave evidence against him.

Strangely, none of the pub regulars who knew Archie saw anything...

After his first court appearance he was remanded in custody at the local prison to await trial within the one hundred and ten day period set by Scots Law. During this time the boxer was interviewed by both the police and the Procurator Fiscal (the prosecutor in Scotland) but refused to identify Archie as his assailant. In addition, Archie's relatives 'visited' the boxer's witnesses and they too withdrew statements they had furnished to the police. Accordingly, the fiscal had no alternative but to drop the charges against Archie and give him his freedom.

On the occasion when Jimmy visited Archie he was well aware of his background and there seemed little chance he would be willing to become a prime thoroughbred in his tout stable. Still if you don't try you don't get... and Jimmy was a persistent trainer.

It transpired that Archie was locked up for a fairly minor assault and Jimmy felt that if he came across with some quality info then he could speak nicely to the duty uniform Inspector in charge on the shift and have Archie released to appear, by means of a summons, at a later date. This was not as easy as it seemed and a lot depended on who the duty Inspector was. On this occasion it was an ex-detective who had somehow managed to get promoted twice in uniform.

Armed with this belief, Jimmy approached Archie in his cell, complete with what detectives referred to as standard issue, i.e. a supply of cigarettes. Giving neds a cigarette nearly always resulted in a trade-off for information, which in Jimmy's mind could be compared to giving a quality racehorse a treat, thus getting their attention. He didn't know what response to expect from Archie and was surprised when, after he supplied him with the cigarette, he said he had heard about Jimmy and his reputation for fairness. The ice was broken and it turned out each had a mutual respect, within boundaries, for each other.

During the subsequent conversation in the smoke-filled room Archie asked why he was being held on such a minor matter which in all likelihood would be dropped before it ever got to court. Jimmy played the game and told him it was a mindset of some uniform cops to lock up people on minor issues, especially those with a reputation like his, just to show them who was boss. This brought a knowing grin and a nod from Archie.

As a show of goodwill Jimmy said he would put a word in with the duty Inspector to see if he could get him released and summoned to appear at a later date. Archie, being worldly wise, asked what Jimmy wanted in return and he replied that maybe some time Archie could repay the favour. Archie said nothing but again nodded.

Now the hard part was to sell this to the Inspector which would be difficult without any guaranteed supply of information.

Jimmy gingerly approached him, stressing that the assault charge against Archie was really a trivial offence. He asked, just this once, to release Archie and they would later get a return. The Inspector knew the workings of the CID but wasn't convinced Archie would ever tell the police anything. Undeterred, Jimmy badgered him and he eventually agreed to Archie's release. However, he stated that when his bosses, some of whom disliked the CID and their 'Jack the Lad' attitude, asked why he was released then Jimmy had better have some good answers. He would be telling them the CID had cleared crime through the release and Jimmy would have to confirm this.

Jimmy returned to Archie's cell and told him to get his mattress and blanket as he was being released. Archie smiled but didn't really believe it until he was walking out the door thanking Jimmy for his assistance.

The next day Jimmy was summoned to see DI McLaren and asked to explain why Archie had been released. McLaren had attended the morning briefing which took place daily between the CID, uniform and traffic officers to discuss the last twenty four hours activities in Newholm. Number one on the agenda had been Archie's release and why this had happened. The DI had received a verbal ear-bashing and questioning by some of his senior officers over Jimmy's ability to remain a detective when his judgement was so flawed.

Subsequently, when Mclaren returned from this meeting he left Jimmy in no doubt as to his opinions and Jimmy's foolishness of putting any trust in somebody like Archie. In his view Jimmy had now made a number of enemies within the force, especially those officers who already hated CID and those who had been on the receiving end of Archie's violence. His last words to Jimmy were to keep watching over his shoulder to see where the knife was coming from that would stab him in the back, stressing that it would be most unlikely that a ned would be the first to deliver the blow.

Jimmy was left questioning the wisdom of releasing Archie but was convinced he had acted correctly. It was a matter of trust and he would just have to sweat it out and hopefully get a return.

Three days before Archie's arrest there had been a robbery at a small jewellers shop in the High Street in Newholm. The culprit had his face covered with a scarf and was wearing a peaked cap, partially covering his eyes. On entering the small shop he had presented a hammer to the elderly jeweller, pointed to the most expensive tray of rings in the shop and demanded that he hand it over. The jeweller decided he wasn't giving the robber anything and as a result suffered a blow to his head. Stunned, and in fear for his life, he opened the locked display cabinet and gave him a tray of rings worth £10,000 and the culprit fled from the shop with the goods. By the time the alarm was raised the robber was long gone. When the police arrived they found the jeweller severely traumatised and disorientated. He was quickly taken to hospital to have his injury treated and his family were called, together with one of the force's Family Liaison Officers.

Initial enquiries found that the shop was equipped with very poor quality CCTV and there were no witnesses to the incident. Local media were quickly onto the story and weren't slow to ask the police how the investigation into this terrible crime was progressing and how they intended to protect the public from further attacks.

DS Browne was allocated the role of investigating officer.

He found himself in the department, not through choice, but rather through promotion with the promise of a short stint in CID to improve his CV.

The chances of him solving this crime were remote and his bosses both within CID and Uniform continued to receive flak for their lack of progress. No one had come forward after an appeal for witnesses - there were no leads, no forensic evidence, while door-to-door enquiries had drawn a blank. The press were giving the police a hard time for their lack of action and apparent incompetence.

Two days after Archie's release Jimmy was on late shift (6pm to 2am) in the CID office completing reports when a telephone call was received by a fellow DC. The caller said he would only speak to Jimmy…when he lifted the phone, the caller asked if he knew who was speaking and Jimmy immediately recognised Archie's voice. Thereafter, he told Jimmy that the following afternoon at 2pm a named individual, well-known to Jimmy, would be walking across a football field in the town heading to one of Archie's neighbour's houses. If Jimmy wanted to clear the robbery at the jewellers then he should stop and search this man as he would be carrying the stolen jewellery. The caller ended his conversation by telling Jimmy this was anonymous information and that is what should appear both in the paper and in court.

The next day Jimmy came into work at 9am even though he was rostered for late shift. Bypassing DS Browne he went straight to DI McLaren and told him about the information he had received, though not where it came from. By now Jimmy had quite a number of touts and as a result of the past quality of his information he had some credibility with McLaren.

After hearing what Jimmy had to say McLaren told him

he would have to pass this information to Browne as he was the investigating officer and would therefore do the intercept with his team. He did confirm that if the information was correct and the crime cleared then he would make sure Jimmy received the credit. This would go some way to taking the heat away from him with the bosses.

At 2pm, as the tout had promised, a local drug dealer with a long record of violence, appeared in the football field and was intercepted by Browne and his team. He put up a fight, breaking Brown's nose with a head butt in the process, but once restrained and handcuffed, he was searched and found to have most of the jewellery stolen from the elderly jeweller.

He was taken to the police station, where he was interviewed by Browne's team and admitted responsibility and also named a friend who had been acting as lookout. He too was later detained and admitted his involvement. The thief refused to disclose who was to be the recipient of the jewellery, but Jimmy had more than a sneaking suspicion that it was Archie, who was known to reset (receive or handle) stolen property.

The police bosses were relieved and there were some promotion hopefuls waiting to front the media with this good news story. Sadly, DS Browne couldn't meet the media as he was having his broken nose attended to. The task of talking to the media fell to McLaren, who was as good as his word and ensured that Jimmy got the credit internally.

As far as Jimmy was concerned he had now recruited a true thoroughbred criminal informant and the quality of his stable had improved. Not only this, but Jimmy had been recognised by some other officers as the one who had really cleared this nasty crime and this enhanced his reputation in the force as a thief taker. He had now gained some grudging respect from officers who could so easily have become enemies.

'CHOCOLATE TREAT'

Jimmy first met Chocolate Treat when he had been locked up for a break-in at a pub. One of the duties of CID officers on day shift was to fingerprint and photograph people in custody before they went to court. On this particular day Jimmy was doing so with a ned who would soon become 'Chocolate Treat', and they were having some good banter. Jimmy knew Chocolate's mother, who was an alcoholic but, nevertheless, likeable. Normally, she was abusive to the police when they were called to her house, which happened regularly, especially when she had consumed too much vodka. She hated a lot of cops, especially those who were 'knocking-off' some of the local, available women whose boyfriends were in prison and who lived nearby. Jimmy, however, was different and when he went to her house there was always good-natured banter about the 'bad boys in blue'. One story she loved retelling related to a night when she found an off-duty cop sneaking through her garden en route to a young female neighbour whose boyfriend was completing a three-year jail term. She confronted him, broke a brush shank over his back and told him to get back to his wife and stop behaving like a dog in heat.

Anyway, when Chocolate went to court he was bailed and returned to his home in one of the poorest areas in Newholm. The next night Jimmy came across him as he was walking to his local pub in the pouring rain. Jimmy offered him a lift in the unmarked CID car. This was frowned upon by the bosses but appreciated by Chocolate, and their conversation on the journey got round to business and the fact Chocolate was quite prepared to take the 'King's Shilling'.

He told Jimmy that a number of cars had recently been broken into in Chapel Street in the town, and that CD players stolen from them were now in a shed at the rear of the culprit's home. Chocolate had been offered one and said he would get back to the thief. He then asked Jimmy if he was interested in this information and Jimmy, who was aware of these crimes, confirmed that he was.

After noting the culprit's address he told Chocolate he would do something quickly with the information he had supplied and get back to him the next day with a suitable reward, providing the stolen property was recovered.

After Jimmy dropped Chocolate off, he picked up his late shift colleague and they went to the local Sheriff's house at 11.30 pm. The Sheriff was not amused at being disturbed at this hour but, after giving Jimmy a grilling, he granted a warrant to search the house and shed of the suspect.

When they got to the ned's house and told him they had a warrant to search his house and shed, he was gob-smacked. In the shed were eighteen CD players and a variety of discs. The ned was detained, taken to the police station and, during interview, admitted these multiple thefts as well as forty others. He was kept in custody but told by Jimmy, who was hoping to recruit him to his stable, that he would not oppose bail at court the next day.

The next morning Jimmy appeared at DI McLaren's office and told him about the number of crimes he had cleared the previous night and the stolen property he had recovered. McLaren was well-pleased and agreed that Chocolate would get £200 from the tout fund once the appropriate paperwork and receipts had been completed.

As promised, that night Jimmy met Chocolate and handed over the money, which more than met with his satisfaction. When they went their separate ways he assured Jimmy there would be much more information coming his way, provided amounts of cash like this were forthcoming.

Chocolate Treat was now in the yard and Jimmy would train him to his true potential in the hope he would become a 'course and distance' winner in the 'Crime Fighting Stakes'.

'HASTY LAD'

Hasty Lad was a 15-year-old tearaway from a very dysfunctional family when Jimmy first came across him. There was no known father in his household and Jimmy doubted whether any of the four kids knew who their dad was. Their mother was constantly drunk or absent and, as a result, social services had a lot of contact with the family.

At this time Hasty's younger brother, aged fourteen, had been charged with indecent assault on two 11 year-old girls. His oldest brother was twenty-five and living with a 15year-old girl, while his 18 year-old sister had been involved with boys since she was thirteen. As for Hasty, he had been in minor trouble since the age of eleven and came to the notice of the police for acts of glue sniffing, vandalism, assaults and break-ins.

It was during his arrest for a break-in that Jimmy first really got to know him. Even at this young age he was worldly wise, had a lot of front and even more attitude. More importantly for Jimmy, he knew what was going on in Newholm among the active young criminals and was prepared to trade information for the 'King's Shilling'.

Accordingly, he was recruited to Jimmy's yard and was in fact an excellent tout for about a year. He could be relied upon and would obey Jimmy's instructions to the letter. This left Jimmy thinking that in Hasty Lad he had a good novice who could eventually become a classic contender.

When Hasty turned sixteen Jimmy saw less of him and he

often failed to turn up at pre-arranged meetings. Jimmy heard he was drinking heavily and had a 14year-old girlfriend who was also heavily into drink.

He did sometimes manage to contact Hasty, but even this was becoming increasingly difficult. In the next four years he only kept contact with Jimmy occasionally, and the tout found himself getting involved in more and more fights and scrapes. This resulted in his regular arrest and serving four prison sentences. Strangely, with all the fights he had been in, he didn't have a reputation as a hard-man, which was probably because most of his victims were either weaklings or younger boys and, on some occasions, girls.

Once, when he was out of jail and Jimmy hadn't heard from him for five months, he was considering Hasty's future in his stable, when out of the blue he was contacted by him.

The result of their subsequent meeting was that Jimmy got enough information from him to arrest two guys for numerous break-ins, two for major fraud and one for reset.

As normal, he received a good financial reward and, just as Jimmy was thinking that that was him back on track, he was arrested for breaking into a cottage hospital. This was a nasty crime, and during the break-in he was disturbed by a nurse whom he beat the living daylights out of and tried to rape...

For this crime he was given four years imprisonment and among the criminal fraternity he was now classed as a 'beast'.

As far as Jimmy was concerned Hasty was now out of his stable and out to pasture. He knew that at some later stage there might be a time when he would require information from him. For the greater good you had to put some of the heinous crimes committed by your charges, not forgotten about, but on the back-burner.

Dealing with touts was indeed a dirty business.

Nonetheless, the stable door was left slightly open on his release for this really nasty crime, and again he supplied good quality information which led to other, equally bad people being locked up.

After this he seemed to disappear off the scene and Jimmy didn't know where he was or what had become of him.

'GOLDEN LADY'

Golden was a 34-year-old female who was married, held down a good job and was well-respected in her local rural community, some thirty miles from Newholm. What the locals and the police didn't know was that she was also a drug user and dealer in amphetamine…

One night, driving her car home on a back road, she was stopped by some traffic cops who were concerned that her car was swaying from side to side. On stopping the vehicle they could smell a strong aroma of cannabis coming from inside the car. Accordingly, having 'reasonable suspicion' that she was involved with drugs, they detained her and her vehicle and took them to the nearest station to be searched.

As luck would have it, Jimmy was at this station investigating the theft of a lorry and its load from a nearby goods yard.

When Golden was brought in both she and her car were searched, but both searches ended with negative results. The traffic cops were baffled. Jimmy offered to help and, on a further search of the car, he found what appeared to be an unopened packet of cigarettes lying on the front passenger seat. The plastic wrapping round the packet was intact and on first glance seemed normal. However, when he lifted the packet up he felt its weight was too heavy just to contain cigarettes.

Consequently, he opened it and found twenty wraps of white powder. Golden would later tell him she used a Stanley blade to cut evenly round the cellophane wrapper on the packet and then re-seal it using her car ignition key which she heated against her cigarette lighter.

Golden was in trouble now and Jimmy took the lead. Along with a female police officer he cautioned and confronted her with the cigarette packet and its contents. She admitted it was amphetamine and also that she had been smoking hash in the car though thrown it away before being pulled over.

Jimmy and this officer then noted her replies and confirmed them with her in a tape recorded interview. She was charged with possession with intent to supply amphetamine.

Once the interview and the charging processes were complete Jimmy spoke to her on her own, and it became obvious she was horrified about her secret life now becoming public knowledge. In true negotiator fashion he told her that if she agreed to keep him informed about the local drug scene then he would release her to be reported by summons and speak to the prosecutor on her behalf. She agreed without hesitation and after exchanging contact numbers left the station, much to the chagrin of the traffic cops who had stopped her. Jimmy had already told them the drugs would need to be analysed to confirm that they contained amphetamine before she could go before the courts and there was no way the forensic laboratory were going to receive a call out for only twenty wraps. They were still not amused but knew that he was probably right. This suited Jimmy perfectly.

Three days later he received a call from her asking to meet at a rural forest area. He dropped what he was doing and went, perhaps unwisely, on his own to meet Golden, though not before telling McLaren where he was headed.

In the car park at the entrance to the forest Jimmy found

Golden in her car. After confirming visually that she was on her own and ensuring, as best he could that they were not being watched he entered her vehicle. At the back of his mind was the earlier advice he had received about being taped by the neds. In keeping with his other tout meetings, he made a mental note to make sure that what he said was legitimate and leave his position uncompromised.

Golden asked when she would hear about the court case and Jimmy said it would be at least six months before she received a summons. He then asked her to step out the car so that if the conversation was being recorded in the vehicle then he was outwith its range. Golden, of course, could be wearing a body microphone but that was the chance he had to take and anyway his conversation would remain circumspect. He then told her he had spoken to the prosecutor on her behalf though in fact he had not.

She went on to tell Jimmy about a very rural location where three men were cultivating both cannabis and opium on a large scale. One of the men was a professional, an artist, who owned the land where the cultivation was taking place. She described how they operated, who they distributed to and the exact layout of the premises. Apparently, all the cultivation was taking place within a commercial-sized greenhouse, and the distribution was outwith the local area to other members of the 'arty' fraternity, along with close associates and friends of the cultivators. Jimmy left this meeting on a high as it wasn't every day you might unearth the cultivation of opium in Scotland.

The next day, armed with suitable surveillance authority, DI McLaren and Jimmy were joined by three other DCs from the CID and two drug squad officers who had been trained in surveillance. They identified a suitable observation point and kept watch on the premises indicated by Golden. Early enquiries with the local police and the force's intelligence section had revealed that the artist had only been residing there for a year. Little was known about him, other than he came from Lancashire. He had no criminal record, nor was there any intelligence, nationally, linking him to drug distribution. All that could be ascertained was that he was well-regarded within the U.K. and internationally as a painter.

When Jimmy assessed the 'plot' he found it was a mini estate and, at its perimeter, there was woodland, adjacent to which was a greenhouse measuring approximately fifty metres by ten metres. The woods afforded partial concealment of the greenhouse from one side, and the landowner had erected a two metre high wooden fence on the other to ensure no-one could see inside from a distance at any angle.

The main house on the estate where the artist lived, was a large, detached, five-bedroom sandstone building located just inside the entrance road and gate. As a result, you couldn't enter the estate road without the householders detecting your presence.

Quite a nice set-up thought both Jimmy and McLaren.

After six hours of taking covert photographs of the occupants, vehicles and people coming and going within the estate, particularly those entering and leaving the greenhouse, Jimmy felt now was the time to apply for a search warrant. He duly applied to the local Sheriff and, while waiting for it to be sanctioned and signed, the detectives carrying out the surveillance completed owner checks on the vehicles in the estate via the Police National Computer.(PNC).

One car was 'flagged' by Lancashire police as being used by a drug dealer involved in the importation of heroin.

The warrant was duly granted, and Jimmy's surveillance officers were relieved by other surveillance- trained officers who kept an all-night vigil on the premises, photographing the comings and goings of individuals and logging the surveillance. At 7am the next morning an exhausted Jimmy, whose mind had been on the job for most of the night, along with McLaren and their team, attended at the premises equipped with cameras, spades, battering rams, protective masks and drug field-testing kits. His surveillance team updated him on activity during the night and McLaren and Jimmy agreed that now was the time to execute the warrant.

The artist, a very well-spoken individual with a mild manner, answered McLaren's knock at the door of the estate house. He got the shock of his life when he saw all the cops and heard Jimmy's explanation for being there. He was then cautioned and the contents of the search warrant were read aloud. On being shown the warrant he immediately capitulated and actually took McLaren, Jimmy and their team to the greenhouse. Prior to this visit by the police he had been living on the estate with his girlfriend and their two children in relative peace while trying to keep a low profile in the local community.

McLaren, Jimmy and the drug squad officers had seen home-grown cannabis before, but it was nothing compared to this. It reached two metres in height and half-filled the greenhouse. They had only seen opium being cultivated on TV but they now found that the other side of the greenhouse was full of lavender coloured opium poppies (papivar somniferum), all with their heads incised and with gum dripping.

McLaren arranged for everything to be photographed and then the estate owner and all his 'friends' who had been rounded up were taken to the house. After obtaining their true identities they were all cautioned and interviewed. Jimmy who was to be the reporting officer, was eventually left with five accused persons, including the importer from Lancashire who had been found in the greenhouse, 'out of his face' and in possession of heroin. They were charged with the cultivation of opium, its derivatives and the cultivation of cannabis, and taken back to Newholm Police Station for further interrogation. The result of these interviews and the search of the estate house revealed they were part of a network operating across the U.K. Interestingly, during the house search, documentation had been found showing that two of those detained in the estate were directors of an importation company which imported artisan goods from the Far East. McLaren arranged a meeting with Customs and Excise staff and they agreed they would approach the procurator fiscal and ask him not to oppose bail. If the fiscal agreed, then Customs and Excise would carry out surveillance on the team once they were released and also conduct in-depth investigation into the importation company.

After a night in the cells they attended at the court and, thanks to the co-operation of the fiscal, they were all bailed. Eventually, they appeared at Edinburgh High Court where they received sentences ranging from three to eight years imprisonment. Meanwhile, Customs and Excise had been successfully gathering enough intelligence on the team and their associates for a further prosecution for the importation of heroin.

All in all, as a result of Golden's information, the team had disrupted a major drug distribution and cultivation network which, in Jimmy's mind, was a top quality detection,

The local and national media ran the story, which was unusual as no-one in Scotland had been charged with the cultivation of opium for more than twenty years. This brought Jimmy into the limelight and he and McLaren gave numerous media interviews relating to the case. Jimmy was even the subject of a broadsheet's Sunday supplement. This pleased him, but not all of his colleagues, some of whom were increasingly desperate to see him take a fall.

However, more important than kudos or media attention for Jimmy was the fact that he now had a pedigree 'filly' in his stable. She could have a classic career ahead of her and she was well-pleased when she received her 'winnings' of £1000 from the tout fund.

THE JOYS OF A TRAINER

Jimmy now had four thoroughbred touts but continued to operate a number of what he would class in horse racing terms as 'point-to-pointers', those who were unlikely to become top level charges but would enable him to clear a lot of lower-level crime. The information supplied by all his informants ensured he was well acquainted with the current 'form' of many local criminals and their track records. As a result, he became an increasingly popular figure with those officers whose task was to deal with individual crimes because, like a well-informed horse racing trainer, he usually had an 'inside tip'. Even some of his uniform bosses now appreciated his efforts, especially since as he had proved himself less cavalier and problematic than DS Martin.

He was now receiving calls at all hours of the day and night from his stable, and being a trainer had now become a 24/7 job. Increasingly, he was being informed about serious crimes still in the planning stages that would soon come to fruition.

Chocolate Treat had been in regular contact and was receiving good amounts of reward money for the quality information he supplied. However, as racehorses need to be kept under a watchful eye, so too did Jimmy's charges. Chocolate was always on the fringes of crime or committing low level crime. This worried Jimmy as it could not only threaten their relationship but also breach his ethical code of tout and trainer. If he didn't abide by the rules then

Chocolate, like Hasty Lad, could end up being put out to pasture.

Jimmy had often told him to stay away from the commission of crime but he was wise enough to know that good touts, like good racehorses, are only good if they are involved, exercised regularly and associated with their peers. Nevertheless, Jimmy had told him officially that if he breached the code and continued to commit crime then he was on his own.

On this occasion, Chocolate telephoned Jimmy and asked to meet him urgently as something big was going down the next night. Quite rightly he would not say anything further on the phone and a meeting between trainer and charge took place in darkness in a lay-by outside of Newholm.

Chocolate stated that some close 'friends' of his had recently carried out reconnaissance at the largest social club in Newholm. They had an inside lead and knew about the alarm systems and the timings and movements of the club steward. More importantly, they knew that on the following night there could be as much as twenty thousand pounds in the club's safe. They had already learned it was a floor safe set in concrete, and could be removed with the use of a jig saw, long cold chisels, mufflers and some other tools. Furthermore, their source on the inside had told them how to disengage and immobilise the alarm system.

The potential culprits named by him were all known to Jimmy as active housebreakers with a lot of form and expertise behind them. Jimmy's mouth was watering at the thought of catching the culprits on the job, which does not happen too often in a detective's career.

It was at this juncture that Chocolate told Jimmy he had been asked to take part in this crime...

Jimmy was now in a dilemma. How could he sanction

Chocolate's involvement without him being classed as 'agent provocateur', and where did Jimmy stand if he allowed him to participate? Irrespective of the way you looked at it this was going to be problematic.

Sometimes it is hard for a trainer...

He considered telling McLaren about Chocolate's proposed involvement but decided against it. However, he couldn't avoid telling him about the job these neds were planning.

Accordingly, he briefed McLaren, telling him that he had good information about this break-in which was due to take place the following night. The D.I. must have had suspicions because he asked Jimmy how good the source was, to which Jimmy said he was reliable and a proven course and distance winner.

Thereafter, authority for surveillance was applied for and granted. McLaren decided that Jimmy and a colleague would man the observation post, while he and his team of four detectives took control of the social club from within the building. There, they would be ideally positioned to arrest the culprits if they entered the club.

In the meantime, Jimmy shot off to see Chocolate and instructed him that his involvement would be minimal, this being the only way he would not be regarded legally as 'agent provocateur'. He would conceal his identity and the only role he would be taking in this break-in would be as look-out. Further, once the first member of their criminal team had entered the club he would be immediately apprehended, and Chocolate, along with his cohorts who knew nothing of this plan, should make good their escape.

Jimmy reminded him to stick to his script and the designated role. Chocolate smiled in agreement.

At 11pm that night Jimmy and his colleague were in the

observation position and McLaren and his team were in the club, which had shut early at their request. It was the middle of winter and the ground was covered with snow. Outside the front of the club were three one-and-a-half metre high hedges which bordered the club green. Jimmy couldn't help but think that these well-kept hedges reminded him of racecourse hurdles.

Chocolate said the job was due to 'come down' about midnight and sure enough, at five past midnight, four men wearing dark clothing and hats and scarves over their faces, appeared at the perimeter fence surrounding the club. After looking all around the club and its surroundings they went into a thick hedge adjacent to a domestic garage at the rear of the club, and re-appeared with three bags containing the tools for the job.

Jimmy immediately radioed McLaren and told him the culprits were outside the club. He then watched as they spread out around the building. Chocolate stuck to his instructions and acted as look-out while the other members of the team cut phone wires and bent back the hammers on the bell alarms. They obviously had help from the inside because no alarms were activated.

The most experienced crook, after satisfying himself that the alarms were not functioning, approached a large window with a glass cutter and started to cut an aperture big enough for him to enter. He then stood back from the window and again no alarms were activated. All this activity was being relayed by Jimmy to McLaren and his team inside the club.

After a short interval the crook entered the club through the cut window and almost immediately the lights in the club came on. Instinctively, Chocolate and his buddies knew something was wrong and they hurriedly began to make their escape, each clearing the fences surrounding the club. For

Jimmy it was like watching a hurdling race but, like many 'fixed' races, only very few knew the race tactics and in this case only Jimmy and Chocolate knew that Chocolate was one of the 'runners'. Nonetheless, Chocolate and his two friends were clearing these snow-covered hurdles in a manner that would make any trainer proud.

The culprit who had entered the building had been restrained after a struggle and was quickly handcuffed. Jimmy and his colleague then ran to the club and quickly realised that this guy wasn't going to make any trouble.

They returned to the office with him, where he was interviewed by two of Jimmy's colleagues and refused to name his associates, much to Jimmy's relief. He was charged with the break-in on his own. With the number of previous convictions he had for breaking into commercial premises there was no doubt that he would get a heavy sentence. He eventually did receive three years in custody. His associates were never caught nor was the 'inside' man, which really bothered Jimmy. Chocolate, however, received a decent reward, which was what he was looking for as he now had a live-in girlfriend to support.

PROMOTION

As well as catching thieves and other miscreants, Jimmy had made it a priority to pass his police promotion examinations. Maybe by getting promoted he could make his grandfather and father proud and, in the process, show them that hard work could be rewarded. This might prove that the class system was not as all-pervading as they, and he, had first thought.

This was always going to be a difficult task, made more problematic by the fact that he had little in the way of formal education, and working all the hours he did in CID was not conducive to study. Nevertheless, he took the task on and, after three failed attempts, managed to pass both his Sergeant's and Inspector's exams. In theory he was now qualified for promotion to every rank in the police service.

What he didn't like to dwell on was that through this selfish approach he hardly spent any quality time with Doris or his son Derek. This was something he would regret in later years. Only then would he realise that he couldn't get back these crucial periods in his family's life. In effect he had put his wife and child into his 'stable.'

His reputation as a thief-taker was growing all the time but, as in every business, jealousy creeps in and the police service was no different. Jimmy found on speaking to members of his stable that, when they couldn't contact him with 'hot' information, they were leaving messages with the CID using the nom de plume Jimmy had given them. After the incident in the dark room, for some reason no-one was now trying to steal his touts. Nevertheless, these messages were not being passed to him and break-ins and robberies took place which could have been prevented or disrupted.

His bosses in CID knew his worth though, and he was by now the most proactive detective on the shop floor. Similarly, within the force hierarchy, Deputy Chief Constable Cobble, unlike most of his peers, had been a detective, and still had a thirst for crime-fighting. He showed a real interest in the CID and, on many occasions, would appear unannounced and make a bee-line for Jimmy to ask him how things were going. He shared Jimmy's view that one of the major police tasks was to take the bad people off the street.

Probably as a result of his support, Jimmy received a call to see the Chief Constable in his office. Fearing the worst, he attended and, after being ushered into the office by the Chief's secretary, he was given a seat and the Chief himself poured coffee and offered him biscuits...

The Chief went on to say he was very impressed by Jimmy's work and he had decided to move some staff around. As a result, DS Browne would be leaving CID and returning to uniform duties. This meant there would be a vacancy for a Detective Sergeant in CID, and the Chief then offered Jimmy this promoted post. Jimmy could hardly contain his glee as this meant he would now be in charge of a shift and able to motivate and direct them, and would have more influence on how his criminal charges operated. He felt Martin's war could be won, especially now that he was Detective Sergeant McBurnie.

When he returned to the office he couldn't wait to tell DI McLaren the good news but, as he began speaking to him, it was obvious he already knew. It turned out DCI Chambers, and DI Stewart, the DI mainly responsible for administration within the CID also knew. Jimmy was summoned into Chambers' office, where the DCI took a bottle of whisky from his desk drawer. He toasted Jimmy and told him how delighted he was at having him as a DS.

After finishing his drink, Jimmy was about to return to the shop floor, where some of his colleagues were waiting to congratulate him, when Chambers asked him to wait a minute. He reminded Jimmy of what he and DI McLaren had told him when he joined the CID. and about how dangerous touts can be. This danger, he said, increased when you had more clout and influence. Subsequently, Jimmy should ensure he abided by the rules and, if there were any problems, he should let him know 'before the shit hit the fan'. If Jimmy didn't know about possible problems then there was little he, or the other CID supervisors, could do about them. Jimmy would then be left on his own and hung out to dry.

These words dampened Jimmy's euphoria. Nonetheless, he was still delighted and agreed to join his colleagues for a drink after work, though not before he phoned Doris to let her know the good news, not to mention that he would also be getting a pay rise. DS Browne, understandably, was unavailable to join Jimmy but was still pleased to be getting out of CID which he knew would only hamper his promotion prospects the longer he stayed.

At the pub next to the police station, Jimmy was in good form but did not let his guard down even after consuming eight pints of beer and a couple of whiskies. When he arrived home Doris was concerned with his drunken state but nevertheless pleased about the promotion. The extra money would come in handy and she hoped this might mean he would not be on call all hours of the day and night, meeting touts and arresting criminals, but rather, at home more with his family..

If only she knew…

On the first day in his new post Jimmy moved into DS Browne's old office. At first it was strange having an office of your own when you were used to sharing a desk in an open plan environment, but Jimmy liked it because it gave him quiet thinking space.

As was normal at coffee break he went to a nearby baker's to get a filled roll. Sometimes, on this short journey, he would meet his criminal clientele whom he always made a point of speaking to, even if they didn't want to speak to him. Those who didn't want to speak still had a grudging respect for Jimmy, though not through fear as had been the case with DS Martin. They classed Jimmy with having guile, and they were worried, because he always seemed to be too well-informed about crime in Newholm.

Jimmy now knew why his old village cop, PC Agnew, was well aware about who was committing crime in his area; like Jimmy he also had a 'stable'.

This morning, as he entered the baker's, he came face to face with a prominent drug dealer and violent criminal. This ned stopped him and said he had heard that Jimmy had been promoted and would be moving to a uniformed sergeant's position, somewhere in the sticks. When he and his 'colleagues' first heard this, he said, they had a wee party. Jimmy laughed and said he was sorry to disappoint but he had been promoted to Detective Sergeant and would be remaining both within the C.I.D. and Newholm. The look of disappointment on the ned's face was only too obvious, and Jimmy apologised that he hadn't lived up to their expectations though guaranteed that they would be seeing more of him. Heading back to the C.I.D. office Jimmy thought to himself that if the neds were having a party to celebrate his removal then this was really a compliment. There was no doubt he was becoming a real thorn in their side.

In his sergeant's post he felt he was now a 'licensed' trainer and in a position to expand the size and quality of his yard. With this new supervisory role he would not only be managing touts but also cops, and he would soon find out that one group was as difficult to control as the other.

One of his detectives was a cop called Green. A man, of diminutive stature but a gregarious personality and, importantly to Jimmy, an ability to work hard. Accordingly, he took this officer under his wing and made more use of him than some of his other colleagues, making him his corroborating officer. All true thief takers, and especially Scottish detectives who by law, need corroboration of evidence, need a good 'second man/woman' as their corroborating officer, although more importantly, one you can trust.

Green fitted that category.

The news of Jimmy's promotion spread quickly and it wasn't long before he received a call from ex- DS Martin, who congratulated him and told him to keep winning the war, taking no prisoners. He still had the utmost respect for Martin's detective skills, even though a number of colleagues described him as 'off the wall'. Jimmy ignored such comments and kept in regular contact with his ex DS who was by now nearing retirement, though showing no signs of slowing down. In fact, in the town he was now policing all the neds were scared of him as they had been in Newholm, and he was still clearing crime. Some of the older cops he was working with now, respected him and were keeping an eye on him to ensure the alcohol he was consuming didn't come to the notice of their bosses. They, like Jimmy, just wanted to see him cross the 'finishing line' of his career before he had a fall or was pulled up as a result of alcohol abuse or a misdemeanour.

Jimmy asked Martin what he thought of his young Detective Green. He got a positive response and confirmation that he had what it took to be a good, trustworthy detective and thief taker.

Green was now an apprentice trainer in Jimmy McBurnie's yard.

All of his charges were now producing quality information, whether their motive was revenge on opponents, to get legal help from Jimmy or for the 'King's Shilling'. Remarkably, he had managed to exercise enough caution to keep all their identities relatively secret under their respective nom de plumes.

Following his promotion, the major crime problem in Newholm was a spate of break-ins at commercial premises which held high-quality, valuable industrial tools and equipment. Some of the articles stolen included diggers, JCBs and generators.

For some reason, none of Jimmy's stable was able to shed any light on who was committing these crimes or where the stolen property was being disposed. Accordingly, both divisional and CID bosses were 'getting it in the ear' from those higher up in the force, who themselves were under pressure from both the media and community representatives. Many of the victims of the crimes were prominent business people in Newholm, who carried local influence. They were not slow, when meeting the Chief Constable at the Rotary Club, to tell him how disappointed they were in the police's lack of response and success.

As you would expect, these comments were soon passed down to senior officers who, in turn, ensured the CID bosses knew that they had to get this sorted out and the culprits locked up. This would have been hard for some to achieve as they had never investigated a crime. DCC Cobble, who was now second in command of the force and an experienced detective, knew the difficulties and pressures of criminal investigation and he brought some reality to the situation.

However, Jimmy was caught off-guard when Cobble appeared at his office one morning, by-passing the CID bosses and making a bee- line for Jimmy who was only the DS. Immediately, he asked Jimmy what the hell was going on and what his touts were saying. Jimmy was honest and admitted there was little feedback from the tout world and little in the way of evidence left at any of the crime scenes. Nor were there witnesses to any of the break-ins. Some of these had been the result of noisy 'ram raids', where considerable time had been spent violating the premises, yet there were no witnesses. Even stranger, some of the property stolen was bulky and would have required heavy transport to remove it.

Jimmy said it appeared they were dealing with professionals and out-of-town professionals at that, who had the means to move their stolen booty. Cobble then, in an attempt to motivate Jimmy, told him that there would be an opportunity to get his name in lights and be brought to the attention of the chief, among others, if he could solve these crimes.

When he left, Jimmy didn't feel motivated, but rather under more pressure and, to an extent, feeling sorry for himself as he wondered why the rest of the department were not getting this direct flak. He didn't know that both the DCI and DI McLaren had been getting it in the ear on a daily basis at the force's morning briefings. He then removed this thought from his head and, using his reason, he could see that his tout stable offered the best chance of getting information on who was responsible for these break-ins. Cobble really was trying to motivate him just as Chambers had been in telling the whole department that they were all in this together. Together they would solve these crimes and take the thieves off the streets.

Three weeks passed and there had been three more break-ins at commercial premises. Plain clothes officers in unmarked cars, surveillance and rapid and repeated checks of vehicles by the traffic department had all failed to unearth the culprits. With £750,000 worth of stolen property the situation was now critical, and even the offer of a substantial reward, provided by the victims and their insurance companies, was not enough to put a stop to the crimes.

Jimmy had to admit they were stumped.

WELSH RAREBIT

One Saturday morning, during the height of these break-ins, Jimmy was helping transfer prisoners from their cells in the police station to fingerprint and photograph them before they appeared at court the following Monday. For any ned, a weekend lock-up was dreaded and one to be avoided at all costs. Some custodies that weekend had been locked up for pub fights, minor thefts and misdemeanours, while others had been arrested for drug dealing and robberies. Most were repeat offenders as evidenced by their conviction lists.

A normal day, thought Jimmy...

While fingerprinting a 28 year-old Welshman who had been locked up following a fight in a pub, the man engaged Jimmy in general conversation and asked for a cigarette, which he duly supplied. Jimmy didn't know him but continued the conversation with the prisoner who said he had a sister in Newholm. Jimmy knew his sister. She had been in Newholm for five years and had a reputation among the neds as a loose woman. As well as being a petty crook, she supplied a safe house and alibis for criminals on the run from the police.

The Welshman then started to tell Jimmy about local guys who were stealing from her, beating her up, getting her drunk and having their way with her. Seeing an opportunity to help and maybe get inside this criminal family, Jimmy offered to look into it and promised to interview the sister that day. The ned then asked if it would be okay if his sister visited him in his cell. This was a common request but not one often granted by custody officers. They had enough on their plate looking after prisoners, feeding them, getting them ready for court and allowing their solicitors access without dealing with family visits, which would have to be supervised. However, Jimmy saw an opportunity in meeting this request and agreed to the visit, promising the custody office sergeant he would supervise it.

After finishing his fingerprinting duties he called the sister and asked if she wanted to visit her brother. She was taken aback as this had never happened before when she tried for a visit, and she had already asked and been refused a visit to her brother on this occasion.

Jimmy told her he was in charge of her brother and she should come to the station at 2pm where he would personally supervise the visit. She turned up on time armed with cigarettes for her brother, Jimmy listened in to their conversation in the smoke-filled detention room.

Before the visit ended, the ned told his sister to speak to Jimmy about the guys who were stealing from her. When she left the cell she supplied him with this information and made a statement which could be corroborated. This was enough to allow Jimmy to detain and later arrest a local worthy, who, as well as being a thief, was violent towards women and children. When later searching this ned's house, Jimmy and his colleagues recovered some of the Welshman's sister's jewellery and the ned was arrested. You can imagine the Welshman's surprise when he saw the guy who had been beating and abusing his sister in the next cell.

Fortunately for the Welshman he was bailed from court on the Monday, without Jimmy's help. By this time Jimmy had carried out some checks on him. These checks revealed he was, as expected, a bit of a rogue with a long list of convictions in Wales for crimes ranging from minor assaults to break-ins and robberies.

Jimmy now knew where he lived, and after further contact with the local intelligence officer he learned he had been in Newholm for nine months. Jimmy could cope with more charges in his stable and was considering calling in the favour. Before he could do this he received a telephone call at the CID office from the Welshman, who asked Jimmy to meet him at a spot next to the river Ure, which snaked through Newholm. He told Jimmy he had something for him. Being cautious, Jimmy contacted DC Green and told him to come along. En route he told Green who it was they were meeting and the young detective said he knew the Welshman, and in fact had a fight with him while arresting him during a fracas in a pub. Green said this ned was a 'right bastard' and there would be no way he would be talking to the police.

Jimmy just gave him a wry grin...

When they arrived at the road next to the river the Welshman appeared from the bushes and jumped into the rear of the unmarked car. He lay across the back seat and Jimmy drove off at speed with a somewhat bemused Green, who was in the front passenger seat, wondering what was happening.

The ned told Jimmy to drive to a derelict outbuilding at a farm next to the river, some three miles upstream. During the journey he had antagonised Green by asking him how his head was. Apparently, during their earlier confrontation, he had head-butted Green causing a lump the size of an egg to appear on his forehead. Green looked at Jimmy but the knowing look he got back meant he should bite his lip.

Once they got to the outbuilding the Welshman walked through the rickety door secured only by a bolt. Once inside he removed some of the old railway sleepers from the floor to reveal a sectioned pit measuring some one-and-a-half metres deep and three metres square. Contained within this pit was a vast array of industrial power tools which Jimmy knew came from some of recent break-ins at the industrial estate.

The ned then asked to speak to Jimmy on his own and Jimmy nodded to Green, who left the outbuilding to keep watch at the car.

In the conversation that followed his new charge told him the culprits were a team from Merseyside who had met a local ned in Durham prison while they were serving prison sentences there. Their friendship had continued once the Newholm guy was released and they had gone into partnership. The Newholm ned's role in this partnership was that of a 'recce' man'. He would target industrial premises, carry out reconnaissance, and get inside information about the respective firms' security and pass it to the Scousers. Meanwhile, they would provide the technical expertise to overcome the security of the premises, suitable vehicles to move the stolen property, and arrange for the sale (reset) of the booty. Once the property was sold the Newholm ned would receive his share.

Jimmy knew now why there was little information locally about who was committing these crimes and why there was virtually no chance of recovering any of the stolen property, which, in all likelihood, had disappeared south of the border.

The position, if any, of the Welshman in this team was nebulous and Jimmy, wisely, did not pursue this matter. He was grateful at this potentially huge inroad and he was hopeful about taking them off the street. He was even more pleased when the Welshman told him the stolen property in the outbuilding was due to be uplifted in two days' time by the Scousers.

Jimmy then told his new tout there was a big reward for information that would clear these crimes and recover the stolen property. When the Welshman asked how much, Jimmy said about two grand. The tout then nodded appreciatively, telling Jimmy that not only did he want some of that but he could put some more 'business' his way, provided his anonymity was maintained.

Jimmy's trainer's mind was now working overtime and he knew that this new charge'could definitely turn out to be a 'classic champion'. They both left the outbuilding and Jimmy told DC Green to stay where he was, but hidden, till he dropped off the Welshman.

That done, Jimmy telephoned DCI Chambers and told him about the stash of property and that they would have to put 'obs'(observation) on it for at least two days. Both Chambers and Jimmy knew that, with the rural location of the outbuilding, it would not be easy to keep watch on it without being 'clocked'. In fact it would require nationally trained undercover obs men, with appropriate surveillance authority, who could dig in and remain concealed. Jimmy figured the granting of the Chief Constable's authority for this type of surveillance would not be a problem given the bad press the police were getting over these break-ins.

Once the scene was secured he returned to the CID office with his young detective and briefed DCI Chambers and DI. McLaren. It was cause for celebration, and whisky was retrieved from Chambers' drawer and shared around. Chambers, however, told his colleagues they were only having one drink, and that the real celebrations wouldn't begin until this travelling team from the south were locked up.

Jimmy was given the responsibility for the operation.

This meant a back-up team of detectives being available twenty-four hours a day, with support from uniform colleagues, to respond promptly when contacted by the specialist obs men whose use had been sanctioned by the Chief.

Sure enough, at about 11pm, two days after the meeting with his new tout, one of the obs men radioed Jimmy to say five men had arrived at the outbuilding in a small lorry and a van, none of which had any lights on. They had now entered the outbuilding and were removing property into their two vehicles.

Jimmy was excited and called in the 'strike'. Cops appeared from everywhere, taking the Scousers by surprise. However, they didn't just put their hands up and surrender, in fact quite the opposite, and fights broke out all over the place. The fracas was brief, though, as there were too many cops and it was only a matter of time before the scousers were overcome and arrested.

When they were taken to Newholm Police Station, Jimmy arranged for pairs of detectives to interview each of the five neds arrested. He had a word with them first and they displayed their professionalism by refusing to discuss or divulge anything, even their names. Jimmy thought that in keeping with the 'war' he was fighting, they should be classed as 'dog tag' men. In other words, they would provide nothing other than name, rank and serial number when captured. However, they were not even playing by these rules and were certainly not bound by the Geneva Convention.

During the interviews, again not one word was spoken by any of them. This didn't bother Jimmy as he had caught them cold and they would all be remanded once they appeared in court. This would give him time to make follow-up enquiries, the first of which would be with the scousers' local Newholm contact who had been in prison with them.

Early the next day Jimmy appeared at this guy's house

with Green, and told him he was being detained in connection with the break-ins he was investigating. On the way into the station in the unmarked car, Jimmy put the wind up the Newholm ned by telling him how his five mates were locked up and the property recovered. Using a bit of poetic licence he said that the scousers were now desperate to get the one who had shopped them.

The local ned wasn't daft. He believed that he was the only local contact the scousers had and the only other person who knew the whereabouts of the stolen tools. He knew that, if he wasn't arrested, they would think he was the grass.

Jimmy didn't let him think otherwise but just gave him a knowing look...

He had already arranged that, once this ned reached the back door of the police station, he would see the Scousers leave in a prison van for court. Perhaps, more importantly, they would see him being brought into the station, not handcuffed and engaged in conversation with Jimmy.

It happened as Jimmy planned and the local ned started to break out in a sweat on seeing the cuffed-scousers entering a prison van and drawing him dirty looks.

Accordingly, it wasn't long before he was not only telling Jimmy and Green about the commercial break-ins and his and the Scousers' involvement in them, but also supplying them with details of where the stolen property had gone. Having supplied evidence against them, he was now frantic with worry that he would surely be a marked man for the rest of his life.

Jimmy reassured him that his 'assistance' with the other crimes, identifying associates of the Scousers, and where the stolen property was, wouldn't appear in any written record of evidence. However, Jimmy did say he would charge him with the same crimes, lock him up, and he would appear in court the next day, just like his former buddies. This would go some way to giving him credibility with them once they knew he had been charged with the same crimes and anyway he had been involved in these crimes. They would never know where the initial information came from and would presume that someone had grassed them all up, including the ned from Newholm.

Jimmy had never seen a ned so eager to be locked up and he wasn't slow to tell him that he was now one of his stable, and he would be calling on him as and when required. So another charge was admitted to McBurnie's yard, under the name;

'NERVOUS BOY'

After some sterling work from his colleagues and with some support from the cops in the Scousers' home area, most of the stolen property from the break-ins was recovered and a number of neds from south of the border ended up facing charges in a Scottish Court.

'Nervous Boy' wound up on remand with his Scouse pals who, when they saw him there, charged with the same crimes as them, ruled him out as being the grass. His credibility with them was further strengthened when police raids took place in England while he was still on remand.

When it was time for their trial the Scousers, not surprisingly, all pled not guilty, while the local ned pled guilty and received four years imprisonment. Luckily for Nervous, before the trial began the crown had enough evidence to proceed without his contribution, and he was not called as a witness. The Scousers were found guilty after trial and each received six years in jail. Jimmy had again prevented crime by taking career criminals off the street and this time had also managed to add two 'thoroughbred' touts to his stable. Wisely, perhaps, he didn't question himself too deeply about how the Welshman knew so much about these crimes. Having said this, Jimmy knew his geography and was well aware that Merseyside was not too far away from Wales...

The bosses were well-pleased, all except DI McLaren's new counterpart, aptly named DI Pratt, who had replaced DI Stewart after his move to divisional duties. He had heard all about Jimmy and he didn't like what he heard, nor did he like mixing with neds. He was on a career path which had, at some stage, however fleetingly, required him to show that he spent time as a supervisor in CID. He considered his forte to be administration and training and he never ever had a tout.

Jimmy was by now well-known for clearing crime and he came into conflict with Pratt early on. Pratt invited Jimmy into his office in his first week in post and left him in no doubt that he was his supervisor, and that Jimmy must share his touts with the rest of the CID. As if this wasn't bad enough, he further aggravated Jimmy by telling him that successful crime fighting required a 'team effort and ethos'. Before leaving, Jimmy responded in the only way he could, demanding that the DI tell the rest of the office that it was a team effort.

It was obvious that Pratt would like to see Jimmy take a fall, but Jimmy, being the trainer, would not allow this to happen. He certainly wasn't going to share his touts with anyone - they had been gained after a great deal of hard work, and trust which had had to be earned. He now, somewhat arrogantly, viewed himself like some of his charges, as a winner over both 'course and distance', and Pratt was merely a hurdle he would clear.

On the home front, Doris had given birth to their second child, Stephanie, not that Jimmy had been very involved. He was so engrossed in crime fighting that he missed seeing his child being born, and Doris had been left to look after the children's needs. He was now addicted to crime fighting and too busy managing his stable to notice the folly of his behaviour and the harm he was causing his family with his constant absence.

Sometimes he was brought back to earth when he attended post-mortems, especially ones carried out on children. At times like this it was easy to share a parent's grief and be thankful you weren't in their situation. On many of these occasions Jimmy said a private prayer for the parents of the lost child as well as for his own family. There is no doubt that the reality of death brought him back to his faith, and belief that God had a plan for him. At these times he made a vow to be a better father and husband, though at the back of his mind he still hoped God's plan included his role as a trainer. He partially ameliorated his lack of contribution to family life by telling himself he was doing good for society as a whole, making Newholm a safer place for his kids to grow up in.

If Jimmy was honest with himself he had to admit that he got a great buzz from being a trainer. He wished he could be a normal dad but realised, tragically, he couldn't switch off from looking after his charges and recruiting new ones. Worryingly, he knew that he would slightly bend the rules if it meant getting guilty criminals off the street. Thankfully, and he didn't really know why, on the occasions where he felt it was necessary to step well outside these boundaries something always pulled him back.

He knew this was God in action and he hoped and prayed that, with his help, he could maintain his conscience and work within or only slightly out with the rules of engagement in the war between criminal and cop.

'CAPO'

In Newholm there was a family at the top of the criminal tree whose activities didn't stop with the sons and daughters but extended to include their widowed mother.

Since joining the police, Jimmy had had a lot of contact with this family. In the early days when he was in uniform, his contact with them was through the three sons and two sisters, all of whom were involved in crime from a young age. He regularly attended one of the local secondary schools to interview these kids who were, among other things, extorting money from their peers and breaking into houses. So frequent did these visits become that the school's headmaster, Mr Wallace, often joked with Jimmy and asked him if he was back again to interview the junior Mafia. The majority of the teachers at the school hated this family as they too had become the victims of their crimes. Quite often their cars were vandalised in the school car park or had property stolen from them. Never were there any witnesses to these crimes, though everyone knew who was responsible and, through fear, nobody grassed. Similarly, each time the police arrived at the family home to detain the kids, the mother always had an alibi ready and it was delivered with dog's abuse.

Consequently, most cops dreaded going to their house either to search it or detain family members. Jimmy in fact quite enjoyed it as he saw it as a real challenge or, in other words, yet another hurdle to overcome. There was no doubt the family hated the police, and they never came quietly. Even at nine and ten years of age the kids were organised, worldly-wise and they made sure their peers all adhered to the Mafia code of 'Omerta' by saying and seeing nothing.

As they became teenagers they started committing more serious crimes. Then followed the natural progression to drug-dealing, where profits were greater and the risks of capture were less, especially when no-one was prepared to speak against them in their role as dealers.

One Saturday morning Jimmy was on day shift when, as usual, he went to the cells to help some of his officers fingerprint the large number of people in custody. This was always a good opportunity to speak to the neds and Jimmy, now a Detective Sergeant instructed his staff not to miss these opportunities to recruit new charges. As normal he made sure he always had the 'carrot' of cigarettes and a lighter with him.

This morning in custody there were twelve males, who had been locked up for a variety of crimes. After fingerprinting and photographing eleven and gaining snippets of information in return for a fag, Jimmy went to take the last one from his cell to the fingerprinting and photography room housed in the cell area.

This man in custody was the eldest son of the criminal family. On this occasion, he had been locked up for beating a known drug dealer with a baseball bat, probably as a result of bad debt or because the dealer wasn't adhering to the rules the family had set for operating on their turf.

The drug dealer had sustained some visible injuries but, after a visit to Accident and Emergency at Newholm Hospital, it was confirmed that he had only bruises and no broken bones. He would never have made a complaint against this ned as this was sure to result in more serious injury. When he arrived at the hospital, the police were there on another matter and also an independent witness who was related to him. She was not local to Newholm and was unaware of the influence the family had over the community. She had accompanied the victim in the ambulance after witnessing his assault. Consequently, she had no hesitation in providing a statement for the police even though her relative had pleaded with her not to say anything. He had already made a statement saying that he had been assaulted after bumping into someone in the pub and that he could not identify who had caused his injuries.

Nevertheless, in evidential terms there was now just about enough to arrest this member of the family, and the local cops, who hated him, wasted no time in arresting him, charging him with serious assault and locking him up. In all likelihood the injured dealer would disappear before the trial or retract his statement, and there was no doubt that his female relative would be 'spoken to' and she, too, would not provide evidence. This didn't matter to the local cops because here was an opportunity to get this bastard off the street, albeit temporarily, and they were not going to miss it.

This hatred was mutual, and he deeply loathed the police, who, he felt, had always gone out of their way to arrest him, leaving him with convictions in his younger years for police assault, robbery and a few break-ins. He was now twenty-three years of age and difficult, if not impossible, to catch, especially now that his role was that of orchestrator of serious crime as opposed to hands-on. He liked sneering at the cops as they tried to pin things on him and he wasn't slow to get his solicitor to lodge formal complaints against them. He had learned this was a good tactic to get the police off his back, because the last thing a cop wants is to be under investigation.

As a result, he had only one adult conviction for violence, and the victim who gave evidence against him on this occasion had to leave Newholm in fear for his life. Like the

Mafia, there were very few, if any, witnesses willing to testify against him.

The police had still managed to gather limited intelligence on him, and they knew he ordered crimes to be committed either to pay off debts owed to the family for drugs or for his family's assistance, financial or otherwise. For example, every Monday he would pick up local drug users who owed the family money or favours, and take them to the post office to collect their weekly allowances. He kept the allowance books from week to week and only gave them to the rightful owner to collect the allowances they were due. Once collected, they then handed the books and the allowances to him. Locally this was known as the 'Monday Club' and although a number of people knew about it, no-one complained. It meant for some of these unfortunates that, for the rest of the week, they had no money to live on, let alone feed a drug habit or a child.

The intelligence also indicated that he provided 'options' for some of them in the form of highlighting houses or buildings they could either break-in to or individuals they could rob or, in the case of women, times when they could sell their bodies to repay the debt owed to his family.

Jimmy knew that when the armed robbery figures rose and intelligence indicated local neds were to blame, on most occasions it was the orchestrator who had put them up to it.

Jimmy named him 'Capo'.

Jimmy had known him quite well since he was 13 years-old and, on occasions when he had been caught thieving, sometimes it was Jimmy who dealt with him. As a result of one crime he had committed he had a sort of grudging respect for Jimmy. This crime took place when he was 15 years- old and accompanied by a close criminal associate. Wearing masks and armed with knives, they robbed a courier who was carrying a substantial amount of money for a local bookie. Jimmy was on the scene early and had an inkling of who was responsible, though at that stage he had no evidence. Undeterred, he made contact with a member of his stable whom he had given the name 'Tarnished Beauty'.

He had known Beauty since she was 12years old. She came from a dysfunctional family and both her mother and father were heavily into drink and drugs. She was a bright girl at school and, if she had been given the right support, Jimmy felt she could have had a professional career. He recruited her when she was thirteen, after she provided him with the names of two youths who had robbed her granny in her home. He had tried to keep her on the straight and narrow but it was only months after he recruited her that he learned she had been taking heroin.

You can guess who the supplier was...

She was now hooked and on a downward spiral, where she became more and more subservient to Capo and his family. Jimmy felt for her, and had even managed to get support from a counselling service to deal with her drug problem, in the hope that she would get into rehab. She did receive treatment, but to no avail, and she was now a helpless addict. In the past, even when very young, she had been forced to sell herself to pay the family off for a drugs debt. When she was only 15 years-old Capo used her regularly when she needed heroin but couldn't pay for it with cash...

For Jimmy, dealing with girls of this age brought his own family to mind and he briefly questioned whether or not it was time to get out of this job and do something else. In reality, he knew that he was like Beauty and addicted, though not to heroin but to crime-fighting.

She hated Capo with a vengeance but never showed it because that was where her next fix came from. She did, however, trust Jimmy and was one of very few prepared to say anything about Capo or his family.

On this occasion, when she tipped Jimmy off about Capo's involvement with the robbery, she was terrified of what would happen if it became known that she had grassed, but she wanted revenge on him. To keep her identity secret Jimmy arranged for her to make an anonymous telephone call to the CID office, naming Capo and his buddy as responsible for this crime and requesting that the information be passed to Jimmy.

When he commenced the enquiry he interviewed the courier who had been robbed of the bookmaker's money. He was terrified, and the first thing he said was that he didn't want to go to court and he couldn't identify the men who robbed him as they both wore masks which concealed their faces.

However, Jimmy's tout had learned quite a bit of detail about the robbery, and was able to supply him with specifics which would normally only be known to the culprits. As a result, he detained both Capo and his buddy and he spoke to them independently. He left each of them in a quandary as he was able to describe specifics about the robbery which they felt only they knew. Each was left thinking the other had grassed. This was unnerving for both but especially Capo, because in his mind nobody grassed on him, and that included his buddy. He had now lost control and reckoned there was a likelihood that he would be taking a fall. Just how hard a fall, Jimmy had told them, was up to each of them. They asked to speak to one another, which normally would not be allowed and Jimmy said he couldn't sanction this request. However, he left the trap door on each of their cells down. They were not in adjoining cells and they could only speak to each other if they put their heads through the trap door aperture. They had to raise their voices to be heard and Jimmy was able to listen, covertly, to their conversation.

After some deliberation and threats by Capo against his co-accused, who denied saying anything to the police, they both asked the custody officer if he would contact Jimmy. Jimmy again spoke to them individually and each asked him what would happen if they admitted their involvement. He said if they both admitted their guilt he would try, but couldn't guarantee, to have them put before a lesser court with a maximum sentence of six months. Normally, for a serious crime such as robbery, the culprits would go before the High Court and could receive a hefty sentence. He left them to contemplate this for a short time and thereafter both made statements admitting their involvement.

Jimmy didn't have any witnesses to this crime, and the only evidence he had against them was the word of a tout, which he would not put before the court, and now their own admission. He seriously doubted if their statements alone would be strong enough to convict them. Nonetheless, he would attempt to meet his side of the bargain. Subsequently, and very unethically, he spoke to the duty prosecutor before the court procedures began. He provided her with the details surrounding their detention and arrest and confirmed that he had no independent evidence or witnesses, only their admissions. He told her he feared that if they were put before the High Court they might be given a remand period of three months, but after this the case could be dropped due to a lack of evidence and witnesses. On the other hand, he suggested that if they were put before the lesser court then they were prepared to plead guilty to robbery and could receive the maximum six months sentence. The fiscal even questioned whether there was enough evidence to put them before any court never mind the lesser court, but nonetheless agreed with

Jimmy that having this pair off the street for six months would be a bonus. More importantly, it would leave Capo and his pal, with a conviction for robbery which they would otherwise have avoided. If they were then convicted of anything in the future, this would ensure they were not dealt with leniently.

Consequently, she put them before the lesser court and was really surprised when they both pled guilty. They each received a sentence of six months which was still Capo's only conviction for robbery.

Capo hadn't forgotten this favour that Jimmy had done, and now he was in need of another favour, this time in the form of his liberty. He asked Jimmy what the chances were of him being released on a summons to appear at court at a later date as against turning up at court from police custody, where he might get remanded again. Jimmy promised nothing but said that if he was in a position to clear some serious crime then he would do what he could. Capo had never been known to 'tout' before this and the proposal put him on the spot. After some musing he said he could clear a high-value crime, but Jimmy would have to ensure his involvement and identity remained anonymous.

Well, this was good news, but it also posed a real problem for Jimmy. How could he convince the duty inspector to release somebody with Capo's reputation? Every cop in the division had some experience of dealing with this notorious family, and Capo's release would be met with anger, and questions as to why he was released would be asked. Jimmy knew there would need to be something 'on the table', accompanied by evidence, if he was to be released.

How to achieve this without every cop in the station knowing that Capo had 'fingered' somebody was going to be equally difficult.

Detective Inspector Coulthard from the neighbouring division of Strathsouth had just been promoted to uniform Chief Inspector and Deputy Divisional Commander in Jimmy's division at Newholm. Jimmy knew him well and they had often worked together on crimes that crossed both divisions. Throughout the preceding five years they had sometimes ended up in the High Court as witnesses against neds who carried out cross border crimes. As a result they had mutual respect for each other, even though they were of different ranks. Coulthard knew the score: that to achieve success in solving serious crime you had to negotiate with the neds. This was something he had done in the CID.

Jimmy went to Coulthard's office and asked for a quiet word. He appreciated that, with Coulthard's recent promotion, the last thing he wanted was the reputation of being soft on his local neds and still following the CID practice of negotiating with criminals. His responsibility was now for uniform policing in the division and if he was seen to favour CID then he would make some dangerous enemies. He already had enemies in the division, who thought that they deserved the promotion he achieved and now held a grudge.

Jimmy told him he could clear a lot of crime if Capo was allowed his temporary freedom. He was sure he would supply some information, as his part of the bargain that would clear some high-value crime. The only problem Jimmy could foresee was how to provide a smokescreen for his release, which was dense enough to ensure he was not unearthed as a tout.

Coulthard was well aware of Jimmy's prowess as a detective and also the likelihood that Capo would be able to clear serious crime. He agreed in principle, providing the arrangement with Capo was all it was supposed to be and didn't reflect badly on him. Jimmy thanked him and made haste to converse with his new charge.

Capo said his girlfriend was pregnant and had already been admitted to hospital showing signs of a miscarriage. Thankfully, she was OK and was now back home. With this in mind Capo suggested that his sister should be allowed a visit to him and, between him and his sister, they could formulate a plan where his girlfriend was admitted to hospital displaying worrying signs again. Who could then refuse to grant Capo his temporary release on compassionate grounds to be with the mother of his yet unborn child?

Jimmy accepted that this was a legitimate ground for his release and the plan was put in place.

Once this was arranged Capo told Jimmy where to recover a B.M.W. sports car worth £40,000 and he named the culprits responsible for its theft. However, Capo insisted it should not be recovered until at least three days after his release in order to avoid suspicion that he had grassed. Jimmy agreed and sent DC Green to an old farm barn eight miles from Newholm. The adjacent farmhouse was occupied by some shady carpet dealers and Capo had told Jimmy to be discreet and not to alert the farmhouse occupants.

After some two hours Green radioed back to Jimmy confirming that he had found the stolen car hidden under some straw bales in the barn, and he now had the premises under observation.

Jimmy then went to Coulthard and explained the potential problems with Capo's baby and the recovery of the vehicle. The B.M.W. was, in fact, owned by the Lord Lieutenant of the region, who had been appointed by the Queen, and there would be political 'brownie points' to be gained through its recovery and the arrest of the culprits. This was not lost on Coulthard and, consequently, he agreed to

Capo's release on compassionate grounds.

When the custody sergeant and his cops were informed Capo was being released, as expected there was anger, disbelief, and questions were raised about the new deputy divisional leader.

Jimmy went to Capo with the good news and as with the rest of his stable when he recruited them, he left him in no doubt that he was in his debt. Capo was certainly of classic potential, but Jimmy was under no illusions that he was one charge who would require constant schooling, if, that was, he ever heard from him again.

SELF-PROMOTION?

Jimmy had now been a DS for five years and had helped the CID to clear a number of serious crimes. His reputation as a detective was growing, but somebody somewhere was 'black-balling' him in the promotion stakes. He spoke to DCI Chambers, but he could shed no light on why this might be, nor could DI McLaren. They both said he was more than ready for promotion to Inspector, and his contribution to both the CID and the force in general was exceptional. In addition, his yearly appraisals were consistently given an overall mark of six, with seven being the top mark on the scale. This more than qualified him for inclusion in any promotion panel or for straight promotion, but for some reason Jimmy never got off the starting blocks.

Jimmy frequently thought about his grandfather's and father's advice to him that he had no betters and should always maintain his self-respect. He should be in no doubt that it would be an uphill struggle to beat the class system. He knew they were referring to the inequality of the old class system of bourgeoisie and proletariat class inequality, which now existed under a different guise and categorisation within the police service. He was aware that, with his background, and more recent reputation as a 'bad boy' through being a member of the undisciplined yet necessary evil called the CID, he would be facing an uphill struggle on the police playing field of inequality. In his heart of hearts he felt there was no way he would advance in the service purely on merit.

Nevertheless, he told himself that he would maintain his respect and never become a lackey or a 'yes' man.

The more he thought about promotion, the more he kept thinking about a few high rankers who had achieved their status without ever spending any time as a detective or, indeed, any of their service within the CID. In DS Martin's vocabulary they had 'never seen the whites of a man's eyes', and even more absurd was that some had never been to court. Jimmy knew that they and their cohorts now had a stranglehold on advancement to senior rank. If you weren't one of their 'class', founded on political correctness, image, appearance, and administration ability, then your chances of reaching senior rank were slim. It was obvious to him and any genuine detectives like him, who had to mix with the neds getting their hands dirty, that they were excluded from this group.

This untenable situation was always in the back of Jimmy's mind. He became even more annoyed when thinking about the majority of the public that he had contact with. They all held the view that advancement in the police was related to experience and that experience included detecting crime and dealing effectively with criminals.

If only they knew...

He often tried, unsuccessfully, to put these thoughts to the back of his mind by throwing himself even more enthusiastically into his work. On the few occasions when he wasn't on duty or on call he would try and spend quality time at home with Doris, Derek, and his new daughter Stephanie. This was easier said than done as he found it impossible to unwind and relax. Consequently, he became even more addicted to his 'stable of touts', using the buzz he got from being a tout trainer as a means of blocking out inequality in the police system.

Doris was a very understanding woman and a great mother to their children, but even she was at her wits' end and stumped in her attempts to assuage her husband's addiction and his apparent depression.

Occasionally Jimmy took stock of his situation and thought that maybe he could advance in the service if he adopted a strategy of self-promotion, rendering himself indispensable. He had been exposed to situations where particularly nasty crimes, or crimes where the victim had influence, were not detected quickly. They attracted the most heat from the media and always resulted in poor headlines and questioning of police failures to get early detections. At these times some of the force's senior officers appeared at the CID office, and Jimmy had seen them putting pressure on the DCI to get a result. They never provided any advice on how he was to achieve this, other than what Jimmy believed they had seen on cop programmes.

On reflection, Jimmy found these situations hilarious, but also shocking examples of the managers' naivety. However, when and if these crimes were cleared these same officers were quick to front the media. By being first to notify the victims that their crimes had been solved and the culprit(s) apprehended by their staff, they got themselves in the spotlight.

Their brand of self-promotion appeared to be effective, so Jimmy thought why not him? He would front the media when possible but would, unlike them, not ride on the back of others' endeavours. He would get there on his own merits.

He was now a top tout trainer with almost half of all CID informants in his yard. Arrogantly, he felt that, without him and his touts, crime would get out of hand. The administrators would then feel the heat first-hand and have to deal with it themselves. Jimmy decided that with his strategy for self-promotion with the media and by keeping both local and national politicians updated, he could get himself further up the promotion ladder.

He already knew the local MP quite well, and had given him some advice when his son began running with the wrong crew and ended up being detained by the police. At that time he had given this teenager a good fright by telling him he knew, which he did, about the soft drugs he was misusing and who was supplying him. This knowledge left the son in a state of shock and deeply worried about what would happen if it wound up in the public domain. The source of Jimmy's information was a tout who knew a lot about the MP's son's pals, and once Jimmy had received this information he wasn't slow to let them know they could be locked up whenever he felt like it. After receiving this advice they stopped mixing with the MP's son, who complied fully with Jimmy's wishes and turned over a new leaf. It appeared to the father that his son was now both respectful and reliable. The MP told Jimmy he couldn't believe the change in his son and, although he neither knew nor wanted to know how Jimmy had achieved this, he would always be in his debt.

He was also well-acquainted with three local reporters, two of whom worked for the local newspapers, the other a free-lancer. These reporters were aware of his success on the crime front and regularly contacted him looking for stories and progress reports. Obviously, Jimmy decided what information he would release and when, and this was always founded on what assistance they could offer him to benefit his specific investigations. He knew they needed him more than he needed them and this he used to his advantage. Nevertheless, they could prove to be of great benefit to him when incorporated into his self-promotion strategy.

At the start of his sixth year as Detective Sergeant, a fatal fire occurred in Newholm where the victim was a 70 year-old spinster who happened to be the sister of the town's Provost and one of the main sponsors of the local MP. The lady lived on her own in a five bedroom, detached sandstone villa in a quiet residential street. Her parents before her had owned property in the town centre and overseas, and she was known to be a wealthy woman.

This had not been missed by some neds, and Jimmy had heard from Capo about six months previously that two local criminals Jimmy knew very well had 'cased' the place. They had heard the old woman kept some very expensive jewellery and a substantial amount of cash in the house. Apparently, it was well-known that she did not trust banks and it was rumoured that she kept at least £10,000 in a safe on the ground floor.

After completing their reconnaissance the pair enlisted the help of two Glasgow neds they had met in Barlinnie Prison in Glasgow. Their plan, thereafter, involved breaking into the old woman's house, tying her up and threatening her until she opened the safe and gave them the money and jewellery.

Jimmy contacted the old lady and the Provost and ensured they had substantial security installed in her house. Two senior officers from Headquarters who were on the self-promotion trail, were aware of the woman and the influence her family carried. Subsequently, after being briefed by Jimmy about this proposed robbery they left their offices and ventured outside to visit her. Once there they made sure she was supplied with extra police security alarms and assured her that the police would check on her and her house every day.

Both left cards with their details before they left.

In the meantime, Jimmy brought the two neds who had, allegedly, been casing the house, into the station for a 'friendly chat' at which he told them he knew of their plans. Of course they denied it, but Jimmy left them in no doubt that if anything happened to this old woman or her property then they would be his first port of call and, once detained, they wouldn't be leaving. They had heard of his reputation for dogged determination and, for the next six months, there was no activity in or around the old lady's home.

However, complacency eventually set in and the senior officers, who had initially reassured this old woman, instructed that all the police security alarms and checks now be withdrawn.

Two weeks later, at about three in the morning a neighbour noticed smoke billowing from the old lady's bedroom and heard the sound of glass smashing. She raised the alarm and, on arrival, police and fire crews found that a ground floor window had been smashed and somebody had used the opening to lift the interior window lock and enter the house. Using breathing apparatus, the firemen forced entry to the house and extinguished the flames emanating from the elderly lady's bedroom on the first floor. It would later be confirmed that the fire was started deliberately and an accelerant had been used to hasten its spread. After putting out the fire they carried out a search of the bedroom and found the spinster dead in her bed. She was bound and gagged, and a further search of the house revealed a combination safe lying open in a room on the ground floor.

This was now a CID matter and DCI Chambers was called.

After ensuring the crime scene was preserved and contained by uniform cops, he contacted the fiscal, who arranged for Professor Browning, an experienced pathologist, to attend. In the meantime, a scenes of crime team, DI McLaren and Jimmy made their way to the house. On their arrival, Chambers appointed DI McLaren Senior Investigating Officer and Jimmy as his Deputy. He then informed the force control room staff that they were dealing with a murder and that the senior police officer on call should be notified. After giving the pathologist what little information he had, he briefed McLaren and Jimmy on the requirements for a major crime administration team, crime scene manager, an enquiry team of detectives and a forensic scientist. During this hectic initial stage he was joined by Chief Superintendent Scott, the senior officer on call.

Scott was one of the officers who had decided to withdraw the police checks at the house. He was only twenty-nine years of age, had no investigative experience and all his promotions had been fast-tracked. He had never been in CID and had spent little time on the street. His experience was gained through stints in personnel, administration and training departments, and being a 'batman' or staff officer to one of the two assistant chief constables.

Jimmy considered him an administrator in the true sense of the word, though Scott thought he knew about crime investigation, and offered advice to Chambers on how to tackle this enquiry. Jimmy thought that it had not dawned on him the amount of flak that would follow from dropping the surveillance on the house, but that was a matter for him. Anyway, thought Jimmy, the last thing Chambers needed was advice from this particular officer. Chambers was well aware that the 'shit was going to hit the fan' and, more than likely, he would be the one taking the heat. As Jimmy had expected, Scott's advice went in one ear and out the other. The reality of the situation was that Chambers, McLaren and Jimmy all knew they would be the ones who would be under pressure to get an early result for this despicable crime.

The forensic scientist, two scenes of crime officers and the crime scene manager, who was one of Jimmy's fellow DS's and who had undergone specialist forensic training, were all fully kitted out with specialist suits to prevent contaminating the scene. Once inside, they were able to confirm the findings of the fire service team, and the crime scene manager used a camcorder to record the scene inside the house and would later show the recording to the detectives at the briefing.

Professor Browning examined the body and confirmed she was dead. He noted the victim's hands had been bound with Scotch Tape and she had bruising on her forearms and throat. Though she was a frail old woman it looked like she had been roughly treated by her attackers and died when her throat had been compressed.

At the request of the DCI the local fiscal attended the briefing.

Chambers knew it was good practice to have the prosecutor at the scene as early as possible, as it meant they had a flavour for the nastiness of the crime, and would pull out all the stops to help the investigating detectives with legal advice. This fiscal, Mr Leigh, was old school and he and Chambers, although widely experienced, both shared revulsion for crimes of this nature. Accordingly, Leigh would become part of the team and, as long as the detectives didn't keep him in the dark, pull any strokes, or take legal short cuts, he would take great delight in helping to prosecute those responsible. As the briefing ended, Scott appeared again and stressed to the troops that it was their duty to get the culprits for this crime without delay.

After the briefing the CID staff were split into teams for door-to-door enquiries, intelligence gathering, interviewing witnesses and preparing a 'time-line' detailing the old lady's last known movements. In addition, specialist search teams, assisted by search dogs, were given the task of carrying out a fingertip search of the house and surrounding area. Good practice stipulated that detectives focus on events before, during and after a crime, and this tactic was a crucial aspect of the strategy drawn up by McLaren and recorded in the senior investigator's policy book. This would show the decisions taken during the investigation, when they were taken, and the justification for taking them. In Jimmy's view the policy book was one of the few positives to come out of the Murder Manual, an English police publication. It had been adopted by the Scottish police and Jimmy felt it portrayed the investigation of murders as an easy to follow, tick-box procedure. He and seasoned detectives knew that murder investigations were individual in nature and, although you could tick the boxes in the various sections of the manual to show you had completed necessary procedures, this did not allow for individualism. Nor did it differentiate between detectives who wanted to get a result and others, whose main concern was to show they had ticked all the boxes and could therefore withstand any subsequent review of their investigation.

Once the body had been removed under escort from the house to the local mortuary, then Chambers, McLaren, Jimmy, the fiscal and Professor Browning attended the post-mortem. The examination was to be conducted by Professor Browning assisted by Doctor McEwan, a local pathologist from the hospital at Newholm, thus meeting the Scots Law requirement for corroboration. Post-mortems are a dirty part of a detective's job, but Jimmy had been present at twenty and had the stomach for it. For Jimmy, this post mortem would confirm just what sort of bastards they were dealing with.

After the PM, the Professor was able to say that the old lady's throat had been compressed and that strangulation was the cause of death. In addition, he had found five bruises on her right arm and three on her left, suggesting she had been roughly handled. Leaving the mortuary, Jimmy received a call from a local free-lance reporter, Dave Armstrong, followed shortly thereafter by calls from the two local journalists, Jamie Kerr and Tom Buchan. All were now on the trail of this horrible crime, which was of even more interest to them, considering the victim was well-known in the community. They wanted the inside line and confirmation that the old lady had been strangled, neither of which Jimmy would offer. He did say, however, that their assistance would be needed to help find witnesses and that their help would be reciprocated.

DC Green had been given the task of obtaining further information about the crime scene, and he was able to confirm that the safe had been opened using the correct code. This indicated that the old woman had passed on the code to her attackers before they killed her and set the place alight. Speaking to the Provost, he had learned that approximately £8,000 and identifiable jewellery, in particular a ruby and emerald necklace valued at £10,000, had been stolen. The Provost told McLaren he had always warned his sister against keeping money and valuables in the house, but she was stubborn and would not listen.

CID bosses know that investigations of this nature can become protracted and costly. McLaren was more aware than most, as the Senior Investigating Officer, that he would have to work to a budget, and there was every likelihood he would need Chambers' support to lobby the bosses, including Chief Superintendent Scott, for sufficient funds. Jimmy, being a bit of a cynic, felt this would be difficult as Scott, and some, though not all, of his cohorts had never been a senior investigating officer. In Jimmy's biased opinion, Scott expected that neds who had committed nasty crimes like this, would surrender themselves to ease their conscience or possibly 'fall out of trees with their hands up'. Jimmy's CID bosses, and Jimmy himself, knew differently.

It wasn't long before McLaren was asking Jimmy to contact his touts and see if they could provide an inside line. Jimmy, firstly contacted Capo, who denied any knowledge of the crime. However, after a covert meeting where some of its horrific nature was discussed, Capo said he would put some feelers out and get back to Jimmy. Even neds as violent and nasty as Capo have a degree of revulsion when it comes to the unprovoked and brutal murder of the elderly.

A major crime administration team had been set up and the slog of door to door enquiries began, along with appeals for witnesses, and trawling through criminal intelligence, both locally and with other forces.

By now the press were hot on the detectives' heels and Mclaren and Jimmy were receiving calls from the three journalists, all of which they were ignoring. Chief Superintendent Scott, for some reason, didn't want to front the media just now and it was left to DCI Chambers to take a grilling at briefings with TV, radio and press. On each occasion he was asked about the nature of the old lady's injuries but refused to confirm any details which would prejudice the investigation or cause stress or trauma to her family.

Jimmy, being a bit insular, was glad the CID were left to get on with it without any internal interference, especially now when there were no good news stories to be told. This suited Jimmy's bosses, but it still didn't stop some of those higher up in the force demanding constant updates on the state of the investigation and pressuring the CID officers to get a result.

At one of the subsequent briefings there was feedback

from the intelligence section showing three Glasgow neds, each with some 'form', living in Newholm and working as sub-contractors, completing road repairs in the town. Intelligence confirmed they had been mixing with local neds and were alleged to be using and selling hash, speed and coke. Far more interesting for Jimmy was the fact they had been seen in Capo's company and at his home address.

Immediately after the briefing Jimmy contacted Capo again and told him to meet right away at their usual place. Jimmy arrived first, followed shortly thereafter by his charge, and it wasn't too long into the conversation before he raised the issue of the Glaswegians and their contact with him.

For the first time in his meetings with Capo, Jimmy could see he was really troubled. He asked Jimmy where the Glasgow neds were featuring in the investigation and Jimmy, using his gut instinct, told him they were the main suspects. He then told Capo he knew he had been in their company and that whoever was involved in any aspect of this crime was going down for murder. Capo paused for a while and said he got to know these Glaswegians through a cousin of his and it was obvious that they were active on the crime front. They had been at his house on two or three occasions for a drink and, on the last occasion, one of them said he had a bit of 'hot gear' which needed hidden for a short period before it could be sold on.

Capo didn't ask any questions about where it came from but said he would hold it for him.

The Glaswegian then borrowed a screwdriver from Capo and hid the bag containing the jewellery under the floorboards in the toilet of Capo's house. Capo was quick to realise that he could be in deep shit as he now had some jewellery which probably came from a murder victim. However, he insisted he didn't know if it came from the old woman as none of the Glaswegians mentioned the murder. Jimmy told him it looked like he had a lot of explaining to do. If he didn't come on board then he was finished and would have to take his chances in court. So he had a choice of either handing over the jewellery or being charged with murder, or with being an accessory to murder.

While pressurising Capo, Jimmy's mind was working overtime, and he was thinking that, if it proved to be the old lady's jewellery, then he would need to arrange for its legitimate recovery. Capo might have to say where he got it from and become a witness. Capo had already said that this would pose him a real problem, and not just for his reputation, because these Glasgow neds were well-connected, with friends who had shooters and took no prisoners. However, Jimmy left him in no doubt as to what the alternative would be if he didn't hand over the jewellery. Capo indicated that he understood.

Jimmy then asked him to confirm if the jewellery was in a container or bag and he said it was in a clear, polythene bag. It was hidden under the floorboards in his toilet by one of the Glasgow neds, and he had never handled the bag or opened it to inspect it closely.

Between the legal ramifications of the recovery and keeping his tout out of the investigative loop, Jimmy needed to confide in a boss, but which one? After mulling it over, he chose to tell both DCI Chambers and DI McLaren, though withholding the name of the tout. When he told them about the circumstances surrounding the recovery of the jewellery they, too, knew it would be a problem ensuring that neither the tout nor Jimmy appeared in court as a witness. That said, they both agreed that nothing was more important than getting these bastards for the murder. They confirmed they would support Jimmy but the tout would have to take his chances.

Jimmy was eighty per cent sure the jewellery belonged to the old lady, but he needed to recover it and have it positively identified. To achieve all of these things, the three detectives knew, would mean having to slightly bend the rules. Jimmy, although thankful for his bosses' support, felt that his position was almost now as uncomfortable as Capo's. It was time for some serious thought about placing this level of trust in a tout, something which his bosses had insisted was a recipe for disaster, but what was the alternative?

Jimmy said a silent prayer, trusting that God would somehow help him out of this awkward position. Surely, he thought, support would be forthcoming when you considered the severity of the crime.

At his next meeting with Capo, Jimmy asked him who else was privy to the fact that he had the jewellery, to which he said only his girlfriend. This didn't help, and Jimmy was still left with the problem of recovering the jewellery without putting Capo in to the category of a witness and also exposing him as the tout. Even if he did come up with a solution, Capo still stood a chance of being charged with resetting the property, being an accessory to murder or murder itself. His involvement meant there was even a chance he could be murdered..

This was a dilemma for a trainer...

Jimmy asked him again if he had handled the bag containing the jewellery. Capo categorically denied it and said he hadn't touched it, that one of the Glasgow neds had put it under the floorboards, not him.

Then it struck Jimmy. Get Capo to move the bag with the jewellery to a field near his house, making sure he had no unprotected contact with it. Thereafter, Capo, on Jimmy's instruction, would make an anonymous telephone call to the police from a public call box, stating that he had seen someone acting suspiciously and dumping a bag in the field. Once the bag with the jewellery had been recovered, Capo could explain to the Glasgow neds that he had been visited by the CID and, fearing a house 'turn', had hidden their booty in the field. His story thereafter would be that somebody must have seen him hiding it and contacted the police.

Jimmy wasn't sure that this would work, but discussed it with his CID. Bosses, and they all agreed it was the only course of action left to them if they were to clear this crime. Jimmy contacted Capo again and ensured that he knew exactly what his instructions were and left him in no doubt that, even if he followed this plan, there was no guarantee he would avoid charges. That said, this plan should at least afford some protection against the Glasgow neds...Capo confirmed that he understood and would stick rigidly to the plan.

Jimmy prayed that when the bag and jewellery were recovered they would be identified as belonging to the murder victim. Hopefully, they would contain some forensic evidence which tied the Glasgow neds into the murder. Jimmy was well aware that, if his involvement in the recovery became known, he would have a lot of explaining to do. He could find himself subject to an internal investigation and, if Capo's prints were on the bag, he could be in the dock and would be relying on Jimmy to be a witness on his behalf. Whichever way you looked at it, it meant trouble.

Jimmy hoped God was on his side.

The next day an anonymous call was made to Newholm Police Station stating that a man, not further described (NFD) was acting suspiciously in the field near Capo's home. The caller said it looked like he was dumping something in the neighbouring field, which might be of interest to the police.

Two uniform cops went along to the field and easily found the bag containing the jewellery. Being forensically aware and well-briefed on the on-going murder enquiry, they left it untouched and contacted DI McLaren, who recovered it and brought it back to the CID office.

Contact was then made with the provost and another relative of the murder victim, both of whom positively identified the jewellery as belonging to the old woman.

Now it was time for Jimmy to sweat.

After the jewellery was identified, some staff higher up the force started to hover, but Jimmy's CID bosses kept his involvement in the investigation concealed from them. Everyone, though none more than Jimmy, was now waiting for the result of the forensic examination.

God must have been on Jimmy's side as, two days after the recovery, the forensic lab and Identification Bureau in Glasgow rang DI McLaren, and confirmed that one of the Glasgow neds' fingerprints were on the bag. He was a well-known face in Glasgow's criminal fraternity and had recently escaped an attempted murder charge on a technicality. In addition, DNA belonging to a second member of the Glasgow three was found on two pieces of the jewellery. He, too, was no stranger to the law and had recently completed a nine-year sentence for armed robbery. There was no DNA or fingerprints found that related to Capo.

DCI Chambers was delighted when he learned of these identifications and made plans to detain the three Glasgow neds. With the identifications supplemented by quite a bit of local drugs intelligence against these three, they now had justification for both their detention and search of their flat in Newholm.

On Chambers' instruction Jimmy took no part in the investigation.

During a thorough search by a specially trained police team at the neds' address, a quantity of cocaine with a street value of £10,000 was found inside two light sockets. The litter bins both inside and outside the house were searched and all the floorboards were uplifted, though nothing further was found. Nevertheless, with the drugs recovered, the CID officers had enough to detain these three neds for possession with intent to supply Class 'A' drugs. They were duly taken to Newholm Police Station and interviewed by detectives about the recovery of the cocaine.

All three were subsequently arrested and charged with possession with intent to supply.

In keeping with their reputation in police circles as 'Dog Tag Men', the accused would tell the police nothing other than their name, date of birth and address. During the interview they remained cocky, obviously thinking they were dealing with 'country cousin' cops.

However, this changed when they were interviewed a second time, this time for the murder and theft from the old lady. Once the first ned was interviewed, he was shown the jewellery and questioned about why his fingerprints had been found on the bag containing the jewellery. He knew he was now in a difficult position so decided to play the percentage game by getting in first with his version of events. He wasted no time telling the officers he had been the look-out for the break-in but hadn't been a part of anything else. It was, apparently, his two compatriots who entered the house of the old lady and returned with money and jewellery. He even offered to hand over his share of the money and told the officers where his two co -accused had stashed their share.

DCI Chambers and DI McLaren, who had been remotely monitoring this interview were cock-a-hoop and immediately recovered the stolen money identified by the first interviewee.

This money, details of where it was recovered, and the jewellery was then presented to the two remaining suspects at their respective interviews. Surprisingly, their bottle crashed too, and lo and behold all three had been look-outs on the job. They incriminated each other and, with DNA and fingerprints, the recovery of the jewellery, the money and their admissions, there was more than enough evidence to convict them.

When the case went to trial at the High Court in Edinburgh the strategy of impeachment was put forward by each of the QCs representing them. The jury believed none of it and they were all convicted of murder, the break-in and possession with intent to supply Class 'A' drugs. Each received the mandatory life sentence with a recommendation from the Judge that they should each spend at least eighteen years in custody before being considered for release.

Neither Jimmy nor Capo was called as a witness, which was a great relief to both.

Equally importantly, the Glasgow neds bought Capo's story at their de-brief in prison, and no fingers were ever pointed at him. DCI Chambers received some plaudits but had difficulty fronting the media because this was now a good news story. Chief Superintendent Scott, since the time these three men had been arrested, had been in contact with the media, holding regular briefings stressing how well 'his' officers had performed and reaffirming how safe a community Newholm was.

To his credit, the DCI had spoken on a one-to-one basis with the MP and provost, and had let them know, though avoiding any detail, that without Jimmy's help the case would never have been solved so quickly. Both men already held Jimmy in high regard and this was sure to further enhance his reputation with them. They told Chambers that in future discussions with the Chief Constable, Jimmy's contribution, not just to them and their family but also the local community, would not be understated. DCI Chambers fed this back to Jimmy, who was pleased, though even more-so because he hadn't been called as a witness and Capo's involvement had remained secret.

On the home front Doris had gone quiet, which was no wonder considering Jimmy was engrossed in his work, spending little time with her or the children. His life was managing his 'stable of touts' and getting that adrenalin rush when he got to the bottom of a crime. It never dawned on him that his lack of attention might encourage Doris to leave him to his obsession and, along with their children, start a new life away from him and his touts.

Things would have no doubt deteriorated to such a stage more quickly had Jimmy not been taken aside one day by McLaren. The DI told him he didn't know how to put it, but there was no easy way of telling him that Doris's loneliness and subsequent vulnerability had been noticed by a uniform Sergeant in Newholm. Apparently he had been calling in at Jimmy's house while he was on late shifts. McLaren said he didn't know how often this had happened but stories were now making their way up from the shop floor, which was no surprise, considering Sergeant Breen, who had a reputation as a womaniser and sexual predator, was the one making the house calls.

Jimmy's force was relatively small with an establishment of only one thousand police officers but it had a terrible reputation within its own community and in police circles for officers having affairs and 'playing away from home'. The divorce and separation rates were high and the reputation of the force was suffering. The old discipline codes based on duty, ethics, and morality, where miscreants could be disciplined for bringing the force into disrepute or for behaving in a manner unbecoming of a police officer, were hardly ever invoked now.

That said, there had still been a lot of internal movement sanctioned by the force to distance the 'bad boys' from their prey, and this was in the form of a transfer. It was still protected by a clause, signed by all officers when they joined the police, which agreed that they would serve anywhere in the force. The bosses really had no other means of dealing with these officers, and they usually disguised the real reason for a transfer, branding it an opportunity to broaden an officer's experience.

Subsequently, a number of officers were having their experience 'broadened' in places resembling the outback, where potential female victims were not so easily identified. To date, the force had been unable to pin anything on Breen, probably because he was being protected by relatives in high places. However, there was little doubt that he was 'at it'.

When Jimmy learned of his visits to Doris he lost the place, stormed out the office and headed home. Livid, he kicked his front door in. Doris rushed to see what was happening and found him red-faced and standing in the hall. He made his way over to her and when they were almost nose to nose, he asked her, "what the fuck's going on?" Stricken by his anger, she asked him what he was on about. He immediately confronted her about Breen visiting her at home while he was at work.

Doris said he had only been around twice and the visits only lasted ten minutes at most. Each time he said he happened to be nearby and had heard that she was experiencing difficulties, which he understood only too well. Bringing up children on her own while Jimmy was so dedicated to his work must be difficult. She said Breen was extremely courteous and told her that she and Jimmy needed to get out more. He mentioned some social events that were coming up that he intended to attend with his girlfriend. He promised that, when the events were due, he and his girlfriend would arrive unannounced at her home, with a baby sitter and offer to take Doris and Jimmy along. Jimmy would then be left in position where he would feel obliged to join them and this would get Doris out of the house for a wee while.

After hearing the story Jimmy asked Doris if she was stupid. Why had Breen not spoken to him, and why had she not told him about the visits? Doris replied that Breen was only in the house for a short time and had asked her to keep the details of his plan secret from Jimmy to ensure the element of surprise. Anyway, he was offering to socialise with both of them, not just her. Jimmy asked her again why Breen never mentioned anything to him, to which Doris just shrugged her shoulders. She then said the kids had been with her on both occasions that Breen had visited and there was nothing going on between them. Meekly, she explained that he seemed to be trying to help both of them to get out more which might bring a bit of relief, especially when he had not conversed with her in weeks. Lastly, she told him that she was far from stupid, and would not dream of getting involved with Breen or any other man and, despite his lack of attention towards her and his children, she still loved him.

Jimmy like most real detectives was suspicious of everybody and Doris was not exempt from his suspicion. However, he had to believe her. He had to admit that some of what she said was true; he had hardly been at home, and even when he was he spoke very little to Doris.

He was totally surprised by his next reaction.

He broke down and wept and apologised to her. Looking at her now he could see how selfish he had been and also how beautiful his wife was. He asked for her forgiveness and promised that he would change. Doris was as relieved as him, because in truth she had considered leaving him, though not for another man but to bring Jimmy to his senses and see what he was missing. As a result they spent that night as close physically and emotionally to each other as they had been for years.

Jimmy, however, was not about to let things go with Breen. He knew that Breen's offer to Doris to attend a 'social function' with him and his girlfriend was just a front. He could see it now. He would have arrived to pick up Doris when he knew Jimmy was working and with an excuse that his girlfriend couldn't make it. He'd then offer to take Doris to a function if she could arrange a babysitter or comfort her in her own home and chance his luck.

When he was back at work McLaren asked him how things were at home. Jimmy replied that they were okay and thanked McLaren again for letting him know about Breen. The DI told Jimmy not to do anything stupid with regard to Breen, especially now that it looked as though Jimmy was up for promotion. Jimmy said he would not jeopardise that, even though he felt like ripping Breen's head off.

Unknown to McLaren, Jimmy had a plan in place for Breen which would probably require, yet again, the assistance of a tout from his stable.

After finding out that Breen was working the late shift, Jimmy sat in an overspill car park near the police station, which some of the cops used. For some reason this was not covered by CCTV and was poorly lit. Having identified Breen's car, he waited in the darkness.

After a short time he caught a glimpse of Breen leaving the station and chatting up a young impressionable-looking female officer. They walked to the car park and Jimmy overheard Breen telling her to drive to a pub some three miles from the station. Breen then made his way jauntily to his own car just as the young female drove away. Breen and this female had been the last two on the shift to enter the car park and as he opened the driver's door of his vehicle he felt a tap on his shoulder. When he turned around he saw a calm and controlled Jimmy. A shocked Breen was expecting a smack on the mouth.

Jimmy asked him how his social calendar was looking, and a shaking Breen said he didn't know what he was talking about. Jimmy then put his arm round his shoulder and told him he would look after his wife's social activities without any help from him. He then asked Breen if he understood. The Sergeant couldn't get the words out and could only nod his head.

Jimmy said goodnight, and a thankful Breen hoped that that was the end of the matter. Perhaps this 'hard man', Jimmy, was going soft or was fearful of upsetting his career plans and of the influence Breen had at senior levels. He breathed a sigh of relief and drove to meet his new lady friend, thinking that was the last he'd see of Doris.

Breen should never have underestimated Jimmy...

Nervous Boy had been released from prison and Jimmy had not waited long before making contact with him to remind him of the favours he owed now he was a lifetime member of his stable. Jimmy was well aware that, during one of their earliest meetings, Nervous had told him that a cop named Breen was 'knocking off' a young female hash user, and that he was using as well. At the time Jimmy was sceptical about the accuracy of this information, and decided to keep it to himself until some of his other charges or Nervous could confirm it. Then he might have to do something about it but it would need to be one hundred per cent accurate before he took any action.

Jimmy now reconsidered this and, in his next meeting with Nervous, he asked if Breen was still seeing this woman. Nervous confirmed that he was, and that the girl was so naïve that she was bragging about it to anyone who would listen. As a result, some of the local drug dealers were putting plans in motion to 'set up' Breen and blackmail him into tipping them off about what the police were planning.

Jimmy couldn't believe his luck and he was sure now that if he played his cards right he could get Breen out of the picture, and perhaps even save him from becoming a charge in a ned's tout stable, not that Breen deserved any such kindness. He told Nervous to do a bit of digging and find out where Breen usually met the woman.

A week later Nervous phoned Jimmy with the news that Breen and the girl usually met on a Friday evening, in a one bedroom flat owned by the girl's cousin, also a drug user. He confirmed that some of the local drug dealers were closing in on Breen and he would soon be trapped into supplying them with information.

Jimmy told Nervous that the following Friday, once it was confirmed that Breen was in the flat, he should make a call to the CID and ask for DC Green. He could then tell Green that drugs were being used in the flat, and Green would ensure the caller's anonymity.

For the plan to work DC Green had to be expecting the call and needed to know if there was any other drug use in this flat. This was not difficult, as both the girl's cousin and the flat were known to the police for drug use.

The following Friday DC Green, who had been well briefed by Jimmy, received the call. There was sufficient intelligence for the drugs squad to get a warrant and make a move on the flat.

Breen was suitably astonished when the front door was kicked in and he was found in bed with the young lady. Fortunately for him, he was not in possession of hash, but the female was, and another half kilo of 'black' was found in the toilet.

Both were detained for possession with intent to supply drugs and taken to Newholm Police Station. Breen now had a lot of explaining to do, though luckily for him his girlfriend accepted ownership of the drugs and didn't incriminate him.

Nevertheless, he was finished, and the best he could hope for was a transfer. Even that would only happen after consideration was taken by the Crown on whether or not to prosecute him for his involvement in the bust. At best, he would be a witness in a drugs case which would disclose publicly his involvement with drugs and drug abusers, and he would definitely be subject of disciplinary proceedings. His reputation was in tatters, and no honest cop would want to be involved with another cop, let alone a sergeant, who was using drugs and associating with druggies.

Breen was suspended from duty for over a year before it was decided not to prosecute him. He appeared before a disciplinary hearing and, without any assistance from those with 'pull', he lost his rank and was subject to transfer to the 'outback'.

Jimmy had no sympathy for him. He was a disgrace to the police and a predator. If Jimmy hadn't acted then Breen would have been in the pockets of the drug dealers, causing more harm. Breen knew better than anyone that he was lucky to keep his job, but he would never learn of Jimmy's role in both his demise and inadvertent rescue.

The other benefit for Jimmy along with quite a few other married officers, and for the reputation of the force, was that Breen became a recluse with little interest in women.

Unsurprisingly he resigned from the force a year later.

After the disciplinary hearing Jimmy was summoned to the Chief Constable and told he was being promoted to the rank of Detective Inspector in Newholm. His first thoughts were for his close friend and boss DI McLaren, and he wondered what was happening to him if he was taking his post. The chief reassured him and said he already had a meeting with DI McLaren that morning and he too was being promoted to the rank of chief inspector in the neighbouring division. Jimmy was now in the dichotomous position of losing a good ally and able detective through taking the position himself. He had mixed feelings but knew that movement in police circles is inevitable and he was advancing in his preferred field.

Jimmy was left thinking, contrary to what his father and grandfather thought, that perhaps you could get promoted on merit after all. He had already achieved the rank of sergeant after his father had said he would always be a constable: now he was to be an inspector.

At the meeting he had been surprised at how much the chief knew about him and his forte for crime-fighting. However, he wasn't surprised to hear that the chief had also had his ear 'nipped' by both the local MP and the provost. Jimmy's strategy of self-promotion seemed to be working, even if his method involved risks, none more than working with touts.

On his return to the CID office he went straight to DI McLaren, shook hands with him and congratulated him on his promotion. McLaren did likewise, then Jimmy asked him why he didn't tell him about the promotion before now. He said the chief had sworn him to secrecy until both had received news of their promotion.

They were joined by DCI Chambers and DI Stewart,

who took it in turns to congratulate them both. Chambers then told McLaren how much he would be missed and, in turn, how much was expected of Jimmy.

Before departing the office for a neighbouring hostelry Jimmy phoned Doris and told her he was now DI McBurnie. The title fell easily from his lips. Doris was delighted at this news and asked him when he would be home to celebrate. He said, out of courtesy, he was going for one drink with McLaren and most of the office, but he wouldn't be too late. Detectives are hopeless at time-keeping especially when it involves leaving a pub, and Jimmy was no different, even when he had such a close call in the incident involving Breen.

He staggered in the front door carrying a bunch of flowers at midnight. Derek and Stephanie were in bed and Doris merely gave Jimmy a knowing look, told him his supper was in the kitchen and went to bed.

Jimmy was left on his own feeling slightly nauseous, still well under the influence of alcohol and somewhat bemused. However, it didn't stop him from opening a bottle of whisky and toasting his father and grandfather, with the good news they never expected to hear. Jimmy then made a vow to them that he would continue to follow what he saw as the socialist principles of equality and honesty, though admittedly with a slight twist when he needed to capture really bad neds.

The next morning at work he was still nursing a hangover with a cup of coffee and a pang of conscience about the previous nights activities. He decided to go to the nearest travel agent and book a fortnight's holiday in Spain for the family. This would be a surprise for Doris and the kids, as would the meal he had booked that weekend for them both, and his gift of a sapphire necklace.

He hadn't told anyone in police circles, but after the incident with Breen he had spoken to his old minister. The minister was now retired but still delighted to hear that Jimmy's marriage was back on solid ground, and that he was now DI McBurnie. As usual, he received good advice and they prayed together, asking God to watch over Jimmy and his family. Jimmy left the meeting feeling uplifted. His promotion had not been on his radar at this time but with hindsight he was now convinced that God was indeed watching over him and had a plan for him. That, he told himself, was why he hadn't heeded his father's and grandfather's advice about joining the police nor had he packed in the police college or, for that matter, followed ex DS Martin too closely.

Back in the office, he received a number of phone calls from other officers who had now heard about his promotion. The first to call was Martin who told him he had been a good apprentice and he had always expected Jimmy to get on. Jimmy was pleased to hear from him. Martin was due to retire soon and was happy that Jimmy would continue fighting the 'war'.

In his new position, Jimmy took with him his 'stable of touts', comprising some novice charges who showed good potential and some classic contenders like Hasty Lad, Capo, Nervous Boy, Wise Archie, Chocolate Treat, Golden Lady, Welsh Rarebit and, potentially, Tarnished Beauty.

All were, in his mind, like thoroughbred racehorses for whom he had the utmost respect, capable of winning in style and producing results. He knew that, with care and handling, they could achieve success, but they needed constant attention. The main differences between racehorses and his charges, were that his charges could refuse to run and could leave the stable.

They all had their own motives for being members of the stable and, as a result, they required meticulous monitoring, reprimanding and schooling.

That said, they each one had proved invaluable to him, and Jimmy, as their trainer, accepted that the problems they brought were part of training and handling touts.

At this stage he thought it would be prudent to do a review of his charges and check their 'form' via both the national and local criminal intelligence systems.

As expected, this research showed there was intelligence submitted by other cops against nearly all stable members: none more-so than Capo and Wise Archie, but there was not enough to arrest any of them for any specific crimes. Their criminal activity still worried him, but he knew he was unable to diminish their involvement in crime. Anyway, only through their contact with crime and criminals could Jimmy stay in touch with crime in Newholm.

He made arrangements to meet them all in the first week after his promotion and gave them the official line, as he had done when he first recruited them: they were not immune from prosecution. If they committed a crime, he told them, they were on their own, and not protected by him. As expected, they all claimed they were not committing any offences, but he knew differently and in truth expected no other response. What they didn't seem to realise was that the composition of his stable wasn't static and that Jimmy was regularly recruiting other up and coming touts who were telling him and other cops about their activities. This access to new informants gave him increased control and put him in a position where a 'charge' could be removed and a replacement allocated a stall.

Such is the life of a tout trainer...

The media had been notified of Jimmy's promotion and it wasn't long before three local reporters were calling him, offering to take him out for a meal and a drink to celebrate his good news. Jimmy always declined because the last thing he wanted was to become part of their stable of sources. He would hold the 'trainer's licence' and control them, just like his charges, by feeding them what he wanted, when he wanted, and always to benefit of his investigation.

During the summer Jimmy and his family went to Spain and enjoyed a fortnight in the sun. The holiday brought him and Doris closer and gave him an opportunity to become a bigger part of his children's lives. That said, even in Spain he was receiving calls to his mobile from some of his touts and the CID.

One of the calls in the second week of the holiday was from DCI Chambers, who said that while Jimmy had been on holiday there had been a murder in Newholm. Chambers apologised for interrupting his holiday but, with a shortage of information about the murder coming in, he needed Jimmy to make contact with his tout stable. He then replayed the story of the investigation so far.

The victim was an elderly female shopkeeper, Mrs Allen, who was known to nearly everyone in the town. She had been robbed and hit over the head with something while in her sweet shop and later died. She had put up a struggle, but this had not been enough to prevent her death, and the culprit or culprits had escaped with the till takings of £150. A trivial amount to have cost this lady her life.

He said that, as usual, he was getting a lot of grief from the bosses as the murder had happened a week ago and there were still no clear leads. The media in particular were having a field day, claiming the force was stumped. A local free-lance reporter, Sean Cairn, had sold his story to a national paper, heavily emphasising the age and local reputation of the victim. Her face was now plastered across every newspaper on both local and national TV.

Chambers reluctantly confirmed there was no information coming in suggesting the culprit was local, and enquiries nationwide had also yielded no results. Jimmy asked him about forensic evidence from the scene, to which Chambers told him the only blood found related to the victim. No fingerprints were left and no weapon recovered, and the only disruption to the premises was the scattering of a pile of A4 sheets of paper. Door-to-door enquiries hadn't given the police any new information and little response was forthcoming, even after renewed appeals for witnesses. Chambers ended the conversation saying that this did not look like it would end in a good news story and for that reason not many of the police bosses had their heads above the parapet. As a result, as with other enquiries, he was left fielding the press and getting the flak.

Jimmy told Chambers he would be more than willing to get back to work as soon as he got home, even though he had four days annual leave left. In the meantime, as requested, he'd contact his touts and pass on anything he gleaned. After the conversation he contacted all his charges but none of them knew anything specific about the crime. He called Chambers back and broke the bad news, but confirmed that as soon as he got back he would be straight into the office. This did not please Doris when she overheard the call, but she understood and was as disgusted as everyone else that Mrs Allen should be so brutally murdered. Doris went into this old lady's shop once a week and bought sweets for the kids. Mrs Allen always had plenty to say and used to tease the kids before presenting them with a free sweet in return for them saying 'please'.

Jimmy was only back in the house a few hours before he made his way to the CID office. There he met with Chambers, who was showing the strain of both internal and external pressure. He briefed Jimmy on the enquiry to date, which differed little from the details he had furnished Jimmy with on holiday.

The DCI, although nearing retirement, was a very capable detective who was determined to solve this horrible crime. He was now living with the crime night and day and, as a result, he went through the enquiry meticulously and showed Jimmy a video and photographs of the scene. From these pictures Jimmy could see how badly beaten about the head Mrs Allen had been and he, like his boss, was livid when he saw the heavily blood-stained shop floor.

He told Chambers that it must be a right bastard who had done this, to which Chambers nodded in agreement. The DCI admitted the enquiry was not bringing in many new leads, but his gut instinct told him a loner was responsible. With the shortage of information or witnesses he had sent out his door-to-door teams again. This time they were armed with specific questions to put to each person they spoke to and this was supplemented by personal descriptive forms (PDFs) which, when completed, would show detailed descriptions of these people. This might prove beneficial if they unearthed an eyewitness.

Initially, the officers had covered all addresses within a square mile of Mrs Allen's shop; now their enquiries extended to two a mile radius. Chambers said they would continue until the whole of Newholm was covered if that is what it took to find the murderer. Specialist search cops had also been utilised by Chambers and they had done thorough sweeps in the area but had found no evidence that might relate to the case.

Jimmy asked the DCI if there were any potential candidates and he said the only things they had gleaned through this blanket coverage was that there were three young men living alone in bed-sits close to the shop. He had checked them out but none had any previous convictions and there was no local intelligence relating to them. Chambers was nothing if not thorough and had them all interviewed about their movements before, during and after the attack. Again nothing was gleaned, except that one had an alibi, while the other two could only confirm they were alone in their bed-sits at the time of the murder. Consequently, there was nothing at this stage to put them into the category of suspects.

On the national level nothing had been forthcoming to assist the investigation, even though the neighbouring forces were sympathetic to the DCI and his team. Enquiries with, bus, train and taxi operators had also drawn a blank, as had checks with prisons, hotels, guest houses, B&Bs, doss houses, the ambulance service and A&E at Newholm Hospital. The media had been constantly updated to appeal for witnesses but still nothing.

Jimmy looked at the photographs again and like Chambers he too was puzzled by the scattering of paper on the floor. He told himself they were going to get this animal, but this might mean having to infiltrate the three men living in the bed-sits. Perhaps this is what made him think about past cases where undercover cops had been used to gain a suspect's confidence and get them talking about the crimes they were suspected of. However, when these cops' actions were later scrutinised in court it was deemed to be entrapment, resulting in the evidence they had gained being inadmissable and the guilty guys escaping justice.

Then he thought, 'what about touts doing the same job as these undercover cops and still remaining anonymous?'

After noting the particulars of the three loners, Jimmy set to work, calling in his stable members one by one. None of them knew any of these guys personally, but Wise Archie knew about one of them, who, he claimed, drank in Archie's pub, the Green Dragon. He said the guy didn't mix with anybody and sat in a corner on his own, nursing a pint. He was local to Newholm but, as far as Archie knew, he didn't work, and a pint usually lasted him a good two hours. He was looked upon as a weirdo according to Archie.

Jimmy then made the difficult decision to get some of his touts to infiltrate the three loners and attempt to find out more about them and, if they could, try to get them talking about the murder. This was a risky tactic which he would have to keep to himself. He knew he was slightly bending the rules and it could be classed as entrapment if it was disclosed. That said, he had no intention of it ever being disclosed and could think of no other way to learn the movements of the three, especially when they didn't mix with anybody. Accordingly, he asked Wise Archie to befriend the guy who went to the Green Dragon and get him talking, providing Archie with expenses to ensure this loner's tongue was well-lubricated.

Chocolate and Nervous were allocated the other two and also given cash to get them talking.

Jimmy knew the process could take some time so he would have to be patient. He hoped Chambers would remain patient as well, especially when he had guaranteed that, if any of these three were responsible then, through his touts he would get to hear about it. How they were going to get this information was another matter which Jimmy kept to himself.

After four days Jimmy met with each of his three touts...

At times like these where he had meetings with more than one tout, Jimmy would hark back to his betting days. He needed a sense of humour when asking touts to carry out this type of work. Consequently, he smiled when he thought that it was possible, unlike in horse racing, to have a stable where the charges don't train together and never meet!

At the meetings, both Chocolate and Nervous said their targets didn't have the bottle to murder anyone let alone Mrs Allen. They had got them drunk and put pressure to talk but it was obvious they knew nothing of the crime.

Wise Archie told him his man, who was called Craig Norton, was starting to get a bit more confident and was happy that he was now one of Archie's 'pals'. With Archie's reputation as a hard man in Newholm, this gave him a bit of street cred and he was loving it. Archie said he was buying him a lot of drink and the budget was taking a hit.

On the third night they were together, this 'weirdo' starting talking about the murder, stating that the old woman was a bitch, and that she had shopped him to his mother when he was kid, for stealing some sweets. Social work had become involved because of his age, and this resulted in a fall-out between his parents. The end result was that a local cop was called round to give him a 'word in his ear', but he wasn't charged with theft.

Although this wasn't a big deal, Archie learned that the subsequent relationship between mother and father was always strained. The father, a strict disciplinarian, belted his son regularly and distanced himself emotionally from him. He was affronted to have a son who was a thief and he regularly accused his wife of being over-protective and seeing no wrong in him. Her lack of discipline, in his mind, had indirectly brought embarrassment to the family from which they could never recover.

On hearing this update, Jimmy could see potential in fostering this new relationship between Archie and Norton. He told the tout to get himself into the bed-sit and have a good look around. This was anything but correct policing procedure and if it became known it was unlikely to stand legal scrutiny. Furthermore, if Archie's involvement was highlighted it would cause all sorts of problems for him and Jimmy, but Jimmy knew that on occasion you needed to use all your resources, and he classed the members of his stable as a resource.

He met Archie three days later and he told Jimmy that the bedsit was a mess, wallpaper was hanging off the wall, dirty dishes were lying everywhere and the place stank. Archie said there was a wedding photograph of Norton's mother on the wall but her husband's face in the photograph had been deleted. Jimmy took a mental note of these facts and asked Archie if Norton had said anything about the murder. Archie said that he had continued to supply him with drink and, during the subsequent conversations, Norton did open up a bit but he never admitted responsibility for murdering Mrs Allen, although he did re-affirm his hatred and lack of sympathy for her.

By now the bosses were all over DCI Chambers pressuring him to get a result. The strain was showing on the DCI, who was pulling out all the stops, working sixteen-hour days, constantly making crucial decisions and all the while fronting the media and getting the flak.

Jimmy, without going into much detail, reported that he was making some inroads into one of the loners but there was nothing to confirm he was the murderer. Nonetheless, he had now established a loose motive for the crime which was a good start.

Help must have been coming from above because the next night Jimmy received a call from Archie asking him to meet him right away at their usual covert place. He told Jimmy he didn't want to talk further on the phone...

Jimmy now had an adrenalin rush, ran out the office and hurriedly drove to their pre-arranged venue. On meeting Archie he could see that he too was excited but also worried.

Jimmy couldn't contain himself and asked Archie for the update. The first thing Archie told him was that he would not be a witness at any cost. Jimmy said that was never the plan and he would see to it that Archie kept his anonymity and would certainly not be a witness.

Then it came out...

Archie had been in the bed-sit the previous night and his new pal had passed out on the floor after a drinking session. This gave him the chance to have a good look round. Initially he found nothing of interest but, when he moved the bed, he felt something move inside it. He investigated further and found a very crudely constructed compartment in the bed frame and within it a blood-stained hammer. Archie was left wondering why the bed had been adapted and why a hammer had been hidden in it.

After his search he had managed to rouse Norton and, to avoid suspicion, he invited three of his friends and their girlfriends round for a party. Archie supplied the cash for the drink from the money Jimmy had given him for the infiltration. Norton, still drunk, couldn't believe he now had a whole group of new friends and a seemingly unlimited supply of free drink.

Jimmy was straight on to DCI Chambers with a sanitised and shortened version of the information he had, which suggested the loner had a concealed weapon in the flat. Chambers decided that it was a good lead and one which they would pursue. However, even if it was the murder weapon, with no further evidence or intelligence that they could use, they were unlikely to be granted a search warrant for the bed-sit.

Consequently, Chambers told Jimmy to see if Norton would agree to come into the station voluntarily. If he did, then Jimmy should interview him to see if he would grant them permission to search the bed-sit without a warrant. It didn't take too long before Jimmy and one of the DCs were at Norton's door. When he answered it Jimmy told him he had two choices, he could either agree to come with them voluntarily for interview, or he would detain him to be interviewed in connection with the murder of Mrs Allen.

Norton was hung-over but said he had nothing to hide and would accompany them to Newholm Police Station voluntarily. Unknown to him, Jimmy had positioned another DC where he could watch the bed-sit during the time the loner was being interviewed, to make sure no-one entered or left. He knew there could be more than one culprit involved in the crime and he was trying to cover all the angles.

Once inside the station he got Norton to sign a form confirming that his attendance at Newholm Police Station was voluntary and he could leave when he wished. Norton didn't know then, but if he had decided he was leaving, Jimmy would have to detain him. This was the last course of action Jimmy wanted as it meant they could only keep him for a total of six hours. During that period if he didn't admit to the murder they would have to release him and under Scots Law they couldn't detain him again for the same crime.

Jimmy was especially careful during this interview. He already knew, but could not disclose, that this guy had a motive, and he was hoping to fill the rest of the evidential boxes with his responses. This, he hoped, would show he fulfilled the criteria the police had been trained to use to identify a guilty man: motive; ability; guilty knowledge; intent; conduct before, during and after the crime; opportunity to commit the crime; and preparation/planning (MAGICOP).

The interview lasted three hours and the suspect was now sweating profusely and frequently asking for drinks of water.

Jimmy knew this would be the result of the hangover that the force had indirectly paid for. It was clear he didn't have an alibi nor anyone who could vouch for his whereabouts at the time Mrs Allen had been attacked. He had already admitted he lived close to the shop but denied knowing her.

During the interview he had tried to put Norton at his ease by confirming the police were interviewing a number of people about this crime, not just him. Jimmy managed to build some rapport using this approach but Norton still denied all knowledge of the crime. Towards the end of the three hours Jimmy asked if he would have any objections to the police searching his house. Norton appeared stumped at this request but nevertheless agreed, and they all left the station together, but this time with three more DCs to help with the search.

When the bed-sit was being searched one of Jimmy's colleagues moved the single bed and heard something moving inside. This DC then checked under the bed and see what was causing the rattling.

Surprise, surprise, he found a blood-stained hammer within a roughly made compartment in the bed base.

Jimmy pulled Norton towards him, pointed to the hammer in the compartment and cautioned him. Apparently unsurprised, Norton said it was his, as was the blood on it. It had resulted from him hitting his hand while repairing a fence at the rear of the bed-sit. When asked by Jimmy about the construction of the compartment, Norton said it was already in the bed when he bought it from a second hand shop. Jimmy told him he was seizing it for forensic examination but Norton made no comment. After the search was finished, Jimmy informed him that he would be in touch after the hammer had been examined, and told him not to leave town.

When he returned to the CID office he showed the

carefully protected hammer to Chambers, who then authorised an urgent examination at the forensic lab.

To put further pressure on the suspect and tick another evidence box, Jimmy instructed DC Green to routinely interview his mother and father about their son's background and movements. His other task was to make sure they confirmed in writing the story Archie had told him about this guy's hatred of Mrs Allen and, indeed, the fact that he knew her.

Green, as expected, completed a thorough interview with both parents, which corroborated what Archie had said. In addition, he confirmed the father's hatred for his son and the fact that their relationship was so bad that, when the son reached the age of 16, he was thrown out the house. This was apparently why he lived in the bed-sit.

The following day, the lab called and confirmed the blood on the hammer belonged to Mrs Allen. In addition, the scientist was able to confirm that one of the A4 sheets of paper which had been sent to the lab previously had been examined and had a footprint on it with a distinctive impression (this would later be identified as the footprint belonging to the loner's training shoe, which had a hole in the sole in the exact location shown on the footprint on the paper). On hearing this news, Chambers instructed Jimmy to detain Norton for the murder.

Before Jimmy left the office Chambers gave him a look, and told him he would not, as requested, be contacting Chief Superintendent Scott or any of the bosses with the developments before he got back with his man.

Jimmy and DC Green found the door of the bed-sit open and the suspect's mother standing behind the door crying. She kept repeating 'Craig', 'Craig', stamping her feet on the ground and screaming, 'Oh my God'; she was inconsolable.

On entering they found out why she was in this condition.

Her son was hanging from a door lintel on the end of his belt.

Both officers immediately cut him down and checked for a pulse, but there wasn't one. Jimmy then made a quick call to Chambers and told him the boy had hanged himself.

Trained crime scene officers were contacted and asked to go to the bed-sit while DC Green, with the assistance of a family liason officer, took the boy's mother home. This left Jimmy in the room on his own with the youth, waiting for a doctor to arrive and pronounce him dead, a seemingly strange but necessary aspect of protocol. Even though he had committed a horrible crime, part of Jimmy's heart went out to him and he began questioning himself again about whether he was in the right job. His stable had once again produced a 'classic' winner in the form of Wise Archie, but Jimmy was left flat in what should have been a win against all the odds.

He had wanted to bring this guy to justice but had now been deprived of that opportunity. All that was left now was to minimise the hurt caused to both the family of Mrs Allen and the family of the murderer.

Once the doctor had attended and the body had been removed to the mortuary, Jimmy made his way back to the office. En route, for some reason he couldn't get a song out his head: 'The Living Years' by Mike and the Mechanics, a song famously describing the fraught relationship between a father and son. When he entered DCI Chambers' office he found him in a heated debate with Chief Superintendent Scott.

Scott was irate, blaming Chambers for not contacting him about potential developments. He was repeatedly questioning him as to why the youth had hanged himself before he could be charged with Mrs Allen's murder. He told

Chambers this was a badly-handled case and a lost opportunity for the force to highlight its success in dealing with a terrible crime.

It had been his intention in the media briefing that afternoon, after hearing of developments from other officers, though not Chambers, to sing the force's praises. This would now have to be cancelled or there would be difficult questions to answer. He would be left looking stupid and he wasn't having that. He stressed to Chambers that he would now arrange another briefing, face the media and explain why the murderer took his own life. As if to emphasise his point, he leaned into Chambers' face and told him he was stupid and a disgrace. He began shouting at him again, repeating the same words and asking Chambers if he understood.

Jimmy had never seen his boss lose his temper before but he knew that he could handle himself. He had been a woodcutter before he joined the police and had forearms like Popeye. He was loyal to the service, and his troops, including Jimmy, had the utmost respect for him. With 28 years' service he was nearing retirement and a well-deserved opportunity to put his feet up.

This situation was different, and Scott hadn't realised you could step over the line with Chambers. He had done it this time and, as they went nose to nose, Chambers punched Scott with a right hook to his head, sending him spinning to the floor, motionless in a crumpled heap...

Scott couldn't believe it, nor could Jimmy, and, while Scott was recovering from the shock, Chambers walked over to him and told him that if he didn't leave his office now by the door then he would be leaving by the 'fucking window'.

Scott got off the floor, clutching the left side of his head and considered confronting Chambers though thought better of it. As he left the office, he shouted to Chambers that he would soon be unemployed and facing disciplinary and criminal charges.

He didn't miss the chance to tell Jimmy that he was now a witness to the assault. Jimmy made no reply...

After the dust settled, the DCI told Jimmy he should do as he was supposed to, and act as a witness to the altercation between him and Scott. He should have known that Jimmy was more loyal than that and wasn't about to break the 'respect' code he had held from his youth, even if it damaged his chances of further promotion.

An internal investigation was duly undertaken at the behest of the deputy chief constable who was responsible for all disciplinary matters. As was normal in such cases, it was conducted by an independent force. Everybody who had been in the main CID office at the time of the incident was interviewed and told it was their duty to speak up.

Nobody did.

When it came to Jimmy, he was taken aside by Chief Superintendent Carmichael who was in charge of the internal investigation. He reminded Jimmy that he must tell the truth and to bear in mind his own career. Jimmy nodded and the recorded interview began. He explained the details of the complaint from Chief Superintendent Scott and stressed that Jimmy had been the only other person in Chambers' office at the time and must have witnessed the assault.

Jimmy then gave his version of events. He had heard shouting between Chambers and Scott as he was about to enter Chambers' office. When he opened the door to the office he was met by Scott, who, as he was leaving the office told him he was now a witness to him being assaulted by Chambers. As far as Jimmy was concerned he had witnessed nothing, and only overheard a dispute between two senior officers which was not an uncommon occurrence.

He stuck rigidly to this line even when Carmichael reminded him about his career and the possibility of him becoming subject to criminal or disciplinary procedures.

After two hours of frustration, Carmichael and his corroborating officer told Jimmy they were disappointed in him but that he was free to leave.

Jimmy smiled and thanked them for their time.

The assault was now the 'talk of the steamie' and everyone was awaiting the outcome of the enquiry, which would be another eight weeks. Much to Scott's displeasure, it was decided that there was no evidence to charge Chambers with assault and he was eventually 'counselled' by a senior officer. Chief Superintendent Scott, meanwhile, was given 'advice' by the force's deputy chief, Mr Cobble.

As usual in these situations there are no winners: Chambers was transferred six weeks later to a uniform position to see him out until his retirement, while Scott's chances of further promotion, like his reputation, looked to be severely dented, though not as badly as Jimmy's.

With Chambers gone, Jimmy got a new boss in the form of DCI Goldie. He had been a DC for a short time at an early stage in his career, but had not been back in the CID for fifteen years. He could hardly be described as a detective and was known as a bit of a ladies' man, who was wise enough to have kept a bit of 'insurance'. This came in the form of knowledge about some of his bosses' philandering, which they could not risk being exposed.

A NEW REGIME

On appointment, Goldie's first port of call was with Jimmy. He tried to keep him onside by telling him that the force bosses would eventually forgive him over the incident with Scott and that he should keep working hard to keep contact with his touts. Once the dust settled he would be considered for promotion again.

Jimmy knew this was crap and that the possibility of him ever being promoted again was virtually nil, as long as Scott remained in the job. He did still love his job but was shrewd enough to know the force only needed him when crime got out of hand. Even on these occasions, he was given little credit or internal support. The incident between Chambers and Scott had ruined any opportunities now for self-promotion. He decided that all he could do was carry on as normal and keep his stable in good shape, while always looking to see what dangers were approaching his blind side or 'coming up on the rails'.

It was now far too dangerous for him to become 'blinkered'...

His ex boss, DS Martin, was now retiring and Jimmy was a guest speaker at his retirement function. There were nearly one hundred and fifty officers there, which was testimony to how highly regarded Martin was. While he was still fairly sober, Martin took Jimmy aside and told him to watch himself. He was aware some of the bosses who had been sponsors of Scott, or others who were looking to Scott to back them for promotion, had it in for Jimmy. Jimmy thanked him but he already knew who they were. At the end of the night Martin came back to Jimmy very much under the influence of alcohol. He told Jimmy, as he had done many times before, not to forget the 'war' was still on, and it looked like Jimmy would be the only one 'going over the top'.

Everybody had a good night and Martin was, in true testimony to a successful Scottish drinking event, carried home.

A year later it was Chief Inspector Chambers' turn to retire. Jimmy was delighted to see him reach the 'finishing post' and, as with Martin, he was a guest speaker at Chambers' leaving function. Once again there were over one hundred officers at this event, again speaking volumes for how highly regarded this old detective had been by his colleagues. As he had done with Martin, Jimmy presented Chambers with a bottle of his favourite malt whisky. The night was a great occasion and it was good to meet up again with old colleagues including ex DI McLaren, as they reminisced and laughed about old cases. As Jimmy was leaving, Chambers came over to him and asked him to meet him out the back of the hotel before he headed home. They met outside, and Chambers presented him with a box which he said contained a 'wee goldie' (Scots term for whisky) and thanked him. He told Jimmy to keep it under wraps and not open it till he got home.

Jimmy agreed and when he and Doris were sitting having their supper he decided to open up the gift. Sure enough it was a bottle of whisky, but had a hand-made label which read 'Silence is Golden' stuck over the original. Jimmy let out a laugh not dissimilar to Martin's, and Doris wondered what was wrong till he showed her the bottle and she too couldn't contain herself. He then removed the label and poured himself and Doris a good measure of what was an excellent 21 year-old malt. They both toasted Chambers and Martin before burning the label.

These were happy occasions, but Jimmy and Doris knew the period ahead was going to be a new beginning for him and that there would be many difficult times without the support of characters like McLaren and Chambers.

Thankfully, there had been little serious crime over the last two years, which was just as well with Goldie parading peacock-like about the office, trying to chat up the young female detectives and typists. He gave the impression of being one of the boys and was quick to take Jimmy and the troops for a drink at the end of their shift but, as far as Jimmy was concerned, he would always be worth the watching. Jimmy knew that he held regular meetings with some of the force bosses, including Scott, and as a result he played by the rules and never let his guard down. He hoped his guarded behaviour wouldn't have to last forever as it was getting him down. The only good news was that DC Green had been promoted to Detective Sergeant . Jimmy was delighted at this news because Green had proved his worth, was a dedicated and capable detective and, importantly, one you could trust.

The situation in the department changed some two months later, when the CID received a call one winter's morning to say the body of a woman, whom Jimmy knew, was lying in a field next to a run down scheme in Newholm. Goldie received the call and told Jimmy to go and take a look at it and report back.

This incident involved an alcoholic called Jenny Palmer. She was known to most of the local police and she had been found lying on the waste-ground near her home. She was 40 years-old and had a history of alcohol abuse going back to her teenage years. So bad had her illness become that she didn't make use of a calendar to ascertain the days of the week. For her, and those who drank with her, Tuesday was when she bought two litres of cheap vodka from the grocery van that visited her scheme. Her and her alcoholic friends then drank it and any other drinks they could get their hands on in her flat. Wednesday was the day she got some allowances which she spent in the local pub, 'The Gargle'. Thursdays, her pals got their allowances and she visited one of their flats and they all got drunk together.

She operated to a weekly routine dictated wholly by drink, and was drunk every day. She was a sad case but had, in the past, while she was still relatively sober, been one of DS Martin's touts, who always took the 'King's Shilling'.

This was how Jimmy had first got to know her and he had always felt sorry for her and her three young children. When she had no money, Martin and he had often bought her provisions and checked up on the kids. When the drink started to take a real hold of her life she ended up losing her children - who all had different fathers - when they were taken into care.

It was therefore with some sadness that Jimmy approached the body, located in the long grass in the rubbish-strewn field. A uniform sergeant was already there and it was she who pointed out the exact location of the body. She told Jimmy that when they found her she was fully-clothed, but it had been a bitterly cold night and it appeared the cold had killed her. Jimmy asked her if any of the cops had touched the body and she confirmed that they hadn't. Being careful to preserve the scene, Jimmy took a closer look, trying not to disturb the body or the ground around it, and then, as was routine, he called the police surgeon to pronounce her dead.

Doctor Bush, whom Jimmy regarded as the most thorough doctor he had worked with, arrived. Jimmy could see his car in the distance and, as normal when he saw the 'Doc' as he was known in police circles, he was carrying his medical bag, and another which he knew contained cameras, tape measures, thermometers and magnifying glasses. The 'Doc' always paid the utmost attention to detail, taking his own photographs and measurements and noting the weather conditions. His reports and statements for court were always comprehensive. He was the only police surgeon Jimmy had known who was supplied with his own police surgeons' register. Normally, these registers were kept in individual police stations for the use of any doctor called by the police to examine people in custody. Doctor Nigel Bush was so well regarded by the police for his professionalism at scenes involving death and serious injury that Newholm Police sanctioned him to carry his own register. Whenever an incident occurred like a murder or serious assault then Doctor Bush was the favoured G.P. for the investigators. Accordingly, with being called out so many times he was allowed to keep his own register and record his findings at the time, instead of having to write them up later when he got back to the nearest police station.

Jimmy had been to the scenes of a number of deaths with Doctor Bush and they had a mutual respect for each other and were on first-name terms. When they met this time, Nigel asked Jimmy how life was and how were Doris and the kids. He told him they were fine, then gave the Doc a bit of Jenny's background. Bush noted the weather and ground conditions before he approached and photographed the body. Jimmy watched closely, as there was always something you could learn from Doctor Bush. In fact, when he was promoted to DI he had asked Nigel to provide a presentation on forensic crime scenes and causes of death to his young CID officers, and he was only too happy to oblige, free of charge.

Bush was able to confirm straight away that she had died and that rigor mortis had set in, meaning that she had been dead for some time. The body was lying face up and there were no obvious signs of injury or struggle. He then took close up photographs of the body in the position it was in, before noting the details of her clothing, measuring her height, taking her body temperature and providing assistance and guidance to the scenes of crime officer. After this he started to turn the body over to check for wounds or injuries on her back, and it was at this time he called to Jimmy to come forward. He pointed to Jenny's right armpit and a wound which he said was a bullet hole.

It was time for the balloon to go up...

This was no sudden death incident or suicide. It was murder and it involved a firearm. Crimes involving guns were rare in Newholm, especially murders involving firearms, and Jimmy was as surprised as doctor Bush to be dealing with such a crime now.

DCI Goldie had never investigated a murder and, when Jimmy called him, there was a pause after Jimmy delivered the news. Jimmy thought he'd been cut off until Goldie spoke very quietly, evidently shocked. His usual cockiness had disappeared and he asked Jimmy what should happen next.

Jimmy said Goldie was the boss and he would have to make the decision. As a firearm had been used, the force executive would have to be notified immediately and they would expect Goldie to personally front the enquiry. Goldie said he wanted Jimmy to lead the investigation at ground level, and he would arrange for administration, investigation and door-to-door teams, while also making sure he read and evaluated all statements as they came in. Goldie would then consult with Jimmy and decide the strategy and priorities for the investigation.

Jimmy knew that this was 'waffle' and that, in reality, Goldie was trying to conceal himself within the administration framework, not getting his hands dirty and avoiding the chance of making any bad operational decisions. These crucial decisions, which would later be subject to scrutiny in a court setting, would be Jimmy's alone. At the end of the call, Jimmy just shook his head, though he said nothing to anyone else.

DCC Cobble was the senior officer on call. He had a lot of CID experience having been a senior investigating officer in both England and Northern Ireland. Once he heard there had been a murder, and one involving a gun, he went along to the scene. When he arrived, the crime scene manager Jimmy had appointed, the Doc, the fiscal, a local pathologist and Jimmy were deep in discussion. By this time, after consultation with these professionals, Jimmy and the crime scene manager had agreed their forensic strategy and arranged for the body to be escorted to the mortuary at Newholm Infirmary. With the unusual circumstances surrounding this murder, Jimmy felt there was merit in having all these professionals at the scene to offer their expert advice and assistance. He had also arranged for a ballistics expert from Glasgow to attend the post-mortem.

In keeping with standard practice, the scene was preserved and cordoned off. Officers were instructed to keep the scene sterile, and to control and record everyone who went in or out. Two uniform cops guarded the outside cordon and were tasked with noting the details of anyone who tried to enter, being sure to notify Jimmy immediately.

These cordon officers contacted Jimmy during his discussions with Doctor Bush and the others to tell him that the DCC was demanding access. Jimmy went to see him and was met by a very excited senior officer who was not too pleased that he had been refused entry to the crime scene. Jimmy explained why and Mr Cobble said that while he understood the need for keeping the scene sterile, the thrill of being a detective again had got to him. He asked Jimmy what he had done about the media, where his contact points were, what he was doing about appeals for witnesses. In addition was he utilising an incident caravan as a focal point for the public near the crime scene, were there any suspects capable of this type of crime in the area and what was the background of the victim? His words came in a continuous question and only after he finished speaking was Jimmy able, remarkably, to supply suitable answers.

Talk about pressure...

Cobble then asked where DCI Goldie was and Jimmy said he was with the administration team and would scrutinise the evidence as it came in. This annoyed the DCC and Jimmy could see the colour intensifying in his cheeks. Once he calmed down, Cobble told Jimmy to front the media and continue doing what he was doing, keeping him up to date with the progress. In the meantime, he would find Goldie and give him some 'advice'.

Jimmy had a soft spot for Cobble who had at least been through the mill. He had first-hand experience of the witness box and the flak detectives often get in court, not to mention the pressure they get from some supervisors with no CID experience. In fact, he appreciated his visit and in answering all his queries he felt reassured he was doing all that was necessary. Furthermore, Cobble's visit meant he would get a reasonable budget for the investigation as well as the support he required.

Once the body was removed, Jimmy and the others attended the post-mortem. There they were joined by a senior pathologist appointed by the fiscal and, together with the local pathologist, she commenced the examination. The ballistics expert was able to confirm Jenny had been shot at close range as there were deposits of soot close to the entry wound. There was only one bullet hole in the body and the bullet was retrieved from the deceased's buttock and found to be of .38 calibre. It was kept for evidence, in the hope that it could be married to the firearm it had come from, if that weapon were ever recovered. The body was fully photographed, swabbed and the victim's clothing was seized for forensic examination.

The cause of death was confirmed as the result of the bullet which had caused irreparable damage to Jenny's internal organs. There were no defensive wounds or marks on the body to show she had put up a struggle against her assailant, nor was there any evidence of a sexual assault. Jimmy was now left with a lot of unanswered questions and a local and national media who now had by now got wind of the murder and were looking for information.

When he got back to the office he briefed a very subdued DCI Goldie, who had obviously had his encounter with Cobble. He listened carefully and told Jimmy to brief the enquiry team and continue to lead the operational side of the enquiry. Jimmy felt slightly sorry for Goldie as it was obvious that his position was now in jeopardy if Cobble had anything to do with it.

He invited the fiscal, the other professionals who had attended at the scene and the ballistics expert to the briefing with his enquiry and major crime administration teams. Here, he provided an update of events so far and set out his strategy, agreed with Goldie, for the investigation. Needless to say, it followed well-rehearsed procedures with built-in accountability as per the policy book. This included the 'norms' of door-to-door teams to include personal descriptive forms, a plan for controlling the media, an appeal for witnesses and local and national collation of intelligence to build a profile of Jenny. They would be supported by analysts who would produce a time line and chart showing the victims known movements and her contact with friends and associates. These documents would become more concise when more evidence was obtained.

Jimmy reminded everyone of the need to remain secretive about how the victim had died. He didn't want the media getting hold of specifics about the murder and in publishing them, possibly prejudicing any future trial.

He then returned to his office for some quiet time, and an opportunity to mull over what he was dealing with and to sort out his priorities for the investigation. He was in no doubt that if he got any suspects identified for the crime he would scrutinise, as he had always done in serious crime investigations, their actions and movements, before, during and after Jenny's murder. This framework had always worked for him in the past and there was no reason to abandon it now.

During this period of contemplation Jimmy received a call from Kerr, the journalist, followed shortly thereafter by calls from Armstrong and Buchan. The media were on his tail, looking for a statement and information about the murder. Jimmy refused to divulge specifics and only declared that it was a murder and he would keep them updated on progress. To ameliorate his stance he told them all he regarded them as part of his investigative team; they would be first to be notified about press briefings and, with their help, he hoped to solve this case. This somewhat naïve statement by him, as expected, didn't mean much to seasoned reporters who had sources of information throughout the community and within the police. It did, however, give him some breathing space, especially when he confirmed he would give them daily updates to supplement what was disclosed at the press briefings. They didn't know how much information Jimmy would supply and that suited him just fine, as it meant he could, to a certain extent, control them.

His investigative team were up for the job and Cobble had provided a substantial budget to finance the investigation, though he stipulated that he wanted regular updates on progress. Jimmy was grateful for his support and his troops were pleased that some overtime was being allocated. This would help those officers with families to support and others without such commitments whom Jimmy classed as 'mercenaries to money'.

After the first day they had gathered enough information to highlight the movements of the victim and begin the time-line leading up to the discovery of her body. She had been murdered on Wednesday and, as usual on that day, she had been in 'The Gargle' with her drinking cronies. At 3pm. she left the pub on her own and, as normal, took a short-cut across the waste ground where her body was later found. When she left the pub she was drunk, as were the two women and three men that she had left in there.

As this group had been the last people to see her alive they were, for the time being, the main suspects. Jimmy had their stories and alibis checked and counter checked which proved problematic, as their collective drunkenness made it difficult to verify. However, the bar staff in the pub were able to confirm that they didn't leave the pub for at least an hour after the victim, and by the time they left none of them could stand unaided.

Public appeals and media releases brought nothing of use for Jimmy and it appeared the investigation was going to be a slog, just like a number of investigations he had led. He knew that, contrary to TV detective programmes and some crime novels, most of these investigations only achieved success with determined effort. This meant going over and over again all the evidence, always seeking new leads and never giving up. The work is mundane, time-consuming, and soul-destroying, but Jimmy knew that if you have a good team and 'help from above' you can achieve success. He hoped that this would be the case with Jenny's murder.

The tout aspect of the enquiry which did not appear in any policy book, Jimmy allocated to himself. He made early contact with his charges, ensuring they knew that the reward for identifying the killer would be significant.

On day two of the enquiry he decided to call on ex DS Martin who had been the 'handler' of the victim when she was a tout. He was following the case on TV and in the newspapers and was delighted to see Jimmy and even more pleased to be consulted by him in relation to the murder.

Martin was able to supply a lot of background information about Jenny which Jimmy duly added to the profile being constructed by his intelligence team. He asked Martin if she had any enemies that he knew off and he said none, although her life was so chaotic with drink that he didn't fully know what she had been involved in. After a second cup of tea and a whisky, Jimmy left the old DS and his wife, promising he would keep him updated on the case, which delighted Martin.

Martin was a perfect example of 'once a detective always a detective'.

Day three of the investigation, much like the others, didn't yield many results other than a growing number of witness statements. Jimmy was also fronting the media and getting the usual flak over lack of progress, both from them, and some of the force bosses. Meanwhile, the DCI, whose ego had taken a bashing, was reading and evaluating the statements that were trickling in.

Following the afternoon briefing on the third day Jimmy received a call from Martin asking him if he had heard of Donny Large, a paranoid schizophrenic, who had only recently been released from the state mental hospital after serving a 12-year sentence for rape. Martin said Large was caught for the rape thanks to Jenny, who had tipped him off. He was pretty sure Large didn't know of her involvement but he couldn't guarantee it with her always being drunk and potentially saying things she shouldn't.

Jimmy knew Large, though not very well. He had been to his house early in his career after neighbours made calls to the police about him threatening to kill them. Any time Jimmy had been at the house Large had initially been aggressive and had the look of a wild man. By remaining cool, somehow Jimmy had managed to talk to him and calm him down. However, before being convicted of the rape Large had developed a reputation as a volatile, unpredictable and violent individual. As a result he had accrued quite a number of convictions for violence.

Jimmy thanked Martin for the heads up and put one of his intelligence teams on to researching Large and producing a profile of him from his earliest criminal years to the present. For now, the investigative slog carried on and Jimmy continued to brief Goldie, the local press and the wider media, in that order. The press wanted a quote about the use of the gun, something Jimmy always refused to confirm. He appeased them by providing snippets of information and they, in turn, ran with daily updates of the story, complete with repeated appeals for public assistance.

On day six, after checking with his stable and finding

nothing, Jimmy received a visit from Andrew Thomason, his best civilian researcher, who was completing the profile on Large. Thomason could be relied upon to be thorough, leaving no stone unturned. He was a frustrated cop and, had he applied to join the force, Jimmy had no doubt he would have made an excellent detective.

Thomason was really excited as he walked into Jimmy's office and said he had found something curious in Large's profile. Thomason told Jimmy that, when he was 14 years-old, Large had been caught with a replica hand-gun with which he was threatening people and he received a police caution. At sixteen he was found with a .22 rifle and a report was submitted to the fiscal, though no action was taken. In three other cases involving breaches of the peace Large had threatened to shoot people, though these facts had only been ascertained after Thomason had dug into each case individually. At first glance these cases were only regarded as breach of the peace, and the detail of the charges would not have been unearthed had Thomason been less thorough. Furthermore, Thomason had contacted the State Mental Institute and spoken to an intelligence officer. He confirmed that, during his time there, Large had a fascination for guns and had regularly purchased firearms magazines. His cell was covered in photographs of high-powered weaponry and soldiers carrying or firing them.

Thomason now had Jimmy's undivided attention and it wasn't long before he instructed him to keep digging and report back. Jimmy then contacted DS Green and told him to get as much information as possible about Large, and to interview him as a witness in order to to establish his movements before, during and after Jenny's murder.

As normal, Green set about this task with gusto and spent a good three hours interviewing Large as a witness and getting the information that Jimmy required. After the interview, to keep Large on-side, he thanked him for his cooperation. Both Jimmy and Green then went over the statement together in fine detail. By the end of this process it was clear Large had no concrete alibi which could withstand scrutiny, but then neither did some of the victim's alcoholic friends. What was significant was that Large had denied knowing Jenny when questioned by Green. Jimmy was intrigued as to why he should lie about this and decided to pursue Large, vigorously questioning him in an attempt to discover why.

Jimmy briefed Cobble on this development, and he, like Jimmy, was optimistic that perhaps in Large they had found their man, though it was still early days.

Jimmy then gave Green the task of knocking holes in Large's alibi and finding witnesses who could tell them more about him after his release from hospital. Jimmy was now feeling more confident about the case and even more so when Capo phoned to say that he had heard through one of his girlfriends that this weird guy (Large), who lived near her, had recently been trying to chat her up. When she had rebuked him he told her she would be getting shot.

Jimmy's problem now was how to get her into the evidential chain without compromising Capo. He would, as usual, find a way round that.

He decided to send a hand-picked door-to door-team, led by a uniform sergeant whom he respected, into her residential area. Jimmy told the sergeant he needed a statement from her about the threat made by Large, and, most importantly, he would need to get it without disclosing that a tout had already provided this information. If this was achieved as a result of a blanket door-to-door investigation then Capo's identity would remain intact.

It worked, and the sergeant presented Jimmy with the

exact statement he had hoped for. It was also corroborated by a neighbour of this new witness. Jimmy thanked him for his efforts and promised him a few drinks for his good work.

The investigation was now making progress, and Jimmy had enough evidence to arrest Large for causing fear and alarm to this woman by threatening to shoot her.

He told DS Green to detain Large for the threats to Capo's girlfriend and reminded him to be careful of Large's violent nature.

Green, who had taken two DCs with him, later returned with an unhappy Large. During the detention Large had threatened to shoot and kill Green and then, almost immediately, he became sullen, shy and withdrawn. These threats made him liable to another charge. After he was interviewed about the threats to Capo's girlfriend and Green, he was arrested, locked up and charged with two breaches of the peace. While he was being searched, and before being put in a cell, he was asked by the custody officer if he was taking any medication. Large said he took tablets for schizophrenia and the custody officer had then asked where this medication was, to which Large replied that he had put it in the bin as he didn't need it now. The officer told Green and he in turn told Jimmy, who made sure the custody officer submitted a statement as it could become useful evidence to account for Large's erratic behaviour.

While Large was in custody, Jimmy checked with the lab for updates. The scientist in charge of the case told him that there were green-coloured fibres found on Jenny's clothing which had not belonged to anything she had been wearing, and some hairs, which were also not hers, had been found on her woollen jersey.

Jimmy had hair samples taken from Large and, along with a DNA sample they had already taken, he sent these to the lab for urgent analysis and comparison.

Large later appeared in court on the two charges of breach of the peace. Although these charges were relatively minor, Large's criminal record was lengthy. Jimmy contacted the fiscal who had attended the crime scene and let him know about Large's suspected involvement in the murder and, thankfully, he was subsequently remanded in custody. While Large was on remand, Jimmy got a call from the lab saying the hair samples taken from Large matched those found on Jenny's clothing. Large now had some explaining to do. However, Jimmy knew that a good lawyer could show that Large knew Jenny and had been in her company earlier, and this would have accounted for the cross transference.

Jimmy knew he needed the murder weapon.

He decided to apply for a search warrant for Large's house and once this was granted he sent in a specially trained search team (P.O.L.S.A.) to take the premises to pieces. They found no evidence other than posters of firearms, and DVDs of the SAS and Commandos. They seized these items as background evidence to demonstrate Large's fascination with guns. Jimmy knew he had barely enough to interview Large as a suspect for the murder of Jenny and, unless he got some other evidence or Large admitted it, there was little chance that the Crown would prosecute him.

The following week Large applied for bail through his solicitor but this was refused and he remained in prison. By now the prison doctor had examined Large and put procedures in place to ensure he was re-supplied with, and took, the medication for his schizophrenia. This should ensure he remained balanced when he was within the prison.

Jimmy was now in a dilemma of whether he had enough evidence to officially class Large as a suspect and then detain and interview him about the murder. In Scotland you only got one chance at such an interview. If you didn't have enough to charge a suspect, you couldn't detain or interview him again for the same crime, until you got enough evidence to arrest and charge. This is very different to the legal system in England where you can arrest on suspicion more than once.

Then it dawned on him...

Wise Archie was temporarily out of commission and in prison, on remand, for three break-ins. Perhaps he could find out more about Large. If this became known, then Archie's reputation and possibly his safety would be at risk. His actions could also be deemed to be entrapment and further aggravated if it was discovered it was being carried out at the behest of the police. For it to be successful and to maintain Archie' anonymity and involvement Jimmy had to ensure any information Archie managed to get didn't feature. This would require things to be kept tight and this could only be achieved with the assistance of a trusted corroborating officer.

Jimmy took considerable time before deciding that he could, as he had done in the case of Craig Norton, get his tout to infiltrate the suspect. These actions, if they became known, would in all likelihood be classed as illegal and the tout's future safety would be compromised. With Large now in prison, access to him was out of the question so how else could he overcome this situation. Jimmy felt that the law always favoured the accused and not the victim. Subsequently, his rationale was that he was dealing with the murder of a helpless alcoholic who had helped the police in the past, and he wasn't letting the murderer get away with it, irrespective of his mental condition. If he had to slightly bend the rules to get him then so be it.

He now had to overcome the problem of getting access to Archie on the inside. Jimmy happened to be investigating a robbery at the time and he knew Archie had some involvement with it. Accordingly, with Archie being a suspect he could get a letter of authority from the duty superintendent to interview him in prison.

After the granting of the authority, Jimmy and Green headed to the prison to interview Archie. Normally, police interviews in a Scottish prison are conducted in the presence of a prison officer, but on this occasion Jimmy gave Archie a knowing wink when they met. Archie then told the warder he could go for a smoke and he was content to be interviewed on his own and he wouldn't be saying anything anyway.

Fortunately, the warder agreed and stood outside the interview room door for fifteen minutes, enough time for Jimmy to ask the tout to befriend and question Large about the murder and try and find out more about the gun. After Jimmy agreed on a substantial reward and confirmed that Archie would not be a witness, the tout said he would see what he could find out. Jimmy told Archie to write to him at a specified address using an agreed nom de plume for the householder. They also agreed on a code for progress or failure to be included in the letter. These safeguards would ensure that the warders who read prisoners' correspondence remained unaware of Archie's involvement on the inside.

Back at the office Jimmy set to work again on the investigation. After checking with his administration team he learned that information had come in confirming that Large had been in 'The Gargle' and had spoken to Jenny the day she died. This particular piece of evidence was being scrutinised by DCI Goldie, who was being very thorough in going over all the statements.

Jimmy could now show that Large both knew Jenny and had been in her company on the day she was murdered. He suspected that she might have spoken out of turn while under the influence of drink, though he needed witnesses to confirm it. He then tasked two DCs with re-interviewing all Jenny's alcoholic friends, along with the bar staff and regulars at the pub to ascertain if anyone had heard her talking about, or to, Large.

This was now classed as a priority action but, because some of these witnesses were alcoholics, they were difficult to trace, and, even when they were found, they often couldn't remember specific events.

Consequently, it took three days to complete this line of enquiry.

However, it was worth the effort as one barman remembered that Jenny and Large had had a brief confrontation in the pub about a week before the murder. During this confrontation she told everyone in the bar that Large was a beast and that she knew 'all about him'. Large had reacted furiously, grabbing her and threatening to kill her before he was thrown out the pub by the staff. Initially, the staff considered this a normal, alcohol-fuelled fall-out and thought no more about it.

Jimmy now had a motive for the crime and confirmation of Large's actions beforehand. Now he just needed details of Large's actions at the time of the crime, after it, and of course the weapon itself. There was still a good bit of work to be done...

Two days later Jimmy got a letter from Wise Archie. In it, by deciphering the code, Jimmy learned that Archie was making some inroads with Large. He had included a sentence in his letter which read 'rabbits laid eggs'. Jimmy had to think about this and what it could mean. Unable to work it out, he decided to go and search through Large's house again. Jimmy was stumped and, just as he was about to leave, he noticed a rabbit hutch in Large's elderly neighbour's garden but thought no more about it.

He went back to the office and told Green to interview Large's immediate neighbours again, going over their statements and asking if Large had ever left anything with them. This caused quite a stir, with twenty householders thinking they were now under 'suspicion' with the police back at their door asking if they had anything belonging to Large. Jimmy knew it was worth the trouble and in carrying out these interviews he was providing a smokescreen which would protect Archie's involvement. A next-door neighbour, an elderly man who feared Large, told the police that Large sometimes left a rabbit and its hutch in his garden when he was going away, and ordered the man to feed it. This was the hutch that Jimmy had seen.

Green radioed Jimmy, out of breath with excitement, and told him about this development. Things were moving quickly now and Jimmy realised why the officers hadn't found any weapon on their search of Large's property.

He instructed Green to ask all the neighbours if they would agree to a search of their houses for a firearm. This procedure would take some time and seriously inconvenience the neighbours, but it was necessary to protect Archie. Thankfully they all agreed.

Then it happened...

Green reported back, confirming that all the neighbours had been helpful but, Jimmy could hear the excitement in his voice and knew something dramatic had happened. He told Jimmy that a search of the rabbit hutch in Large's neighbour's garden revealed that it had a double-skinned floor with a gap of three inches between the two floors. The top floor could be removed for cleaning purposes by pulling it from its two retaining slides, while the bottom floor was an integral and fixed part of the hutch. Surprise, surprise what had he found when he removed the top floor...?

A point 38 revolver.

Jimmy was cock-a-hoop and immediately told Cobble about the recovery. He too was delighted but wise enough not to ask Jimmy where the information about the firearm had come from. Green recovered the weapon after it had been photographed in the position it was found and suitably protected. He then showed it to the elderly neighbour, who re-affirmed that the hutch was Large's and that he, the neighbour, had never seen the gun before.

When DS Green returned to the office, Jimmy shouted him into his room and cracked open a bottle of whisky. Jimmy arranged for the weapon to be sent by courier to the ballistics department of the forensic lab for priority examination and comparison with the bullet found in Jenny's body.

Two days later the lab confirmed that the weapon they received had discharged the bullet which killed Jenny. There was even better news the following day, when fingerprints found on the painted wood making up the two skins of the rabbit hutch were identified as Large's. Things got better still when a partial fingerprint of Large's was found on the firearm.

Jimmy now had his man and he made a point of briefing Mr Cobble and his D.C.I. on what he felt they needed to know. Trainers have to keep some of their tactics secret and some things, especially those involving touts, are best kept within your stable.

The next day, Green and Jimmy attended the prison with a mobile tape recorder to interview Large as a suspect for Jenny's murder. When they entered the room that had been set aside for them they were met by a calm and serene Large. Jimmy felt slightly sorry for him. He was going to be charged with murder and it was obvious through his demeanour that he was a different person when he took his medication. He then explained to Large that he was being interviewed about the murder of Jenny Palmer. Large said nothing.

Once the tape recorder was set up he was cautioned again and the interview, which was to last two hours, began. Large said that he didn't know anything about the murder. He did admit this time to knowing Jenny and remembered a confrontation with her in the pub, but he couldn't remember when that was, nor could he remember being in the pub on the day she died. Jimmy then showed him the revolver which they had recovered and asked him if he knew anything about it, to which Large made no comment. He then asked him about the rabbit hutch. Large said it was his and, when questioned specifically, he admitted he had constructed and painted it. He also confirmed that he sometimes left it in his neighbour's garden and asked his neighbour to feed the rabbit. Jimmy then charged him with Jenny's murder and again Large made no reply.

Both detectives returned to the office and, rather than get drunk, they went for a quiet pint before going home.

The following day, after briefing Cobble, Goldie and his enquiry team, Jimmy hosted a meeting with the media, where he confirmed that a man had been charged with the murder of Jenny and would be appearing in court in three days' time to answer this charge. He thanked the media for their assistance, then spoke privately to his three local reporters and told them they would get more info from him about the case once Large had made his first appearance in court. The following day, the papers and TV carried the story of Large's arrest.

The case never went to trial, which was a blessing as some of the evidence could have been contested. If Archie's involvement had become known, he would be unearthed as one of Jimmy's touts and the case would probably have been abandoned. Large pled guilty to culpable homicide (manslaughter), through diminished responsibility which was accepted by the crown. He received a 15-year prison sentence and was later sent back to the State Mental Institution.

Jimmy McBurnie felt he had earned his spurs as a detective inspector and hoped, though didn't quite believe, that perhaps he had 'tholed his assize' (been dealt with and could now move on) with the bosses over the incident with Scott.

Somewhat naively he told himself that maybe he was back in consideration for promotion.

He should never have underestimated internal politics but he did just that. He had redeemed himself to a certain extent in the eyes of some of the police bosses and certainly with Cobble. In fact, the force executive were considering him as part of a promotion pool for chief inspectors and, after some prompting by Cobble, initially agreed to support him. Chief Superintendent Scott, however, suggested that, although Jimmy had proved to be a capable detective, he needed wider policing experience before he should be considered for promotion to the rank of Chief Inspector.

He proposed that Jimmy should perform a uniform inspector's role covering general policing and be assessed in that position. After much debate by the five-officer panel this was accepted. Only Cobble felt it was folly, and he even said the force would suffer with Jimmy being out of the investigative loop.

At the time Jimmy didn't know of Scott's proposal, but he did know there was a promotion pool being formed and he suspected his future was being discussed. He was hoping to get some feedback, which he eventually did from DCI Goldie. When he heard that not only would he be excluded from the promotion pool but would also be moving to a uniform post to gain wider experience, he was livid. He asked Goldie how it was that, of the five members of the force executive, only one had CID experience. How could these members of the panel be in control of the force and a detective's career without having any CID experience?

Goldie would not comment.

Jimmy was devastated, and when he went home to Doris and the kids they could see the disappointment in him. He became sullen, then angry and voiced his opinion on the bosses. However, Doris secretly hoped this new position would allow him some more time at home to spend with her and their children.

So it was that Jimmy moved to the neighbouring division and the town of Stratshall as Uniform Inspector McBurnie.

GENERAL POLICING

It was strange for him to be wearing a uniform again, even when it had a shiny band round the front of the hat and two pips on his epaulettes, indicating his rank. His new boss, Chief Inspector Parker, had never been in the CID but was still an experienced, no-nonsense cop. He had heard all about Jimmy's detective prowess and told him he sympathised with him having to move out of the CID, though perhaps in the long term this move would be in his best interests.

Jimmy, being Jimmy, intended to give a hundred per cent to his new role, and put those he felt responsible for his move to the back of his mind. He decided he would treat this time in uniform as a training gallop, as he had already told his stable he hoped he would not be away for too long.

His job now involved supervising a number of young and inexperienced cops, some older cops who had little ambition or drive, and some hidden gems who had been overlooked by their bosses, but who were in fact good cops and very capable. In many ways, Jimmy considered himself a trainer, not only of touts, and he intended to train these officers to fit into his stable as apprentice trainers.

He set about his task with relish.

On his first day he toured his new patch, speaking to as many officers as possible. He made particular effort to visit the CID, which was staffed by a detective inspector, two detective sergeants and four detective constables.

The DI was protective of his office, but Jimmy knew that

if he were in his position he would be just the same. All in all, it appeared that they had a hold on the local crime situation; crime levels were respectable and detections seemed to be good.

As third in charge of general policing in Stratshall he now had to represent the police in a number of community forums, and he found that he had little difficulty in mixing with all sections of the community. He also became the force's representative in the Licensing Courts. For Jimmy this meant he could now, on behalf of the force, make objections and observations to the granting of local authority licences which included, pubs, hotels and taxis. This reminded Jimmy of the criminal court, but it was one where you were not bound by the same rigid rules and scrutiny, and as a result he quite enjoyed it.

In no time at all he became a well-known and respected figure in the area, which had a population of around forty thousand. This must have come as a surprise to some of those who had engineered his move, hoping Jimmy would have a hard time and fail as a uniform inspector.

For the first six months he kept coming up with new ideas and operating an open door policy for all his officers and support staff. Chief Inspector Parker gave glowing feedback to the force executive about his new enthusiastic inspector. It had been Scott who had questioned Jimmy's lack of uniform experience and he wasn't too pleased to hear about his progress in this new role.

Obviously, for Scott, supporting Jimmy would always go against the grain after the incident with Chambers and he would never forgive him for that. Now, with hindsight, he thought it would have been better to keep stereotyping and reminding the force that Jimmy was too close to criminals and not far short of becoming one himself. A bitter Scott would now need another strategy to discredit Jimmy and, if possible, get him dismissed from the force.

He decided to phone a friend of his, Alan Gemmill, who was a leading figure in Statshall Council and a member of the police committee. With his help he would find out if Jimmy could withstand scrutiny outwith the police, and possibly even succumb to temptation and speak openly about some of his irregular policing tactics.

Subsequently, it was not long before Councillor Gemmill was in contact with Jimmy, inviting him for lunch. Jimmy knew the councillor, mainly through the licensing court and the police committee. Since his arrival in Stratshall he had found him supportive of the police and their work. He was surprised to be asked for lunch but nevertheless agreed, meeting the councillor at a local hotel. Immediately, Jimmy felt he was being interrogated. He was aware of the bosses' hunger for closer community links and keeping the councillors, especially the police committee members, sweet, but he felt it strange that here he was being asked very personal questions about his social and family life. He was even more suspicious when Gemmill asked him if he had ever been tempted to bend the rules to get a conviction.

Jimmy thought to himself, 'does this guy think my head zips up the back?', but he played along without saying anything out of turn. At the end of the meal Gemmill asked for the bill, but Jimmy insisted he would pay his half. He made a point of doing so in front of the waiter before leaving him a tip.

The following week he got another call from Gemmill inviting him and Doris to his holiday home on the coast for a meal and an overnight stay. Jimmy declined the invitation, making up an excuse. He did however discuss Gemmill with Chief Inspector Parker, who told him he was worth the watching. One of the wealthiest men in Stratshall, he knew he was the 'silent partner' in what Parker referred to as a rough pub in the town. He also knew that he owned two shops in neighbouring villages and a caravan park, though he suspected he also owned or was behind other businesses. Parker said Gemmill had hosted a few functions for the police, had often donated to police charities and enjoyed being photographed alongside senior police officers.

Parker confirmed that Gemmill had friends in the force executive, though he didn't know who they were. This raised Jimmy's suspicions that Scott was playing some role behind the scenes. Parker was also in no doubt that, with Gemmill's presence on the police committee he had extra clout, and some senior officers might be too scared to keep him at arm's length.

Jimmy mulled over what Parker had told him, wondering how to play Gemmill, finally deciding he would pull a stroke of his own. He was still in contact with all his touts and Chocolate had a brother in Stratshall. He got in touch with Chocolate and asked him to find out what he knew of Gemmill's pub there. Chocolate came back a couple of days later and said that the bar manager, who was a cousin of Gemmill's, was using coke and speed along with some of the regulars after hours.

Jimmy decided to raise the stakes, and, holding the element of surprise, he contacted Gemmill, inviting him out for lunch, saying there was a delicate matter which Gemmill could perhaps assist with. When Jimmy got to the hotel, Gemmill was already waiting, obviously desperate to know what the meeting was about and thinking that Jimmy was going to disclose something that might be of benefit to Scott.

Jimmy didn't mention that he knew of Gemmill's involvement with the pub or his relationship with the bar manager. He merely said that he had heard a whisper that there was drug abuse taking place in that pub. He was sure that Gemmill, with his local contacts and membership of the police committee and licensing board, would be able to assist him in gathering sufficient intelligence and evidence to apprehend those responsible. This, Jimmy told him, would not only get rid of some of the dealers but, after their convictions, he would be able to object to the pub's licence being renewed at the next licensing board. Whoever owned the pub would then see its licence to sell alcohol taken away, and the pub might even be closed down. All in all, he told Gemmill, it was a good message to send to the local community of Stratshall, that drug abuse was not going to be tolerated.

To say Gemmill was taken aback would be an understatement, and Jimmy watched, amused, as he found it difficult to eat his lunch that day. Before they parted he promised Jimmy that he would be in touch. His first call was to Scott, to tell him that he would not be assisting him any further. Jimmy was too hot to handle and Gemmill advised Scott that it would be in everybody's interest to get him out of Stratshall. If this didn't happen, then perhaps the chief constable would somehow find out about Scott's motives and actions for Jimmy's somewhat unexpected arrival in Stratshall.

Surprisingly, Jimmy was beginning to enjoy life and the job. He was having much more time with Doris and the kids and he was at last taking an interest in their education, social lives and hobbies, becoming, in fact, something of a family man.

Not long after the meeting with Gemmill Chief Inspector Parker came to see him. He said that he had received a discreet request from a DCI Holloway in London, who was investigating a murder that had happened some ten weeks previously. A shopkeeper had been shot and killed with a Colt 45 handgun during a robbery at his jewellery shop. The murderer had been arrested, and the DCI now had some information indicating that the weapon had been obtained by him from a man in Stratshall. The only information they had about this man was that he owned a red car with a dented rear bumper and a Scottish flag motif somewhere on the vehicle. Parker said it would be like looking for a needle in a haystack.

For Jimmy, the word 'murder', spoken aloud, was like a starter's pistol going off at a race meeting, the stalls flying open and the horses shooting out.

He asked Parker if he could smooth things over with the local CID, then Jimmy would take this enquiry on using the services of a young cop whom he felt had shown potential to become a detective. Parker agreed and Jimmy found the cop, telling him he would be working with him on the enquiry. He knew in his heart of hearts that this was a matter for the CID but, with the information being so sketchy, it would end up at the bottom of their pile of enquiries. It also gave Jimmy the chance to become a detective again.

His first action was to have every shift briefed to check all vehicles on their beats to see if any car resembled the description forwarded by the Met officer. In addition, individual officers would be tasked with visiting the garages, repair shops, M.O.T. and tyre centres in Stratshall.

This was an onerous task but, after two days, a young cop on night shift found a car with similar characteristics to the one they were searching for. Jimmy checked and the car was registered to Shaun Nicholson, the head librarian in Stratshall. He was a well-respected member of the community who lived with his wife and two young children in their privately- owned detached home. His car was left every night in his driveway at the front of his house, where the young cop had found it on his rounds. It was unlikely that a head librarian would be involved in anything to do with a murder or illegally held firearms but, as Jimmy had learned, appearances or occupations count for nothing.

He told his young compatriot to check round the car in the hours of darkness and confirm that it did indeed have the Scottish flag emblem and the dent on the bumper. While the cop was completing this task, Jimmy started digging into the librarian's background.

Jimmy's potential detective later verified that the car was red, had a dent, and also the flag emblem. He had peered into the vehicle, but it looked clean, tidy and relatively empty except for two toy models of military vehicles on the rear parcel shelf.

Jimmy was getting nowhere with his enquiries other than learning that Nicholson was a member of the Rotary Club, did a lot of work for charity and was an active hill walker. He appeared a normal family man with normal hobbies. He legally held both firearm and shotgun certificates which were issued by Jimmy's force.

You couldn't take the detective out of Jimmy though, and he continued digging and found that Nicholson was also a member of the Territorial Army (TA), holding the rank of major in the organisation. Jimmy knew a guy who was a sergeant in the same TA regiment whom he could rely on to remain discreet. Accordingly, he made a call to him and after swearing him to secrecy, he started asking questions about this librarian.

It turned out that Nicholson had been with the TA for ten years. The sergeant described him as enthusiastic for all things military and an avid collector of military toys, uniforms, and historic items relating to the army. The sergeant said that he felt the Major was obsessed with his collection of military toys and he regularly attended military fairs anywhere in the U.K. to supplement his collection.

Jimmy didn't find this information particularly unusual, so he asked the sergeant what roles Nicholson performed when he was on active duty with the TA. It became clear then that one of his roles was that of the range officer, with responsibility for declaring what weapons were allocated, to whom, and when they were used. He was also responsible for signing a declaration stipulating the amount of ammunition discharged during practice on the firearms range. Jimmy was more suspicious now but didn't let on, instead thanking his friend for his assistance, and reminding him not to mention their meeting to anyone.

When he returned to the station he briefed Parker on what he had found and asked if he knew of a sympathetic sheriff who would grant a warrant to search the librarian's house. Parker was on good terms with the local sheriff, who openly admitted he hated crime being committed in his region. This sheriff was a landowner and had, in the past, lost both animals and machinery to theft. Accordingly, Parker was sure that if Jimmy presented a well-constructed case to him, then he would grant a warrant.

Jimmy did just that.

Before approaching the sheriff he contacted DCI Holloway, the officer dealing with the murder, and told him what he had found. He offered him the chance to travel to Stratshall if he got the warrant and be present during the search of the librarian's house. He was delighted and surprised that Jimmy had made progress, especially when he had only provided him with scant information to work with. Most likely, he thought, it would be a meaningless enquiry but, like many officers from large forces, he loved having an 'away day'. This would give him the opportunity to strut his stuff, claim expenses, and to show his country cousins how serious crime was investigated. Jimmy's stereotypical opinion of these police 'spivs' was confirmed when the officer asked if Stratshall had any golf courses and would it be worthwhile him bringing his clubs.

Jimmy politely told him there would be no time for golf.

The next day, he managed to get a warrant to search Nicholson's house and he again contacted his new London colleague, who said he would be with him that night. He would fly up, (business class) to Glasgow and hire a car to take him to Stratshall. He asked Jimmy to book him into the nearest five-star hotel. There was no five-star accommodation in Stratshall so Jimmy booked him into one of the local two-star hotels.

That night Jimmy was at home with Doris and the kids when he got a call from the civilian receptionist at the police station, saying that there was a rather elegant looking DCI Holloway from London in the office hoping to make contact with him and take him for a pint. This was not the plan, as Jimmy had told this officer he would pick him up from his hotel the next morning and take him on the 'turn' (house search).

Nevertheless, he asked the receptionist to make the DCI a coffee and he would be along shortly. When he arrived, Jimmy's stereotypical view of the cop was confirmed by his appearance. He was sporting a dapper suit, complete with silk handkerchief, and wearing shiny shoes. He smelled as though he had just left the House of Fraser perfume department and his confidence was all too obvious.

He asked Jimmy if he could show him the night life in Stratshall and Jimmy decided he would take him to his local, which could hardly be classed as night life. In fact it was a run down wee bar, with no music, T.V, pool tables or fruit machines. Everyone who went in there went for the beer, as it had ten different real ales, which could give you more than a sore head if you drank three or four pints. Jimmy liked this pub because it was not frequented by cops and everyone in it knew who he was. The fact that he was a cop didn't matter. He was always addressed by his first name and he had built up a good rapport with most of the regulars. On the way to the pub, Jimmy dropped his new friend at his two-star accommodation, which obviously was not the standard he was used to while on his travels. After he had booked in they headed for Jimmy's pub.

Holloway stuck out like a sore thumb when they entered the bar, with his snazzy dress sense and smell. Jimmy introduced him to the bar staff and the punters and asked him what he would like to drink. He in turn asked Jimmy what he recommended, and Jimmy suggested one of the weaker ales. Holloway sneered at this and said Londoners could hold their drink as well as any Scotsman and watery beer would have no effect on him. Jimmy ordered a mid-range real ale and, after three pints, Holloway began to slur his speech and after five he was teetering on his stool.

Jimmy decided it was time to get him back to his two-star hotel.

The next morning at 8am Jimmy picked up his bleary-eyed and hungover colleague and, along with his team, they went to the librarian's home armed with a search warrant. The knock on the door was answered by Nicholson's wife who was shocked to see six police officers on her doorstep. Jimmy explained the reason for the visit and showed her the warrant. She invited them in and then phoned her husband at work to tell him what was happening. When she had finished her call she told Jimmy that her husband would be home right away and had told her not to let the police search until he arrived.

The woman was shaking while she explained the layout of her house, which comprised two floors and a basement. Jimmy, seeing her condition, tried to put her at ease by telling her to have a cup of tea and, in keeping with her husband's instruction, said that they would not begin the search until he arrived.

It wasn't long before the irate Mr Nicholson turned up at his home, demanding to know what was going on. Jimmy took him to one side, cautioned him and showed him the search warrant. He explained the reason for the search of his home and the possible connection with the murder in London and cautioned him. Despite his protests, Jimmy told him the house would be searched thoroughly, and he asked him if he held any firearms illegally or if he had ever supplied firearms to anyone. This he denied.

The searches of the ground and first floor yielded nothing of significance. The team then commenced a search of the basement, again in the presence of Nicholson, who was now looking agitated and perplexed. Here, there was a strongroom and, on the wall outside it, a wooden frame was mounted, which showcased a large selection of replica firearms. Nicholson told Jimmy the strongroom was where he kept his legally-held rifle and shotgun. When Jimmy told him he wanted to see inside the room, Nicholson said he had lost the key. By now the guy, like his wife, was physically shaking, and he looked even more alarmed when Jimmy said he would force the door if Nicholson didn't open it. He then conceded that he did have the key and, when he had retrieved it from the kitchen, he sheepishly handed it to Jimmy.

When he opened the door Jimmy could not believe his eyes - the place was like an arsenal. On the walls were mounted about twenty rifles, at least twenty more handguns and, on top of a cupboard, were two hand-grenades. Inside another cupboard was a Thomson submachine-gun, a selection of bayonets and other weaponry. On the adjacent wall were three long shelves, each containing a selection of military toys, and on the floor were four boxes of ammunition, marked to show they were army property.

Jimmy reminded Nicholson that he was still under caution, at which point he nearly fainted. On seeing this weaponry, Holloway couldn't believe his eyes and was about to take over proceedings until Jimmy reminded him, none too delicately, that he was in charge.

Being a seasoned detective and looking for an early opportunity to put pressure on the librarian, he asked him where he'd acquired the ammunition. He replied that it was army property and that he shouldn't have it. That was enough for Jimmy, and he informed Nicholson that he was now under arrest for theft of the ammunition. This meant that further interviews with him would not be time-constrained as they would have been had he been detained rather than arrested. Jimmy then left his team to complete the search and recover all the weapons after they were photographed where they were found by the scene of crime officer. He then took Nicholson to Stratshall Police Station along with DCI Holloway.

On arriving at the station he winked at Parker, who had come to see what was happening. Jimmy told him to watch the rear door of the station because, in the words of his old DS Martin, there was evidence coming in confirming the 'war' was still on. Parker was later astounded to see an arsenal of weapons being carried into the labelling room next to the production store. Jimmy, meanwhile, accompanied Holloway and the suspect to the tape- recording room.

By now, Nicholson had lost his bottle completely, and

during the interview he admitted, when questioned by Jimmy, that he had stolen the boxes of ammunition from the TA. He had achieved this by keeping ammunition which he had falsely declared as 'spent' after rifle practice. Later in the interview he said he had been to a military fair some three months earlier and had taken a fancy to a selection of toy military vehicles which were for sale. When Nicholson had asked the seller how much he wanted for them, he was told he didn't want cash but another commodity. Jimmy questioned him further and it transpired the seller had an interest in handguns, particularly pistols, and would exchange the toys for a handgun and ammunition.

Nicholson was well aware he would be breaking the law but, as he had a large selection of handguns and suitable ammunition and he was keen for the military toys, he foolishly agreed to the deal. The following week, he met this man in a lay-by outside Stratshall and he handed over a Colt 45 hand gun complete with ammunition, and received the military toys in exchange. Holloway then showed him a selection of mugshots, and he picked out the murderer as the person he had supplied with the handgun and ammunition.

When this interview ended, Holloway called his office and told them he had kept his country cousins right, and that they had recovered the murder weapon. They now had a stonewall case against the murderer. After he finished his phone call he told Jimmy he had decided to stay another night in Stratshall and offered to take him for a meal, provided they didn't visit Jimmy's local again. Jimmy agreed but said that he had unfinished business with the librarian first.

In round two of interviews with Nicholson, Jimmy was accompanied by his potential detective. During this interview Nicholson revealed that, as the range officer with the TA, he had been declaring that all ammunition had been discharged after practice sessions and had signed the declaration accordingly. In reality he had been keeping some ammunition back and taking it home to exchange with other people like himself. He confirmed that all the weapons recovered from his home had been obtained as a result of exchanges with people at military fairs and other enthusiasts he had got to know. He had some engineering know-how and had been able to re-activate some de-activated weapons, and most were now cleaned and in full working order.

Jimmy took the seized boxes of ammunition to the TA sergeant, who identified them as belonging to the army, and from the code on the boxes he confirmed they had been issued to his unit. The sergeant was furious about the dishonest behaviour of the major and Jimmy knew the sergeant would have sorted him out had he not been locked up.

The major became the subject of numerous charges under the firearms act in addition to theft from the TA. The seized weapons were photographed, identification details obtained, and their descriptions circulated nationwide. This resulted in quite a few forces in the country now becoming linked to this investigation as the buyers and sellers involved with Nicholson were dotted all over the country.

Nicholson would later receive five years' imprisonment for his actions.

Holloway headed home the following morning after a relatively sober night with Jimmy, who had lost no time letting his new friend know that he had little time for 'know it all' urban cops. Holloway was taken aback, but he wasn't on his home turf and so remained subdued, even when Jimmy began ramming the success of the rural force down his throat. Parker, meanwhile, was delighted, because the success of this investigation had got Stratshall Police, and himself, recognised, both within the force and nationally.

Jimmy was 'adopted' by the local media and he gave interviews about the success of the investigation and the irresponsibility of people like the librarian. As normal, some of the police bosses used this success to enhance their positions, highlighting how well they were managing their officers. Every time this happened Jimmy thought to himself that the actions of this elite police 'class', riding on the back of the efforts of the workers, were little different from that of the propertied and upper-classes of his grandfather's and father's day. However, he didn't dwell on this for too long because he was enjoying the adrenalin rush of being a detective again.

He had now been away from Newholm for fifteen months, and in the meantime serious crime there had crept up. Although there had been notable successes in solving some of the crime, mainly through the efforts of DS Green, a number of cases remained undetected and public unrest was growing.

In Stratshall however, Doris and the kids were enjoying having Jimmy at home, and were able, for the first time, to plan ahead for holidays and other social events. When the family had returned home from their summer holiday Jimmy was checking through his mail and found a hand-written letter addressed to him. The letter was from Cobble. He asked Jimmy to get in touch on his return from annual leave. Jimmy showed this letter to a worried looking Doris and they both wondered what was in store.

He waited till he was back at work and called Cobble, who instructed him to come to his office in Newholm the next morning at 11am. Jimmy made the drive through, wondering what the secrecy was about as Cobble had not expanded over the phone. After waiting outside the DCC's office for ten minutes he was ushered in by his secretary and received a warm handshake. Cobble told him to take a seat and offered coffee, which Jimmy declined.

Jimmy, noted for speaking his mind, immediately asked why he had been summoned. He said he knew it couldn't be about promotion, because in his fifteen months away from Newholm there had been a promotion panel and he couldn't have been considered. Cobble said that he would speak candidly and told him that he was sure that Jimmy knew he had enemies in the force, some at senior level. Jimmy nodded, and then Cobble asked him if he would consider coming back to Newholm as an acting DCI while Goldie was completing a year-long secondment at the police college.

Jimmy, truly the product of a socialist upbringing, and previously a strong trade union member, quizzed Cobble on what would happen when Goldie returned from the secondment. He was told there was no guarantee he would be appointed permanent D.C.I. but the force would look on his position favourably.

Being respectful to Cobble he said he would consider the offer. The DCC told him to remember that the force could instruct him to serve anywhere and, if he refused this offer, then he might find himself in the 'sticks' and forgotten about as far as promotion was concerned.

Jimmy was angered by this comment, but he did have a lot of time for Cobble, so he kept his feelings to himself. Somewhat cheekily, he then enquired if the real reason he was being asked to take up the acting DCI position was because the detection rate for serious crime had significantly reduced, and maybe there was pressure from councillors, the media, and the public.

Newholm police were indeed receiving some very poor headlines in relation to serious crime, and Jimmy was well aware of this. He also knew that anything which resulted in bad PR could reflect badly on some of those officers who had aspirations within the force. They were more than willing to ride on the back of success and this irked Jimmy, especially when some of these same officers would be more than willing to stab him in the back if the opportunity came along.

Jimmy's frankness had angered Cobble, who wasn't used to being spoken to by a junior officer in this manner, especially one that he supported. Cobble had a soft spot for Jimmy which he had never hidden, nevertheless, he told him to take serious consideration of the offer as it was in his best interests. Before Jimmy could say anything further Cobble told him to get going and contact him first thing the following morning with his decision.

Jimmy returned home, broke the news to Doris and asked for her opinion. After a quiet moment she replied that there was no doubt he was being used if he went back to the CID. However, it appeared that Cobble was in his corner and this might lead to further promotion. She also said that both she and Jimmy knew that the CID was where he wanted to be, and for that reason she would, albeit reluctantly, support him. She had real concerns about the children changing schools again, but she accepted that this was part and parcel of a police officer's lot. She hadn't forgotten the contract that Jimmy, like all other cops, had signed which said they would serve where posted. She also pointed out, as Cobble had told him, that he might end up being a lot worse off than being in the CID at Newholm.

Jimmy didn't sleep much that night. He thought about the set-up with Gemmill and the fact the force bosses had made use of him and his talents when it suited them. Sure, he was getting a temporary promotion which would look good on his CV but what happened at the end of his acting stint?

He thought again about the upper classes exploiting people like him and his grandfather's words again rang in his ears.

Reluctantly, he decided that he had no real choice and phoned Cobble the next morning to tell him he was accepting the position. Cobble was pleased he had seen sense and, although not promising him anything, said that if his performance as acting DCI went as he anticipated, he would be well-placed in the promotion stakes to make this position permanent.

Jimmy's first day back in the CID was good news for some but not others. Green was delighted to see him, as he knew the department needed his drive and also thought his return might help his own promotion prospects. Others who had been posted to the CID to have their promotion card 'stamped' were not so happy, and were wary of Jimmy's reputation for not standing for slackers and those who had no real desire to be in the department. These officers knew that 'political correctness' or 'management speak' were not part of Jimmy's thinking or vocabulary.

Privately they thought he was a loose cannon but were too afraid to say so.

His first task as acting DCI was to have a quiet one-to-one with Green and find out the strengths and weaknesses of his new team of detective constables. There had been quite a turnaround of staff in the time he had been away and a few political appointments, one of whom was DI Pratt.

After his chat with Green, where he got the 'inside line' on his new cops, he held an open meeting with all his charges and told them he would not tolerate non-contributors nor officers who were not loyal to the department. However, he stressed that if they proved their loyalty then they could be assured of his full support. He knew that every word he spoke would be reported back to the force bosses so he was careful not to go over the top.

He then invited DI Pratt, who would be his deputy, into his office and between them they went through the crime figures. There had been some serious crimes that were still lying undetected and Jimmy asked Pratt what was being done about them. Pratt said they had pulled out all the stops but nothing was forthcoming. Jimmy asked him what his touts were telling him and, meekly, Pratt said he didn't have any. Jimmy had expected as much.

He then asked Pratt to provide a comprehensive breakdown of the most serious undetected crimes, including any common denominators, distinct patterns or similarities in their MO (Modus Operandi), and to supply Jimmy with this collated information.

When he received what turned out to be a very concise report, including all the newspaper cuttings, from Pratt, he was able to gain an appreciation of the problems the police were facing. Included in these crimes were a few robberies with common denominators. In particular, five 'tie-ups' where all the victims had been beaten, bound, gagged and threatened into handing over money, or disclosing where it was hidden. The media had had a field day in portraying the CID as amateurs. As expected, all the victims had been front page news and some appeared on TV. This had fuelled a climate of fear which the media were doing nothing to quell.

Jimmy decided he would look at these crimes first.

How to address them and get the right result was now his priority and the 'trainer' reined in all the charges in his old stable. Thereafter, he made contact with three local journalists who agreed to re-run the details of each tie-up robbery in the local newspapers and make further appeals for witnesses. When Jimmy saw these articles he found that they had all highlighted his return to Newholm at the helm of the CID.

This was to be expected as part and parcel of the relationship with the media but it would also put increased pressure on him to solve these crimes. If he didn't succeed, then his internal enemies would take great delight in seeing him, and his reputation as a good detective, very publicly shot down.

Shortly after the articles appeared, DCC Cobble called him into his office.

Cobble asked him if he knew the pressure that he had put himself under by appearing in the papers. Jimmy said it was not his doing but he would nonetheless try and use it as a motivating factor. He left Cobble's office after a lecture about the dangers of the media, and being reminded by this senior officer to keep himself from being blinkered and to remain politically alert.

DELICATE GIRL

He soon found out that none of his touts had heard much about these crimes, but 'Delicate Girl', a 28 year-old mother of two young children, whom Jimmy had recruited just before he was transferred to Stratshall, had heard three local drug dealers had been spending money like it was going out of fashion. The three had previous convictions for robbery, violence and housebreakings, before turning to the lucrative trade of drug dealing. Delicate felt they were worth a closer look.

After receiving this information Jimmy asked his intelligence team to do the background checks on these neds. Their previous records confirmed that they were indeed 'serious neds' capable of carrying out these crimes. Jimmy then set about tasking his other touts with finding out what the three were up to.

Some two weeks later he had both his 'official' information and intelligence and his 'unofficial' material as supplied by his tout team. It turned out that Capo knew the three and Jimmy suspected they were only dealing drugs in the Newholm area because Capo had given consent, and was receiving some of the profits. This was the problem with touts, you never fully knew what they were up to and how heavily involved in crime they were themselves. Capo certainly fitted this description and Jimmy was sure that when he provided him with information, it was to get him off his case, keep him sweet or get rid of his competition.

Nevertheless, Capo told him that two other neds who had been recently released from prison had teamed up with this threesome. These two were crazy guys who had just completed a 7-year sentence for armed robbery at a rural post office where they had used a gun, an axe and a knife to threaten the staff before escaping with £20,000. During the discussion, Capo who knew nothing about Delicate being a member of Jimmy's stable, told him that she had been a girlfriend of one of these two neds, before he was imprisoned.

Bingo...

Jimmy quickly arranged a covert meeting with her with the intention of getting her to infiltrate this team. Jimmy asked her about the boyfriend whom Capo had named, and she said that on his release she had reluctantly taken up with him again because he was able to supply her with 'smack'. Situations like these always deeply troubled Jimmy, especially when he believed he was a Christian. He thought about his own daughter and about how he would feel if it was her in this situation. It was always a moral dilemma of tasking Delicate and rewarding her while she was still involved with people who used her and supplied her with drugs. He knew she was a heroin addict and. other than offer her advice or get her into treatment, which he had done on many occasions, what else could he do? He also knew that these guys could end up killing one of their victims, or her, and they needed to be stopped. He eased his conscience in the knowledge that she had already taken up with this guy before he had employed her and hopefully that would be enough to keep her position as his tout uncompromised.

Jimmy's religion often didn't sit well with keeping touts, especially when the charges were as complex as his, but he needed their assistance to get these guys off the street.

Now that he was acting DCI he would have to make

major decisions on his own, without the support of a boss. In reality, he wasn't only asking this tout to obtain information, but her involvement with him meant he was putting her life at risk. As her trainer, he had to weigh up the moral and ethical arguments and the risks to her as well as the odds of success or failure. He opted for the greater good and set up pre-determined times and locations for meetings with Delicate. To protect her identity and involvement, he gave her a dedicated phone number and coded names they would both use when they were in contact. If her boyfriend checked her phone or if it got into the wrong hands then it would not arouse suspicion.

Three days passed and he had heard nothing from her, and she had failed to turn up at two meetings they had planned. He knew only too well that junkies can be unpredictable, but he still feared for her safety. Accordingly, he breathed a sigh of relief when she contacted him that afternoon, using her code name and asking for an urgent meeting.

Jimmy found her in a bit of a state. She was shaking and looked in need of a fix to calm her down.

She told him that the tie-up robberies were being undertaken by the guy who was supplying her with heroin, and another Jimmy knew nothing about. She then dropped a bombshell by announcing that these robberies were planned by a ned whom Jimmy knew as Wise Archie. Apparently these guys, although violent, were scared of him and held him in awe.

Jimmy knew there was always a possibility that some of his stable would 'grass up' other members, but if they did he was still the beneficiary of the information. Nevertheless, this was going to pose both legal and logistical problems which would take all his skills as a trainer to manage. Flippantly, he thought to himself that the tactics he would have to utilise here could now be compared to those adopted by some racehorse trainers in order to fix races.

Delicate explained that these two neds and one of the other three that she had previously told Jimmy about, had planned another tie-up robbery. She had been asked to supply an alibi for one, the guy she was sleeping with, for the time of the robbery. Jimmy asked her if she knew who the 'mark' (target) was and she said it was a female solicitor who had acted for some of the criminal fraternity in the past. Her boyfriend blamed this solicitor for not getting him off on his last robbery charge.

Jimmy knew this solicitor well and always thought she had a high opinion of herself. In court proceedings she made it her duty to try and make the police look stupid in the witness box. This wasn't as difficult as it sounds. Jimmy knew that detectives in particular often got a hard time in the witness box as they usually had the most evidence and facts to relay to the court. The more serious the crime then the more information and detail they had to provide. This left them vulnerable to attack by solicitors with guile and armed with the science of hindsight.

Through personal experience he knew that, in court, detectives were dealing with numerous live cases and investigations. The defence solicitor or QC, however, had the benefit of examining actions after the event, with all the information at their fingertips. Not surprisingly, some cases that appeared certain to obtain a guilty verdict, fell when scrutinised by lawyers, who supplemented their advantage with acting ability in the court room. Some of their performances would not have disgraced professional actors. Jimmy had witnessed, first-hand, these theatrical performances which convinced juries that the Crown had not proved cases 'beyond reasonable doubt', the basis for a guilty verdict. Consequently, guilty people had gone free and Jimmy felt this solicitor had been responsible for a few of them...

Lately, however, she had lost a few trials she was expected to win, and one such case was that of Delicate's boyfriend. At the time, Jimmy had been delighted when he was convicted and the solicitor's reputation took a well-deserved dent.

Now, with the information Delicate had supplied, he had a motive for the planned crime where she was the intended victim. He would have to do the spade work on his own because of Delicate's involvement, and he still had the problem of Wise Archie.

He paid Delicate the 'King's Shilling' and she agreed to keep him up to date with the robbery plans. He knew the money he gave would provide her next hit, but what else could he give her? He had, in the past, managed to get her re-housed, provided her kids with clothes, supplied her with provisions and stuff for her house, but she sold them all to buy heroin. It was always a moral dilemma for him and he was never comfortable with the relationship. He appeased his position by re-assuring himself that what he was doing was for the greater good, and removing dangerous and violent neds from the street was the name of the game.

Jimmy didn't hear from Delicate for another five days and during this time he told nobody about the planned robbery, including the female solicitor. This was a gamble, as it relied on the dependability of a junkie, and the solicitor could have been robbed in the interim period. Trainers are well used to gambling, and Jimmy decided he wanted to wait and tell the intended victim when he had more information and details of the plan.

When he next met with Delicate she told him that the robbery was planned for the following night. The neds had carried out a reconnaissance, and knew that the solicitor had just recently parted from her husband and was staying in her rural and isolated home some three miles from Newholm with her five-year-old son. They also suspected she kept a large amount of money and other valuables in the house.

The planning for this job, under Archie's direction, had gone as far as disabling the house alarm and sending another ned into the solicitor's office to speak to her on a bogus matter. This had allowed them to confirm that she would be at work the next day, not away anywhere, and also to identify her car.

Jimmy could now wait no longer so he telephoned the solicitor and asked her to meet him at the station. She asked what the meeting was about and all he said was that it involved her and that she shouldn't tell anyone where she was headed.

She was in the habit of coming into the station to see clients, so no suspicion was aroused when she met Jimmy. He was waiting for her in the reception area and ushered her into an adjoining interview room. As usual she was aloof and cast him a dirty look when he told her to sit down. She demanded to know what it was about and Jimmy explained the reason for her visit. After hearing what he had to say she was shocked, more amiable and, for the first time since Jimmy had come across her, she looked scared.

He explained that he wanted to catch these guys on the job and for that to happen he needed her full co-operation. Without hesitation she agreed. He then instructed her to carry on as normal for the remainder of the day but, when she got home, she should check that her alarm system was still working and telephone him immediately. He gave her a mobile phone and re-assured her that the police would be checking on her house throughout the night.

The next day she was to carry on as normal, go to work, drop her son off at school and return home at the end of the day along with her son in her Golf GTi. Once darkness fell she would be contacted by Jimmy, and she and her son would leave the back of the house on foot, be picked up by the police and taken to the safety of her mother's house. She was to leave the Golf in her drive as usual and leave the lights in the house on, as she normally did. She could then give Jimmy the house keys and he would make sure officers gained covert entry to her home, to wait for the robbers.

That first night she phoned Jimmy to tell him the alarm covering the house was not functioning and Jimmy knew then that the job was on. He approached Cobble and told him that he had very reliable information that a break-in at the solicitor's home would take place the following night and that the intention of the culprits was to tie-up and rob the householder. He told Cobble he had made plans to ensure the safety of the potential victim. Now he required some public order-trained cops with protective equipment, as he knew the robbers would be carrying knives and other weapons, though there was no intelligence to suggest they had guns.

Cobble agreed to the request but stipulated that a firearms team would be authorised, assembled and ready nearby. Jimmy felt this might mean his troops inside the house could be compromised if the firearms officers were seen by the robbers, but he bowed to his senior officer's experience and instruction.

The next day a very nervous solicitor was trying to appear normal at her office, but couldn't wait to finish work and get her son. She complied with all Jimmy's instructions.

Jimmy had given DI Pratt, whom he was now getting to like, the task of getting her and her son out of the house quietly and safely. Once he had done so, Jimmy and his team would gain access to the back of the house under the cover of darkness. Prior to this, he had met with the sergeant in charge of the firearms team and they knew what they were to do if they were needed.

When he entered the house with his team of six public-order trained officers, all wearing protective vests, they took up most of the living room. They made their way to the kitchen and began devouring the solicitor's up-market cakes, sweets and biscuits. Jimmy then contacted DS Green, whom he had left with the firearms team, and he confirmed they were prepared but well-concealed and ready to respond if required.

All that was needed now were the bad guys...

At 11pm Jimmy switched all the lights out in the house, indicating to anyone watching that the occupants had gone to bed. This was the solicitor's normal bed-time, and it would appear to any onlookers that she had been at home before retiring for the evening.

The cops on the inside were told to be as quiet as possible, which was difficult for some of these 'hand-picked' soldiers, who, because of the amount of goodies they had eaten, were passing a lot of wind. Their position was aggravated when they were refused access to the toilet by Jimmy.

At around 2am there was a slight noise at the rear of the house and the sound of a glass cutter against the kitchen window. You could feel the tension in the house and Jimmy instinctively checked the position of his weapon to ensure it was ready for use.

He had never been known to use his police baton, but he had a reputation for knocking out some of the most violent criminals when involved in a physical confrontation with them, by what appeared to be just a tap on the head. He never disclosed to anyone how he achieved this.

He had, in fact, learned from an old friend from before his police days - a pub bouncer - that if you filled a leather finger bandage which had a long leather thong attached, with lead, then you had a useful weapon. This could be concealed up your sleeve and used to thump rowdies across the head, rendering them helpless before returning it to your sleeve. So proficient had the bouncer become at using this particular weapon that nobody had seen it, and it was widely believed that he was so skilled in the martial arts that a focused tap on the back of the head rendered you unconscious.

He had, however, revealed his secret to Jimmy and, after he joined the police, he had used it, though only on 'special occasions' like this. Had he been found out then he would be out of a job and a defendant in court.

The next thing the team heard was the kitchen window being opened and what sounded like a man entering the house through it, followed by another man shortly thereafter. It was obvious that a third ned was still outside as the other two were whispering back to him. It transpired that the men inside the house were carrying a hammer, a machete and torches. The two who had entered the house were big guys and their shadows in the confines of the interior of the house made them look enormous. They left the kitchen area and made for the living room to access the staircase to the bedrooms where they expected the solicitor to be.

Just as they entered the living room Jimmy came up behind the biggest of the two, who was carrying the machete, and after just a pat on the head he slumped to the floor. Someone switched the living room lights on and the other ned who was still standing, was caught like a rabbit in headlights when he saw six huge cops descending on him. In fact he wet himself and dropped the hammer he was holding, just as he was thrown to the floor while being given numerous cautions that he was under arrest and he should come quietly. The third member of the team was making a getaway after seeing the lights in the house come on. Sadly for him he ran into Green and the firearms team, who had been alerted by Jimmy to the arrest of the two inside the house. He, too, wet himself when he was instructed, at gun point, to lie on the ground face down with his hands in front of him.

After the commotion had died down some of Jimmy's colleagues asked how he had managed to disarm the robber with the machete and render him unconscious. They were astounded when he told them he just tapped him on the head and he fell...

The three neds, including the one with a bump on his head, were taken to the police station.

After interviews, during which the neds never spoke, they were locked up to await their first court appearance. None of the three knew what, if anything, their co-accused had said during interview and Jimmy raised their suspicion of each other by thanking them individually for their co-operation when they were all standing together in the cell passage. He told them all individually that he would now be interviewing Wise Archie.

If you could have seen the fear on their faces when his real name was mentioned, then you would have been in no doubt that they were terrified now by the prospect of Archie's future visits.

Jimmy contacted the solicitor and told her the good news. She was relieved and had lost the aloof attitude she had always shown towards Jimmy. Laughing, she assured Jimmy she would not be representing any of the three at court and would castigate any of her local colleagues who did. This brought a smile to Jimmy's face when he thought about the idea of lawyers being loyal to each other or working under a code of ethics. In his mind the only code they worked to was the one involving cash.

The bosses, with the exception of Scott and Assistant Chief Constable Ramsden, who had a huge dislike of the CID, were singing Jimmy's praises, and the local media who had picked up the story were keen to get the inside line. Jimmy made sure the only person who would be releasing this good news story would be him, and Cobble assured him that if any senior officer tried to muscle in then they would answer to him.

Jimmy was on a high with the arrest of these three neds, but he still had the problem of Wise Archie who had been the brains behind this sequence of tie-up robberies. When he asked himself what would a racehorse trainer do with an unruly charge then there were only two answers: either get rid of it or try and correct its behaviour through 'schooling.' He decided to take the latter course of action but, if that didn't work, then Wise Archie would no longer be a member of his stable.

To distance himself from this aspect of the investigation Jimmy got DI Pratt to detain Archie and interview him for all the tie-up robberies. Archie, who would have known the three culprits for the break-in at the solicitor's house had been arrested, must have been puzzled about who grassed on him and worried when he was detained so soon after their arrest. During the interview with Pratt he denied all knowledge or involvement in any of these crimes as well as denying he knew the three accused. When the interview was complete, Jimmy had Archie ushered into his office and when they were alone he asked him why he had not contacted him about these crimes. Archie said he knew nothing about them and was puzzled about being detained and interviewed.

Jimmy then pressed him on his association with the three arrested neds and the other two neds who had been named to him. Still Archie denied all knowledge. However, it was obvious from Archie's discomfort that he was becoming agitated in answering Jimmy's questions, which, as a result of specific information supplied by Delicate, were much more pointed than those of DI Pratt. The situation was not going to get any better when Jimmy, using a bit of hyperbole, said one of the three who had been arrested had indicated he might do a deal. He told Archie that this guy was prepared to name the whole team, including the planner involved in the entire sequence of robberies, in exchange for a reduced sentence.

Archie, now in a sweat, assured Jimmy that he knew nothing about this team's activities or anything about the robberies. If he had, he said he would have told him right away. Jimmy felt his form of schooling was having some impact, but he knew that Archie would have to take a fall and at some stage he was likely to have to give up his stall. Jimmy had by now put Archie under close scrutiny and had asked all his touts to provide information relating to Archie's criminal activities.

Through a contact in the local prison, Jimmy was supplied with names of visitors to the three robbers who had now been remanded in custody. It was no surprise that Wise Archie was on each of the visitor lists and that he was the first person to visit to all three. Jimmy knew he would now be paranoid about which one was going to talk to the police and give him up.

Shortly after this, his new female solicitor friend contacted him to tell him she had been informed by a colleague that all three were pleading guilty to the crime they had been charged with. Remarkably, all three had, through their solicitors, admitted responsibility for all the other tie-up robberies Jimmy's team were investigating. Now there would be no trial.

Jimmy knew that Archie would have put pressure on them to plead guilty to keep himself in the clear. However, neither could he have anticipated that the three would admit responsibility for all the other tie-up robberies. He realised now the clout and reputation Archie must have to get these guys admitting to serious crimes, knowing it would put them away for years.

Nevertheless, like the victims of the previous tie-up robberies Jimmy too was pleased there would be no trial and no need to attend court. His reputation in the force had been further enhanced by clearing these crimes, but more importantly for him, he had protected Delicate from any suspicion.

SCHOOLING

As anticipated, Archie had proved too dangerous to handle and Jimmy had decided that he would be put out to grass.

Shortly after the admissions, but before the three neds had been sentenced, he received a call from Archie asking for a 'meet'. At this meeting he passed on information about some middle level drug dealing and then started fishing to see if Jimmy knew anything further about the identity of the other members of the robbery team. Jimmy was in control now and told Archie these matters could not be discussed with him, but that others involved in the crimes would be getting a call from the police in the very near future.

Jimmy received another three calls in quick succession from Archie over the next week, each asking for a meet. At each meeting he supplied low-level intelligence about local crimes and repeatedly asked Jimmy if there had been any other developments with the robberies. Jimmy kept the heat on him by stating that things were moving and the deal with one of the robbers could be completed the coming week, just before they were sentenced.

Archie was exasperated and now visibly paranoid, but Jimmy continued to play it cool and told him to keep in touch, before hurriedly leaving their meeting. The following day Archie provided more information about a guy Jimmy had been targeting and whom he knew was responsible for extorting money from junkies. The information supplied was sufficient to arrest this ned, and, having provided quality information, Archie was looking for a reward, though this time not in monetary terms. He was more interested in what the robbers had said about the planner. Jimmy kept him dangling and told him it was getting close now and that somebody would be looking at ten years inside once one of these guys spilled the beans.

Jimmy then met with Delicate and asked her what else she knew of Archie. She, like most of the local community, was terrified to talk about Archie but knew that Jimmy had protected her identity in the past and she also had a motive for providing information about Archie.

She revealed that Archie was one of her main suppliers of heroin, but she hadn't told him this before as it would cut off her supply and be likely to get her at least a beating if not murdered.

Archie, she said, was not normally hands-on in relation to his drug dealing but he did visit her every two weeks to supply her and get his 'reward' as payment. Normally, he brought three or four grams of smack and the same of coke. He used her and some of the coke and left her the rest to feed her habit for the week

Jimmy knew this amount would be classed as a borderline case in terms of 'possession' as opposed to 'possession with intent to supply' but, nonetheless, if Archie was caught with this amount then, with his record, he was likely to be kept in custody awaiting trial. He then asked her who else knew of this relationship, and she said two of the robbers who were on remand but not her boyfriend. He asked when Archie's next visit to her was due and she confirmed it would be the following night. After some deep thought, he instructed her to act normally with Archie and keep to her usual routine, but to make sure she had no drugs on her or in her flat. Jimmy then contacted DS Jones of the Drug Squad.

Jones had been one of his DCs in the CID and was now making a name for himself in the drugs world as a shrewd operator and a thorn in the side of local drug dealers. He had faith in Jones and so told him about Archie's proposed visit the following evening, with the suggestion that he stop and search Archie before he got to the flat and then search Delicate's flat. As always, Jimmy kept her identity as a tout to himself.

Jones told Jimmy he could rely on him and said they already held intelligence on some assets that Archie had accrued through his drug dealing. Subsequently, if he was arrested in possession of Class A drugs, then this would open the door to further financial investigation which could result in a significant seizure of cash and a long holiday for Archie.

Jimmy sat back and waited.

Late the next night he received a call from Jones confirming that Archie had been picked up just before entering the flat. He had put up a fight and it took four officers to get hold of him. They had found him in possession of both heroin and coke, along with some hash, all of which he had stated, as expected, were for his own personal use.

Jones said Archie could argue that in court if he wished, but he had charged him with the more serious crime of being in possession of Class A drugs with intent to supply to others. Jimmy, worried about Delicate, asked Jones if he had searched the flat and he said they had but all they had found was a female junkie, no drugs. Jimmy breathed a sigh of relief at this news and with both him and her flat being searched, Archie would have no reason to suspect her involvement as a tout.

The following morning, the custody officer phoned him and said that someone in custody wished to speak to him before he was taken to court. After confirming it was Archie he visited his cell. Archie had now lost his 'hard man' front and pleaded with Jimmy to do something for him. If he did, then he guaranteed there would be no crimes committed in Newholm that he would not hear about. Jimmy, playing dumb, asked what he had been caught with and who was dealing with the case, and Archie told him it was only personal amounts of hash, coke and smack but that bastard Jones had charged him with intent to supply.

Jimmy said he would speak to Jones on his behalf, but drugs offences were really outwith his remit. Archie promised the earth if he got bail and Jimmy again said he would do his best for him. Needless to say unruly charges need to be taught a lesson and Jimmy had no intention of approaching anybody.

Consequently, when Archie appeared in court he was remanded in custody and sent to prison. He was only there two days when Jimmy received a call from his contact in the prison who said that one of the three robbers who were due up for sentence had been set upon by Archie in the showers and now had bruising to his face. He was not making a complaint about the assault and, when questioned by the warders, said that he had slipped on some soap and fallen into Archie, who had lashed out at him in self-defence.

After a week's remand Archie came up for bail, which was refused, and this meant he would spend the remaining three months in prison before the trial. In the meantime, the three robbers had appeared in the High Court where they pled guilty to all charges. Each was sentenced to ten years imprisonment and, unsurprisingly, none got a reduced sentence. Archie must have thought at this time that his threats, and the violence he had used, ensured that none of the three had spoken to Jimmy.

Jimmy had been successful in clearing up some nasty crimes, preventing another serious crime from taking place, and removing some vicious criminals from the streets for a considerable time. Through necessity, he had to put one of his stable out to pasture. Although he was saddened, this was a necessary evil for trainers when a charge became too strong-willed and unresponsive to schooling. He was sure Wise Archie and his information would be a loss, but at this time he was too dangerous to be one of his charges.

UNCERTAIN FUTURE

DCC Cobble invited Jimmy to his office when he heard about the ten-year sentences and asked him to come at 5pm, when most staff would have left for the day. On arrival Jimmy was offered a good measure of an 18 year-old Islay malt, which he gratefully accepted. Cobble told him that he had been singing his praises to the chief constable who was gradually coming round to the notion that Jimmy should be given more substantive rank. However, the chief had no CID background and would, on occasion, listen to those eager to portray the CI.D as full of 'bad boys' and a necessary evil, who couldn't be trusted to hold senior posts nor mix with the higher echelons of society.

With most of the headquarters staff having left the building, Cobble and Jimmy sat for half an hour with the bottle of malt. Before Jimmy left, Cobble told him that he planned to retire in a year's time, but until then he would continue to support him for promotion to full time DCI. He said he knew what it was like to be a detective, with all the hardship and lack of recognition that came with it. He told Jimmy that he himself was an example of how you could overcome these obstacles and be promoted to senior rank and that Jimmy should 'hang in there.' Jimmy thanked him for his support and his sincerity, but left wondering what his future would be like when Cobble retired.

Following Jimmy's success, the CID office had a buzz about it and there was no doubt that DCI Goldie was not being missed. Jimmy's media friends had all featured the series of crimes and Jimmy himself in the local papers and, through a free-lance reporter, he had gained exposure in some of the national newspapers. On the face of it he should be delighted, as his strategy of self-promotion seemed now to be working, but he was worried about Cobble's imminent retirement and who would get his job.

He carried on as normal and it wasn't long before he had moulded a core team of crime fighters within the CID Those who were in the department on a short-term basis to show they had some CID experience before being promoted, didn't buy into Jimmy's team. This didn't bother him, because he knew who they were and he made sure they were never in a position to compromise him.

But what about his stable?

STABLE FORM

Wise Archie got three years in prison after being convicted by a jury on a majority decision of supplying drugs and police assault. In addition, the force's financial investigation team were able to identify assets he possessed totalling £200,000 which they were now seeking to confiscate.

Archie wrote to Jimmy from the inside using coded language and the postal address he had used in the past. Jimmy was sure he had dealt with Archie without him ever suspecting he was in some way involved in his downfall. Nonetheless, he was still relieved when he got Archie's letter, which gave no indication of a breakdown in their relationship. In fact, it was clear from the content of the letter that Archie didn't suspect Jimmy had anything to do with him being imprisoned. On the contrary, he thanked him for his efforts and confirmed he would be in touch on his release. Jimmy knew now that his story about one of Archie's cohorts identifying the planner for the tie-up robberies was a good example of how effective schooling could be. He looked forward to having Archie back in his stable, though on his terms.

As usual, Chocolate Treat had been in touch regularly, providing Jimmy with information in return for the 'King's Shilling'. He, like most good touts, was involved in some form of criminality, and in his case it was always low level. He wasn't a very accomplished criminal and was caught by the police more often than most of his cohorts. He paid the penalty and had served numerous sentences ranging from sixty days to six months for petty theft, fraud and shoplifting. As far as Jimmy was concerned this allowed him to keep his street cred, and meant Jimmy had a continuous source of information about crime in Newholm.

After completing one short sentence, Chocolate contacted Jimmy and said he was in a bit of trouble. Chocolate had got his new girlfriend pregnant and he wanted to marry her and also wanted the child to have his name on the birth certificate. The problem was he did not have any money for a wedding, and he wondered if Jimmy could supply him with £500 for a small ceremony. This cash would allow him to pay the registrar, organise a buffet at the local pub, and take his new wife away for a couple of nights at a hotel in Blackpool.

Jimmy reminded him that he could only get money in the form of the 'King's Shilling'. Chocolate was well-trained and knew what was expected of him. In the next two weeks he supplied Jimmy with information that led to the arrest of three local criminals who, between them, were responsible for eight housebreakings. Jimmy happily paid £500 for this information from the tout fund.

After Jimmy handed over the money he wondered why Chocolate had never mentioned needing cash for drink at the wedding. This was especially strange as Chocolate and his buddies were known to drink a fair amount of alcohol.

The day after the wedding this query was answered...

On the day of the wedding there was a report of two kegs of beer being stolen from a local hotel. They had been taken from the rear of the premises, which just happened to be adjacent to a railway line. The culprits had shown a bit of ingenuity and had rolled the barrels along the railway tracks into the scheme where, coincidentally, Chocolate lived. The empty kegs were later found on waste ground near

Chocolate's home address and there were reports that there had been a street party near his house to celebrate his wedding.

Jimmy had a laugh to himself about who the culprits might have been and then dropped a couple of names of Chocolate's associates to the cop dealing with the investigation. Jimmy knew that once these neds were captured they would almost certainly name Chocolate, and the beneficiary would then be Jimmy.

Hasty Lad had been in and out of prison, mostly for minor crimes and as a result had had little contact with Jimmy. On the occasions they did meet he supplied information about his family members' criminal activities, which struck Jimmy as strange. Still, you never look a gift horse in the mouth and Jimmy always acted on the information Hasty supplied, paying the 'King's Shilling' when he got results. It did, however, appear that Hasty was becoming more and more of a loner, although he still managed to get girlfriends with whom he usually shacked up until he got bored. Jimmy had heard that Hasty had been violent with some of his girlfriends, although complaints were never made to the police. He had not heard from Hasty for a while now and it was believed he was either in prison in England or had moved away to another area. Jimmy was not too concerned by the lack of contact and felt it might be better if Hasty was retired altogether.

Golden Lady had been fairly quiet, going about her business unnoticed in the small community. She received a £200 fine for the drugs offence which first brought her to Jimmy's notice and he had managed, somehow, to keep her name out of the papers. She hadn't forgotten about his help and had been in touch with him on a couple of occasions about some guys living in a nearby rural community. Nobody had heard about these two who, she said, were using and selling hash and speed. They had now been captured as a result of her information, received through Jimmy who passed it on to the drug squad. By keeping them sweet he could call up some favours if any of his charges fell foul of the system. They would still be prosecuted if they broke the law, but with the help of the drug squad he could occasionally get them bail, or have them released to be reported by summons at a later date.

In his mind, with this strategy everybody was a winner and crooks were captured and taken off the street. In his role as tout trainer he could maintain some control over his charges and if they were involved in drug abuse, which most of them were, he could offer some assistance and schooling when necessary.

Welsh Rarebit was a bit special and, in Jimmy's eyes a true 'classic' tout as far as supplying information went. His contact with Jimmy was infrequent but, when he did call him, it was always to supply quality information about serious crimes. His motives for doing so were obviously questionable but this did not concern Jimmy as long as he got information to clear crime and had the opportunity to get some particularly vile criminals off the street. His information was always 'on the money' and, thanks to him, six of Newholm's nastiest neds were now locked up for considerable periods of time.

Like all his charges, Welsh needed constant supervision and monitoring, but no-one could ever accuse Jimmy of being blinkered, and he kept a close eye on this tout. Often, he would hear of this newcomer to Newholm who was a bad egg and not slow to lift a bat or a pool cue to sort out trouble. Welsh had been picked up by Jimmy's uniform colleagues on numerous occasions for getting involved in pub fights and assaulting other neds. There was rarely enough evidence to keep Rarebit in custody and there was always a shortage of witnesses.

Rarebit was worldly-wise and knew how to run the circuit while keeping the inside line. As far as Jimmy was concerned, he was a winner when it came to supplying information. He had taken the 'King's Shilling' on many occasions but it appeared to Jimmy that money was secondary to his own motives, and that he was using the police to get rid of some of his opposition in the crime stakes.

He was certainly worth the watching but this was all part and parcel of the tout business...

What Rarebit, like the rest of his charges, didn't know and would never know, was that if Jimmy found out about any crimes he committed, he'd pass on the information to other detectives. In his charges' eyes he would remain the good guy but, through necessity, they would still take a fall.

Nervous Boy had been released from prison after completing a short sentence. He had infrequent contact with Jimmy but when he did get in touch it was always with information about some criminal activity that he had been asked to take part in. He had not lost sight of how dangerous Jimmy was and remained afraid of him. As a result, whenever he was approached to take part in a crime his first port of call was Jimmy.

This suited Jimmy who, with the information that Nervous had supplied, had been able to lock up three especially dangerous criminals from Newholm for armed robbery, and he had also been able to disrupt three planned break-ins.

Thankfully, he was able to keep Nervous Boy's involvement in Breen's demise a secret, not just from the neds but from other cops.

Nervous was always rewarded financially for the information he provided even though he insisted he didn't want the money. However, Jimmy was also insistent and, in taking the cash, Nervous remained part of the stable and under Jimmy's control.

Capo was the tout with the most guile in the stable. He was always involved in crime but never hands-on. He orchestrated most of the crime in Newholm, particularly the distribution of drugs. He suspected that Jimmy knew about some of his activities but believed he was so far removed from direct involvement that it would be hard for anyone, including Jimmy himself, to pin anything on him. He had never met a cop with as much guile as him, and he had a sort of admiration for Jimmy and, if he was honest, a real fear that Jimmy could nick him.

Although he was top dog in Newholm he didn't fancy spending any time in prison and, by supplying Jimmy with information, he felt he had taken out some insurance against this. Little was he to know that, like all of Jimmy's charges, he was as liable to take a fall as the next person. Jimmy ran a tight yard and, if he heard that any of them had committed crimes, he was sure to pass the information on to some of his colleagues, in the knowledge that his charges would want to speak to him as soon as they were brought in by the police. He had set boundaries at the start of his police career and, on occasion, slightly crossed them to capture the bad guys, but condoning or ignoring crime was never a consideration.

Tarnished Beauty had been getting further involved with drugs and had been into rehab three times. She had tried to get her children back from social services but, in her present condition, this wasn't going to happen. She had contacted Jimmy with small shreds of information in the hope that she would get a financial reward, which, when she did, usually went on drugs. As always, her situation placed Jimmy in a moral dilemma and he tried repeatedly to get her treatment and support. He even spoke off the record to some drug workers he knew, telling them that he was deeply concerned about her, but every time she got support she ended up back on heroin.

He had just about given up on her when he got a shock, and a welcome one at that. He hadn't seen her for about three weeks when he got a call from her asking for a meet at their usual place. He went expecting to see her in her normal hungover condition, but was pleasantly surprised when she appeared almost wide awake. From somewhere, she had found determination, and the numerous knock-backs she had had from social services seemed to have propelled her into action. She told Jimmy she had been clean for three weeks and was determined to get her children back. Jimmy was delighted but, at the back of his mind, couldn't help but wonder if this was just another flash in the pan. He could see the grit in her this time and offered her support and a listening ear. This was the first meeting Jimmy could remember which did not end in her asking for money.

Before she left, she told him she was going to help him to put two really bad Newholm neds away. She explained to Jimmy that they had messed up her life and she was going to get even, and the best way to do this was to supply information that would be enough to put them away for years. When Jimmy asked the identity of the two he realised she was talking about Wise Archie and Capo. She had already, many years before, provided good quality information which led to Capo's only conviction for robbery. With Wise Archie and Capo both now classic touts in Jimmy's stable this could prove to be problematic but, as he had shown previously, not insurmountable. He had his own philosophy for dealing with touts and, whichever way you looked at it, he was still going to be the winner.

Delicate Girl was the second filly that Jimmy had recruited to his stable. When he first met her she was seventeen years old and a very good-looking girl. However, like many young girls she was impressionable and became infatuated with an older man. In this case it was a 30 year-old drug abuser who had a bad reputation for beating up women. Jimmy never understood what she saw in him. Consequently, she too became a victim of her boyfriend and started to use heroin, which he supplied, and she subsequently became an addict.

Like all addicts she needed money and, because she knew Jimmy, she started to supply him with information about her boyfriend's competitors in the drug dealing business in exchange for financial reward. At first Jimmy didn't realise she was an addict but, after a few meetings with her, it became all too obvious. She was beginning to look unwashed, her hair was never clean and she would shiver, even on hot days.

She began to slide down the slippery slope of drug abuse. In fact, Jimmy was receiving information from another tout suggesting that her boyfriend was making her sell herself to lorry drivers to finance both their habits.

Once he confirmed this, Jimmy made it his business to track her boyfriend's movements. He already knew that he was a creature of habit and frequently out of his face on heroin. One particular night this addict was heading home from a local pub frequented by drug abusers in Newholm, along a rough track in the direction of his house. Suddenly, from nowhere, a man with a scarf round his face walked up behind him, tapped him on the head and he keeled over. Before he fell to the ground he was punched in the eye and nose and kicked two or three times in the ribs. No words were spoken by the assailant during the attack and there was never a report to the police. When Jimmy met Delicate two nights later she relayed the story about her boyfriend's beating, but Jimmy just shrugged his shoulders and commented that maybe he deserved it.

Unlike Tarnished Beauty, Delicate never had any children. At the age of twenty-five she looked more like fifty, and by this time her abusive boyfriend had died of an overdose. She was trying, unsuccessfully, to get her habit under control but Jimmy always felt guilty when he gave her money for information, knowing where it would end up.

There was now quite a bit of intelligence in the police system about her and it was clear that she, too, was associating with the nastier neds in Newholm, including Capo and Wise Archie.

For Jimmy, this association also meant he had another inside line into their activities, but in Delicate also a very vulnerable and confused young woman. She had given him enough to put Wise Archie out to pasture before, and she kept coming forward with information about other Newholm neds, including Capo. Jimmy always feared for her, both because of her addiction and the company she kept who fuelled her heroin habit.

DANGLING THE CARROT

At this time, Doris and the kids were seeing a good bit more of Jimmy, probably because he was not getting the same adrenalin rush he had when he was a young cop and detective. There was no doubt that now he was a contender for promotion. Not long after the arrest of the three robbers involved in the attack on the solicitor, he was visited by the chief constable.

This was a first for Jimmy and, in his own mind, he jokingly asked himself who gave the chief directions to the CID office. Anyway, the Chief congratulated Jimmy on his success and spoke highly of his performance in the role of acting DCI, telling him to keep up the good work. He remarked that DCC Cobble was always singing his praises and he, too, could now see why. Jimmy was elated as a result of the visit but his shrewd head told him to keep his feet on the ground. His grandfather and father had both instilled in him, in true union style, that bosses' words and promises come cheap, while actions are different things.

Over that same week nearly all the senior management took the opportunity to speak to him and express their admiration for his detective work. All, that is, except for ACC Ramsden and Chief Superintendent Scott. They had a joint dislike for the CID, but Scott's dislike was more personal and he would walk past Jimmy without ever acknowledging him.

Jimmy expected nothing more from him. Ramsden's dislike was not personal but rather he had a problem with the CID as a whole. Subsequently, both of them would always be obstacles to his advancement.

In three months DCI Goldie was due to return from his one-year secondment at the police college and Jimmy was wondering what would happen to him then, irrespective of the praise that had been heaped on him. He knew that the bosses were not daft and loved a good news story. The last thing they wanted was undetected serious crime and the ensuing media flak. Accordingly, when Goldie was due back in force, he was informed that he would not be returning to CID but would be going to the neighbouring division where a uniform chief inspector was retiring.

Jimmy felt he had earned the substantive post of DCI and had proved his worth, but Cobble took him aside and told him he would have to wait until there was another promotion pool selected. He then assured him that he would be in it and, in the meantime, would retain the acting position and the extra £8 a week that came with it...

In his heart of hearts, Jimmy didn't hold out much hope that he would ever get promoted again. The only thing that could help him would be if the pool was selected before Cobble retired and maybe, just maybe, that would help Jimmy beat the odds.

THE VIKING

In the meantime, Capo had been in touch to let Jimmy know he had heard a rumour about a possible armed robbery planned in neighbouring Stratshall, where the victim would be a local wealthy business man. The information was sketchy and all Capo knew was that it would involve heavy gangsters from south of the border, who had already carried out such a robbery near Newholm. The CID, under Jimmy's guidance, had investigated the Newholm crime but had made no inroads into identifying the culprits.

While Jimmy had been in Stratshall he had cultivated a new tout, and had given him the title of 'The Viking' when he was added to the stable. This guy was only just out of his teenage years and had never had a job. He was very immature, unpredictable and a bit of a novice in tout terms. Jimmy knew he would require some serious schooling but felt he had potential to become a good tout. After hearing Capo's information he decided to return to Stratshall, look up Viking and question him about this possible armed robbery.

When he met the new tout the atmosphere between them was light-hearted. However, this changed when Jimmy told him that he was hunting for information on the potential victim of an armed robbery by newcomers to the town.

Viking's attitude changed when he heard this. He, like most of the local neds, knew Jimmy was the wrong man to cross or keep something from but, like most touts, he only gave up information when he was under pressure or had an alternative motive. Accordingly, after seeking some reassurance from Jimmy that he wasn't going to be jailed he began to spill the beans.

A few weeks ago he had been in his local pub when he got into conversation with three gypsies doing tarring work in Stratshall. After a few drinks it was obvious they were no strangers to crime. They struck up a rapport, offered him a job as a labourer and told him his wages would be cash in hand. That suited Viking, who never had any money, and he was further impressed by them when they said there could be bonuses that would make him a wealthy boy. He suspected that he knew what was meant by this statement, but he was more than happy to get the wage and, potentially, the accompanying bonus.

After two weeks' work it became clear that tarring roads was only a front, and that his bosses were more interested in finding out whom Viking knew, preferably someone who had plenty of money and who might be worth robbing. Initially he didn't identify a victim, but he became really worried when one of his bosses showed him a sawn-off shotgun that he kept concealed in his caravan. He told Viking they used the shotgun to 'scare the shit' out of their victims, who soon handed over their cash and valuables.

After four weeks they paid him cash for some of the work he had done on the roads and told him they had to return to England for a week, on business, but said they would be back in Stratshall shortly afterwards. Before they left they told him to make sure he had a victim identified before they returned.

It was no coincidence that, during the week they were supposed to be in England, a local publican who lived on his own near Newholm, was tied up, badly beaten, threatened with a sawn off shotgun and robbed of £10,000 by three masked men.

Viking suspected these gypsies were responsible but he told Jimmy he wasn't the one fingering this 'mark'. On their return they didn't mention the robbery and, through fear, Viking never brought it up even though it was in the papers and on the television. When the gypsies weren't contacted by the police, they must have assumed Viking could be trusted.

This was the crime Jimmy had been dealing with. The victim had suffered two broken ribs and a fractured jaw before he disclosed where he kept the pub takings. The police had made no inroads into the crime, but the word on the street was that the perpetrators were not local. Jimmy had tried his entire stable at Newholm but only Capo knew anything about it. In fact all he did know was that the culprits were supposed to have a gypsy connection and it was they who were planning the robbery in Stratshall.

Viking then told Jimmy that, under duress, he had pinpointed a scrap metal dealer in Stratshall who was supposed to be a millionaire. He was a 'bit thick' and lived on his own at his scrap yard. Locally, it was said he owned a racehorse and kept a lot of money in his house. The gypsies were now very interested in targeting him as their next victim and told Viking to do a bit of 'digging' on the scrap dealer. In particular, he was told to obtain the layout of his house and scrap yard, the his telephone number and details of any cars or vans belonging to him.

When Viking had returned with the information, they decided to carry out their own surveillance over a week to confirm what he had found. They said they would also visit the scrap yard using a front of either buying or selling second-hand equipment for the roads. They had told Viking he would be the look-out when they carried out the 'business'. He would then get a share of what they found as his bonus.

Keeping a tight rein on Viking, Jimmy told him to stay

abreast of developments and remember that, even now, he could be classed as part of a major criminal gang. This could end up with all four of them appearing in front of the High Court and, even if the crime did not take place, he could still be charged with conspiracy and would be as guilty as the other three.

Understandably, Viking was now panicking and had no intention of crossing Jimmy, whom he viewed, albeit privately, as more dangerous than the gypsies. Consequently, two weeks later he contacted Jimmy and told him the attack on the scrap dealer was scheduled for three days later. His three employers had already stolen and 'rung' (fitted with false plates) two cars to use as getaway vehicles.

This information put Jimmy in a quandary about what he should do before the robbery took place. After some careful thought he decided he would share some of it, but not the role that Viking was playing, with his uniform counterparts. Accordingly, he briefed Chief Inspector Parker about the planned robbery and he duly agreed to provide extra policing on the dealer's premises, but pointed out that because of its rural location it would be difficult to cover. Jimmy decided then that there was no option but to speak to the intended victim and alert him to the crime. He could then try to formulate a plan to protect him and arrest the prospective robbers.

At the scrap yard Jimmy was greeted by ten geese running freely and noisily around. Jimmy remembered from his history lessons at school that the Romans had used geese to raise the alarm when they were under surprise attack. Perhaps then, the scrap dealer was not as stupid as some of the locals, or his potential robbers, thought. After eventually getting past the geese he knocked the door of the dealer's home and was met by a small, thick-set man in his late sixties who was covered from head to foot in dirt. He did not look like someone who had plenty of money, but Jimmy knew that appearances counted for nothing as far as wealth was concerned.

Jimmy identified himself and was invited into the house by the dealer and offered a cup of tea, which he declined.

Jimmy didn't beat about the bush and told the scrap dealer he had strong information that he was being targeted for a robbery. Jimmy said he was visiting to agree a plan to protect the dealer and apprehend the culprits before they could commit the crime. Jimmy was entirely unprepared for the man's response.

The scrap dealer slowly began to smile and told Jimmy not to worry as the robbery would not be happening. Jimmy, gobsmacked, asked him how he could be so sure of this. The dealer replied that he had 'friends' who would ensure that no harm came to him. Jimmy was puzzled and tried again to convince the dealer to listen to and follow his plan but the man only replied, "Don't worry son it's not going to happen."

At this point Jimmy said he would have a cup of tea. He wanted time to interrogate the dealer further on how he could be so sure he would not become a crime victim. It was a pointless exercise, and all the scrap man would say was that his friends would take care of any potential robbers and they would not get anywhere near him. Before leaving, Jimmy asked if he kept money in the house, to which the man nodded but said no more. Jimmy left and, although puzzled by the dealer's confidence, nonetheless remained concerned for his safety.

In the back of his mind, Jimmy remembered something DS Martin had mentioned to him when he was a young DC, about some local businessmen employing an enforcer from the north-east of England to take care of their business interests. Jimmy decided to drop in on Martin and have a word.

Martin, like Jimmy, could remember neds, the crimes they had committed and their MOs from years gone by. He had no difficulty in naming this enforcer, a Geordie who had no form with the police. Martin said this man operated on his own and probably that is why he had not come to the notice of the police. He had only heard about him from a guy in the gypsy community who, initially, was reluctant to talk about the enforcer until Martin put pressure on him. When he did talk, he said that this guy should be avoided at all costs because, if you crossed him, you could end up dead. This gypsy told Martin stories about the enforcer threatening potential robbers and house-breakers with guns and, in some cases, knee-capping some of them on behalf of his clients. He did not know if the scrap dealer was one of his clients but did know of one businessman in Newholm, a publican, who allegedly paid this guy a retainer to protect him. Perhaps, then, with the publican being a friend of the scrap dealer it couldn't be ruled out that the dealer was paying the same guy for protection.

Jimmy thanked his old DS and told him about the events surrounding the proposed robbery. In turn, Martin, clearly glad to have been consulted by Jimmy, supplied the limited details he could remember about the Geordie.

Jimmy returned to the office and carried out checks on the details Martin had given him. There was no local information about the Geordie and the computer system returned 'no trace' when Jimmy checked the criminal records. Jimmy then told Parker about his meeting with the scrap dealer and confirmed that his staff would not be required to provide blanket coverage of the area. |He did request, however, that they still carry out periodic checks on each shift leading up to the expected robbery. The idea was that the police would be seen in the area and this might prove enough of a deterrent to the robbers. Parker was as dumbfounded as Jimmy by the scrap dealer's response but agreed to have the checks carried out. This brought some relief to Jimmy, who was more worried about the dealer than the dealer seemed to be about himself.

Two days later Jimmy got an urgent call from Viking asking to meet. Jimmy was astounded when Viking told him the robbery would not now be taking place. When he asked why, he was told that apparently the three gypsies had been visited by a Geordie they all knew. He was armed with a sawn-off shotgun and left the men in no doubt that if they went anywhere near his friend they would end up in body bags. He ordered them to leave the area for good and Viking said they had packed up there and then.

Before they left, the threesome told Viking they were well-aware of the Geordie who, like them, had a gypsy background. His reputation preceded him and, before becoming an enforcer, he had been a renowned bare-knuckle fighter. They had no plans on being his next victims. They told Viking they suspected he had murdered some gypsies though this had never been reported to the police. They then hurriedly left Stratshall.

Jimmy thanked Viking, told him to keep in contact if the gypsies returned and, before he left, told him to keep his nose clean.

Back at the office Jimmy rang the scrap dealer and asked if he knew the Geordie. There was a pause on the phone before the dealer responded and even then he didn't reply to Jimmy's question, but merely said he would be in touch.

The next afternoon Jimmy received a call from the dealer asking if he would meet him at one of Stratshall's fancier hotels. He didn't tell Jimmy what the meeting was about and a somewhat bemused Jimmy went along wondering what could be on the agenda. At the hotel Jimmy was met by the owner, who ushered him through to his office where the scrap dealer and a publican, who owned three pubs in Newholm, were seated. The men shook hands with Jimmy and the hotel owner provided him with tea and chocolate biscuits.

Once the pleasantries were over Jimmy asked the scrap dealer what he wanted to discuss, but there was no reply until the hotel owner spoke a short time later. He asked Jimmy how he knew about the Geordie, to which Jimmy replied that that was his business. All they needed to know was that he knew who he was and what line of 'business' he was in. The three of them then took it in turn to speak and, after they were finished, it was clear that none of them was relying on the police for their safety but were paying the Geordie a significant retainer. He, in turn, was ensuring no harm befell them or their businesses.

Jimmy said it was a matter for them if they paid protection money, though the three men seemed to take exception to this terminology. In their view they had a friend from the Newcastle area who was always reliable and available. Jimmy could not believe such a thing was happening in small towns like Stratshall and Newholm . He felt it was more like something you would associate with major cities or gangster books or films. Nevertheless, he accepted the arrangement worked for them and, provided it did not involve any criminality for the police, then he was not too concerned with their dealings.

It was clear that these apparently respectable businessmen were worried about Jimmy, as they continued to question him about how he had come to know of the Geordie. Clearly, they wanted Jimmy onside and, before he left the meeting, there were offers of lunches and, ironically, even tips on three of the racehorses they owned between them.

Jimmy declined the offers...

He knew they all had close associations with various strands of the police, and he wondered to himself how quickly these senior officers would work to dissociate themselves from the businessmen if they knew about their 'arrangement'. Jimmy was sure his name would now come up in conversation between them, and that was bound to puzzle some senior cops. However, that was another matter and Jimmy didn't intend to enlighten them.

As he left, he told the businessmen to let their friend know about this meeting and remind him that if he broke the law in his area then he and his cohorts should be prepared to take a fall. The three looked worried. Jimmy was curious about what the Geordie would be thinking when he found out that Jimmy knew about his 'occupation'. He jokingly thought to himself, 'who needs a crime prevention department or strategy when you have respected and well-to-do members of the public acting like this?'

Jimmy's next action was to locate the three gypsies who had taken Viking under their wing and arrest them for the robbery of the publican near Newholm. This would be easier said than done and, with the amount of work Jimmy was carrying, he passed on all the information to DS Green. As expected, he left no stone unturned and one month later the three were in custody charged with this robbery.

HURDLES FOR THE TRAINER

Two months later Jimmy heard there was to be a promotion pool for chief inspectors and one of the posts to be filled would be that of Detective Chief Inspector; he would be in the pool. For the first time it was decided that candidates would not just be interviewed by the force executive but would give a presentation and compile a 'policing plan' on allocated areas in the force that they had never policed before. This would mean a good deal of research, planning, preparation and rehearsal before the interview in three weeks' time.

Jimmy wasn't looking forward to the new interviewing process as public speaking was not his forte. Still, he was determined to compete and he hoped, perhaps foolishly, that his reputation as a detective, his experience of dealing successfully with serious crime and his success in the DCI role, would count for something. He kept telling himself, albeit naively that maybe he could beat the police class system and be promoted on merit, though a huge part of him did not believe it.

Typical of a detective's life, two days after being notified about the date for the promotion interview a report came in from a cleaner at an old, run-down, garden tool warehouse in Newholm. The cleaner had gone to work as normal at 7am and rang the bell in the heavy front door to alert Jim Cahill, the elderly night watchman, of her arrival. When she got no reply, which was very unusual, she inserted her spare key into the door and felt something behind it blocking her entry. She had to push hard to gain access and once inside she found a fencing post had been jammed behind this solid door. It had never been secured in this manner before.

She then went looking for Mr Cahill and, as she approached the small office in the warehouse where he slept, she got the shock of her life. He was slumped on the ground at the side of the office, blood pouring from his body to form a narrow stream down the incline of the warehouse floor. She screamed, ran to the neighbouring florist shop, and the florist called the police.

The duty uniform sergeant was first on the scene. Finding the watchman, he looked for signs of life, but the man was dead. He had been beaten severely about the head and neck and attacked with a weapon.

This was a murder scene and now a job for the CID.

Jimmy was contacted and quickly went to the warehouse with Green, a trained crime scene manager, two DCs and a scenes of crime officer. After arranging a sterile entry path to prevent contamination of the scene, Jimmy and his colleagues got suited up into protective clothing and made their way to the body.

They found Mr Cahill as described by the uniform sergeant.

Without disturbing the body they could see his throat had been cut and, by the bruising on his face and head, it appeared that someone had stamped or kicked him repeatedly.

Jimmy called for the fiscal, the local pathologist and also Doc Bush, and then contacted the duty senior officer, who just happened to be Cobble, to let him know he was dealing with a gruesome murder.

Jimmy arranged internal and external cordoning-off the crime scene and examined the scene with his crime scene specialists. He also arranged for a police incident vehicle to be placed near the premises as a point of contact for the public, then made appeals for witnesses through his contacts in the media, who had already started sniffing about. Chief Superintendent Scott was duty officer on call and Jimmy had, however reluctantly, to ask him for trained staff for a major crime administration team, uniform cops for door to door enquiries as well as a suitable budget for the investigation. Scott, as expected, treated Jimmy with contempt, but he was aware that if he didn't give him the necessary resources then Cobble would hear about it and give him a hard time. He told Jimmy he would ensure he got some uniform troops, but that he could not have them for long as they had more important uniform duties to perform. Jimmy expected this and he was used to getting uniform cops to assist in major investigations who had to return to their uniform duties within two days due to their bosses' requests. It appeared to Jimmy that outwith the CID. only Cobble took 'serious' crime seriously. He asked himself what uniform duties could be more important than investigating a murder.

In his mind it was now time to nationally split the police service into two branches: general policing and CID. There was a world of difference in dealing with domestic disputes and public order and investigating serious crimes like murder, robbery, extortion and rape. Furthermore, if each branch had its own career path, officers could then build up their experience and expertise and be better able to serve the public. The present situation, where some bosses had no experience of particular policing roles, including the investigation of serious crimes, yet still maintained autonomy over officers with that experience and training, was, as far as Jimmy was concerned, crazy. He knew that as long as the present system continued there would always be flawed decision-making and the losers were always the public.

Jimmy thanked Scott for his 'assistance' and then called out all members of the CI D, including those on rest days, to form an enquiry team.

The Doc and a pathologist attended and confirmed Mr Cahill was dead. Both were of the opinion he had been stamped on the face and head repeatedly. There was bruising to both ears which suggested his skull had been fractured, and his eyes were bleeding. His nose was broken and it looked as though his jaw might also be badly fractured. In their view, however, the cause of death was still likely to have been the six inch cut along his throat which appeared to have severed the carotid artery.

Jimmy arranged for the body to be escorted to the mortuary and told the Doc, the pathologist and the fiscal that he would join them there for the examination. In the meantime Doctor Bush was as thorough as possible. He photographed the body, took relevant measurements including body temperature and noted conditions inside the warehouse. All this information was then recorded in his personal issue Police Surgeons' Register.

The crime scene manager reported back that entry to the warehouse had been through a hole in the twenty foot-high sloping tin roof, which had been the point of entry at previous break-ins at this warehouse. The owner had tried to cover the hole using boarding and barbed wire, but his efforts were amateurish and anyone intent on entering the building through this aperture would have had little difficulty. There had been no sign of force to the external doors and the rest of the premises was secure. The police had found that a small safe in the the office where the night watchman slept had been prised from the wall and was now missing. It appeared that the culprit, or culprits, had placed a fence post they found in the warehouse behind the heavy front door to ensure they would be aware of anyone trying to get in by using this door while they were inside. As a result, it looked like the hole in the roof which was the point of entry was also the way the culprit or culprits had left the warehouse.

Jimmy made sure this information was passed to the crime administration team. He then sent two intelligence officers to get local information together, including details of all previous break-ins, and another two intelligence officers with research nationally. The two officers gathering local intelligence were also asked to obtain as much background information as possible on Mr Cahill and all the people who worked in, or had worked or had access to, the warehouse.

These officers would then carry out an in-depth interview with the warehouse owner to confirm how much money was in the safe and what notes, other monies or items it contained.

With this going on, Jimmy's chief inspector interview was the furthest thing from his mind...

Green, meanwhile, had organised the door-to-door teams and was helping to shield Jimmy from the media. His other task was to make sure that all the cops kept their mouths shut with the media which wasn't as easy as it might seem.

It transpired that Cahill had bled to death as a result of the severed artery in his neck. The post-mortem revealed that this poor man had numerous bruises and cuts on his forearms which, from their positions, indicated he had tried to fight off his attacker/attackers and defend himself.

The senior pathologist who conducted the post-mortem and the local pathologist confirmed that the watchman's jaw was broken, as were his cheek bones, while his head was so badly beaten that it resembled a cracked egg. This had been a frenzied attack and both pathologists said they were among the worst injuries they had ever seen.

Jimmy phoned Cobble with the update and then briefed all members of the enquiry team.

Two detectives who had interviewed the warehouse owner had found out the stolen safe held around £5,000, mostly in Scottish £20 notes. It was a small safe and had been prised from its mounting on the wall by means of a crowbar or similar instrument. As it was not very heavy it could have been removed by one man . The motive for the crime appeared to be theft but Jimmy still wondered why the culprit or culprits had gone to the extremes of brutally murdering the night watchman.

It was clear that whoever they were dealing with was obviously a huge danger to the public. If the media got wind of the details of the attack there would be public panic in Newholm. Keen to avoid this, Jimmy reinforced Green's warning that under no circumstances should any officer discuss the details of the incident with the media. Being a good motivator, he also praised them for their efforts with the case so far and said if they all worked together they would catch the 'bastards' responsible.

Over the next three days the door to door teams identified everyone who had been seen near the warehouse, and Jimmy's enquiry team obtained details of all the people who had worked in, or had connections with the warehouse. The information was fed into the major crime administration team and then individual officers were allocated specific tasks.

Even at this early juncture, Jimmy was becoming frustrated, as he was already receiving requests from some uniform bosses asking for the return of their staff. Jimmy felt there would be an outcry if the public had any idea how half-hearted some cop bosses were in dealing with serious crime and getting dangerous criminals off the street.

Despite the setbacks, Jimmy got on with the investigation. A few good leads were coming in, but those individuals that had been interviewed seemed to have an alibi or corroboration of their movements.

It was time for Jimmy to visit his stable...

Obviously, in a relatively small town like Newholm, his charges had heard about the murder, but none of them seemed to know any details. Jimmy told them individually that the 'King's Shilling' in this case would be unusually high in the hope it would motivate them.

After a week-long enquiry and a vastly overspent budget paying for overtime, Jimmy was beginning to get it in the neck from both Scott and Ramsden and what he saw as some of their 'lap dogs', who held rank equivalent to or higher than his. He was now constantly being pestered for the return of staff, and his position as senior investigating officer was being hampered by the media, who were constantly trying to contact him and get him to provide specifics about the murder. Some reports in the local press were doing little to allay public fears and the police were being castigated for lack of progress. This was to be expected, though Jimmy had tried to keep his three journalists sweet with tit bits of information on how the investigation was progressing. He was well aware that they could only be trusted with so much information but knew he would always need the assistance of the media and for that reason he kept them updated, provided it did not prejudice his investigation. In general terms, his relationship with them was good, which is why, in police parlance, he adopted the tactic of 'feeding the beast' (the media) with these constant updates. The last thing he wanted were headlines constructed, not from facts, but from sensationalism.

It was just as well Cobble still had a thirst for detective work. He protected Jimmy, ensuring the budget would be increased when needed and that officers remained seconded to the enquiry team.

He really did keep the internal wolves from Jimmy's door.

Jimmy made further rounds of his charges, though none of them had heard anything about who was responsible for the murder. He was beginning to feel the investigation was going to be another hard slog and, with pressure mounting, he would need to get a break soon.

The man above was, as usual, looking out for him and the next day one of his seasoned detectives came to him, saying he had a tout who stayed next door to a family named Stevenson, a family with a bad reputation. The tout had overheard one of the sisters of the family talking to her brother, Tommy, who had just completed a 3-year prison sentence for serious assault in England. The sister, Heather, asked Tommy about changing some Scottish bank notes to English notes. He also heard Tommy name a local 17 year-old youth, Brian Straw, who he said had 'crapped himself' and ran away. The DC didn't think it was much to go on but Tommy Stevenson was a nasty piece of work and capable of extreme violence. He had a previous conviction for almost murdering a woman he had met in a pub in Newholm after she rejected his advances. After the knock-back he kicked her till she was unconscious and then stamped on her before leaving her for dead. Jimmy knew Tommy Stevenson, and he was one of the 'potentials' his local intelligence team had turned up. He personally had locked Tommy up for break-ins and assaults when he was just a youngster. He was now thirty-five with ten previous convictions, six of which were for assault or serious assault.

Jimmy thought for a while and decided to take a closer look at Stevenson. There were no other good leads at this time and perhaps with help from above he might be on the right lines. He had enough guile to realise that the best chance of making inroads with Stevenson lay with Straw. Consequently, he told his seasoned DC to bring Straw to the station for a quiet word. This was done quickly and the DC and Jimmy didn't wait too long before putting the boy under pressure. He was interviewed at length about his association with Tommy Stevenson and Stevenson's sister Heather, and where he had been at the time of the murder. The longer the interview lasted the more worried he became. He was sweating and wringing his hands and kept looking at the floor in the interview room. When he was threatened with being locked up for murder he snapped and told Jimmy he knew about the murder of the watchman.

However, before making a statement about his involvement he pleaded with Jimmy to give him a cast-iron guarantee that he would get police protection. If he gave evidence against Tommy Stevenson then he was sure he would be killed. Jimmy gave the guarantee and Straw provided a statement which was noted, videoed and tape recorded. Jimmy was aware that, before a trial, witnesses as fearful as this guy could go back on what they said and claim to have been coerced or beaten into an admission by the police. In meticulously documenting and recording what was said he was ensuring this was not going to happen.

Nonetheless, with this witness's nervous disposition, and even after Jimmy agreed to protect him, it took six hours to complete the statement. In it, Straw said he stayed at an address close to Stevenson's sister Heather. He had been involved with Heather, who was ten years older than him, for about six months. When Tommy was released from prison there had been a party at her house to celebrate his freedom. It was on this occasion he found out just how violent Tommy could be when, after consuming a lot of drink, he went into a rage, smashed two doors with his fists and threatened to kill Straw if he was not nice to his sister. The day after this party he met Tommy again at Heather's house and he was told they would be going out 'tanning' (breaking into property) that night to get him some cash. Straw had only a few minor convictions but was afraid not to agree. That night he acted as look-out while Stevenson broke into a newsagents and stole £300 in cash and ten thousand cigarettes.

The next night, he was again instructed to act as look-out while Tommy broke into a pub and stole £200 in cash as well as a quantity of drink. After each of these jobs they returned to Heather's house and got drunk.

On the night of the murder, Stevenson told Straw he had good info that the warehouse where the night watchman worked had poor security and would be easy to break into. He said that it was an easy mark and that there could be as much as £10,000 in a 'stupid wee safe'. Stevenson also said he had worked there for a couple of weeks when he was younger, and the building had a flimsy roof. There had been a break-in where access was gained by making a hole in the tin roof, through which some of his pals had entered and stole money from the tills. Tommy had been involved and was given a share of the proceeds. The owner had since bought himself a safe for his takings, which he had bolted to a wall. Stevenson knew that it would be easy to get the safe off the wall and he also knew there was no alarm in the premises, because the owner was a miser with his cash and hadn't even fixed the hole in the roof properly after the break-in. The only security measure he had taken was to employ an infirm old guy as a night watchman and pay him a small wage. Stevenson said the watchman, who was a bit of a drinker, would 'shit himself' if they entered and would hide in his wee booth.

That night, they drove to the warehouse about midnight in Heather's old car. Tommy was driving and by this time had drunk about ten pints of lager. Somehow, he had managed to manoeuvre the car into a poorly lit shopping car park next to the warehouse. He told Straw to wait at the front of the warehouse while he went round the back, carrying a crowbar inside his zipped up fleece and a torch, which was stuck in his belt. He climbed an 8-foot high wall which led onto the sloping roof from where he could gain access.

When he was in the warehouse he told Straw he would open the front door from the inside and Straw could then enter. He would then help him carry out the safe, which he would lever of the wall, and they would put it into his sister's car.

After failing to hear from Stevenson for a while Straw began to panic, and was about to run away when the front door was opened from the inside. Stevenson summoned him and, though it was dark inside the warehouse, Straw could see Tommy was covered in blood. When he asked him how this had come about he was told to shut up. Tommy then jammed a fence post from a bundle of posts he had found inside, against the heavy front door. Straw was instructed to follow him to the safe, which Tommy had now managed to remove from a wall.

On the way there, the youngster saw the reason Stevenson was covered in blood...

The watchman was lying on the floor outside the office with his throat cut and blood flowing copiously from his head, mouth, ears and even his eyes. Straw was now out of his depth, he couldn't believe what he was seeing, he felt sick, broke out in sweats and started shaking uncontrollably.

Stevenson however, seemed to be enjoying himself, laughing and telling his 'apprentice' to get hold of the safe and help him carry it to the car. At the front door Stevenson checked outside, satisfied himself all was quiet and the two carried the safe the hundred metres or so to the car. Stevenson then went back into the warehouse, put the fence post behind the front door and left through the hole in the roof. Outside, Straw had panicked while waiting for Tommy's return and had run off into the night.

Two days after the break and numerous calls from Heather, Straw eventually answered. She told him to come round to her house, because both Tommy and she herself wanted to see him.

Straw didn't know what to do, especially since he had read in the papers that the watchman had died from his injuries. He was the only witness to a murder. If he didn't go round, they would get to him sooner or later and he would end up dead. If he did go, he might still end up being murdered. If he went to the police he would be a marked man for the rest of his life and, even then, he could be impeached by Stevenson and convicted of murder.

He decided that he had no option, so he turned up at the Stevenson household, terrified about what was to become of him.

He was totally taken aback when they greeted him like a long lost relative and Tommy Stevenson told him he shouldn't be too hard on himself as lots of guys lose their bottle on the job. He put his arm round him and told him he would be all right if he kept his mouth shut. Not surprisingly, he agreed that he would say nothing and then Stevenson gave him £200 in English bank notes, which he said were not traceable. This money was his share of the cash that he had got out of the safe. He was then ordered to drink to their success.

Stevenson got Straw drunk and, when he awoke on the couch the next morning with a severe hangover, Tommy was standing over him with a machete. He reminded him to keep his mouth shut about the job and Straw nodded in agreement.

He was only too glad to be still alive...

After noting, videoing and tape recording this statement, Jimmy made arrangements to have Straw put on the witness protection scheme and handed him over to the force's trained staff in that field.

Now it was time for Jimmy to get Tommy Stevenson and his sister Heather.

He organised a police posse which included his seasoned detective who had acquired the initial information, and they obtained search warrants for three addresses frequented by Stevenson, including Heather's home.

At each address there was no trace of Tommy himself, but Heather had been found at her home and she was detained in connection with the murder. It wasn't long before she broke down and confirmed what her boyfriend had said. In addition, she admitted changing £4500 of Scottish bank notes that Tommy brought to the house that night, for English notes, at banks and shops across England. These establishments were well away from Newholm, and she had used numerous shops and banks to exchange the money, so it was unlikely there would be any suspicion. She also admitted burning his blood-stained clothes in a bin at the rear of her house and buying him new ones. She stated that initially she had no idea Tommy had murdered someone. She thought it was just a break-in, but, if she had known, she wouldn't have done any of these things.

Like her young boyfriend she, too, was terrified of what

Tommy would do if he found out that she had shopped him. After noting, videoing and tape recording her interview, she too was passed to the witness protection team. Before she left she told Jimmy that he should try an address where a previous girlfriend of Tommy's lived.

Jimmy got a search warrant and, with a team of public order-trained cops, he went to the second floor two bedroomed flat the sister had mentioned. It was 11pm by the time he got there and the flat was in darkness. After knocking the door and getting no reply Jimmy kicked it in and was followed quickly by his team. On entering they tried to switch the lights on, only to find all the bulbs had been removed from their fittings.

They shone their torches as they entered each room, starting with the living room, and you could have heard a needle drop, such was the tension. When they went into the kitchen one of the cops was hit across the head with a brush shank, and he immediately slumped to the floor. Jimmy and the team then saw Stevenson standing in the shadows, brandishing the shank and shouting to them "Come and get it you bastards!"

No-one hesitated, especially the sergeant in charge of the public order team, and within seconds Stevenson had been felled by his baton. He was quickly overcome and handcuffed, before being dragged out of the house and placed in a police van with four cops. The householder, a 28 year-old woman, then emerged from the main bedroom clutching her two small children. She was hysterical and Jimmy tried to comfort both her and the kids. She kept saying that Tommy was crazy and had threatened to kill her if she didn't let him hide in the house.

Jimmy arranged for specially trained officers to look after this distraught woman and her family, and then hurriedly made his way to Newholm Police Station to interview Tommy Stevenson.

On arrival, he went to the main interview room adjacent to the cell complex where a somewhat dishevelled Stevenson sat. He was now wearing a protective all-in-one suit after all his clothing had been seized, and he was flanked by four burly uniformed cops. Jimmy told the four cops to leave as he wanted a word with Stevenson on his own. They were worried for Jimmy's safety if he was left alone with him, but he reassured the men that he would be all right and they left. They couldn't have known that Stevenson posed no threat to Jimmy.

He was in fact 'Hasty Lad'...

Jimmy told Tommy to take a seat and then took out a packet of cigarettes from his pocket. He lit one and gave it to Tommy after telling him that he was out of his depth with the crime he had just committed. Stevenson just nodded and then took the fag and drew deeply on it. He said he knew that what he did was crazy, but when he was pumped up with the drink he never gave anything else a thought. His idea was just to break in and get the safe, but the night watchman didn't run away or hide as expected, and in fact put up a struggle.

The rest was history now.

He asked Jimmy if there was anything he could do for him and the only thing he could suggest was to plead guilty. Perhaps then he would get a reduced recommended period of imprisonment from the judge because the case had not gone to trial. Irrespective, he was still going to receive a life sentence, which was mandatory for murder.

Jimmy then left the interview room and the cops who had been waiting outside, worried for his safety, couldn't believe it when Tommy Stevenson trooped out sheepishly behind him and headed for the tape and video-recording interview room.

Jimmy completed an in-depth interview with Stevenson, corroborated by DC Starkey, a bright, young, enthusiastic detective that Jimmy had taken a shine to. Starkey had never been part of an interviewing team with a murderer and he was astounded when Stevenson admitted all aspects of the crime when questioned by Jimmy. In his admission, he confirmed that he knew of the previous break-ins, and the hole in the roof, and gave specifics about the crime that only the culprit could have known. When asked by Jimmy about the whereabouts of the weapon used to cut the night watch man's throat he said he had thrown it in the sea the day after the break-in.

He also said he was the sole culprit and was wholly responsible. This suited Jimmy as it meant that Straw and Heather Stevenson, now both on witness protection, would not be incriminated further. There was now the likelihood that they would be used as witnesses as opposed to co-accused, provided, of course, the fiscal agreed. In fact, if Stevenson pled guilty there would be no trial and they would not even be called as witnesses. Stevenson could even return to Jimmy's stable, though he would have to be put out to pasture for a very long time.

Stevenson made no mention of his sister's involvement and, once Jimmy heard that, he started making plans to accommodate another filly in his stable.

Jimmy charged Tommy Stevenson with murder and the break-in at the warehouse. He then handed him over to the custody officer who had arranged for the police doctor to examine Stevenson. Two detectives had seized all his clothing and searched him. They would now, with assistance of the police doctor, swab and take fingerprints and DNA samples from him.

Starkey left the interview room, swaggering just like

Jimmy had done when he was a young detective with Martin. He headed straight for the CID office with his chest sticking out. It wasn't every day that a young DC became second man in the interview of a murderer, and he wasn't slow to tell his peers all about the experience.

His actions reminded Jimmy of himself with Martin and he knew that Starkey's real test would come if the case went to trial. The swagger would be gone then, replaced by nerves and sweats when he was cross-examined by Stevenson's defence team.

Jimmy's experience had taught him that there would be no guarantee Tommy Stevenson would plead guilty. Once the defence lawyer representing him knew that it was a murder he had been charged with, then the cash register would start ringing. They would do everything to get him to plead not guilty so they could start the legal aid cash rolling in. Of course, they would state that they had to see the strength of the evidence against him before deciding on what plea they would lodge. Jimmy knew this was just a legal smokescreen. All lawyers knew that representing a murderer and preparing a case for the High Court was a huge money- earner and this one would be no different. As expected, on his first appearance at court Stevenson was refused bail and at his first hearing tendered a plea of not guilty.

For the next two weeks Jimmy was fully committed to preparing, for the first time, a major case against one of his touts. He received multiple requests from the fiscal for updates on the evidence and further requests for forensic analysis. In the meantime he still had his day job of supervising his team of detectives and dealing with other crimes, which meant he was working twelve-hour days.

He had received many plaudits when Stevenson had been arrested but, in the minds of some non-CID officers, including senior officers, that was yesterday's news. They had no experience of arresting a murderer or preparing a case for the High Court, and didn't realise how time-consuming and detailed this was. In their mind the bad guy had been caught, the public and the media had been appeased, and that was the end of the story.

However, Jimmy and all seasoned detectives knew that, if the preparation for the court wasn't up to the mark and if you didn't perform well in the witness box, then you could lose the case. In Scotland, verdicts are not just 'guilty' or 'not guilty', but can also be 'not proven'. Jimmy knew that the latter of these verdicts provided a good get-out clause for a weak jury, something a theatrical QC could exploit to the full.

In these circumstances, Jimmy was well aware that the failure to get a guilty verdict always ends up at the reporting officer's door. It is they who receive the media and public flak and their reputation that takes a hammering. Consequently, Jimmy's reports were always detailed, with all the relevant facts, dates and times, checked and counter-checked. In this case, he would be even more meticulous, especially when the accused was one of his stable. Jimmy knew that, before you entered the witness box, you had to be well-rehearsed and have done your research. He had appeared in the box on a number of occasions and, on some appearances, had found that he was the only witness called for a whole day or even two or three days of a trial. He was used to being slandered in the court by defence solicitors and wrongly accused of telling lies, setting their clients up, assaulting them or coercing them. It didn't matter how many times he experienced these attacks, because the next time he appeared as a witness he was as nervous as the first, even when he knew what to expect. Through these experiences he could concur with ex DS Martin. The witness box for a cop is indeed the loneliest place in the world. Starkey could soon find this out for himself.

While reflecting on his appearances in court, he couldn't help thinking about how some senior police managers achieved their lofty positions without ever appearing in court, never mind spending this kind of time in the witness box. Even more worrying, senior officers from this elite group would be the same ones who would interview him for promotion in two days' time...

Having only two days to prepare for his promotion interview was not long enough, but he felt that, with one of the posts to be filled being that of Detective Chief Inspector, his experience would be invaluable. Jimmy decided he would gave it his best shot in the knowledge that some of his competitors had little or any CID experience but, they had been preparing for the interview since the first notification of the position. They had the benefit of not having to investigate a murder or deviate from their regimented nine-to-five, Monday-to-Friday schedule.

If he thought the odds were against him then this was further reinforced when he learnt that DCC Cobble would not be part of the interviewing panel. For some reason he had to represent the force at a terrorist briefing on that day.

When Jimmy arrived for interview at headquarters all six of his competitors appeared confident, having put in enough study and research for the gruelling interview. The same could not be said for him, as he had only managed to get a hold of basic material about the area of the force he had been allocated. Consequently, his policing plan and his presentation were limited. He was the only detective in the pool but it was still going to be an uphill struggle against his peers, especially when two members of the panel either hated the CID or hated both Jimmy *and* the CID.

Not surprisingly, he was given a torrid time by the panel,

which comprised the Chief Constable, ACC Ramsden, Chief Superintendent Scott and a divisional superintendent. No allowance was made for his recent time spent on the murder case or the follow-up enquiry and little in the way of appreciation seemed evident for his prowess as a detective, a uniform inspector or as a team builder. He left feeling the odds were very much against him.

Three days later he got notification from the head of the training department that he had been unsuccessful, and was offered feedback on his performance with Cobble.

He was disappointed, though not surprised, when Ramsden and Scott made up two of the four panel members. Now he couldn't help but wonder where his future lay. Would he have to transfer to another force? Or apply to join a central service post or even leave the police altogether?

His mind was awash with these thoughts, but he knew he had to provide for his wife and family. He was well aware now that, like his father and grandfather before him, he would always be labelled as a worker. Irrespective of how much he produced or the successes he had, he would get little or no reward and would always be excluded from senior management.

Jimmy was depressed with the outcome after the effort he had consistently put into his work, but agreed to meet Cobble for some feedback.

Cobble apologised for not being at the promotion interview, but explained that the Chief Constable had instructed him to attend the terrorist briefing on the same day and he couldn't say no. He told Jimmy he was gutted that he hadn't got through the panel interview and he was stuck for words as to why he hadn't been successful, especially when one of the posts to be filled was that of detective chief inspector.

He tried to temper Jimmy's disappointment by telling him he was one of the best detectives he had ever worked with and, if he was interested in joining another body such as the Serious and Organised Crime Agency (SOCA) or the Scottish Crime and Drugs Enforcement Agency (SCDEA) or any other promoted position in a central service post, then he would fully support him.

Jimmy admitted he was undecided about what to do and any decision would have to be discussed with Doris. At this time, he said, he could not see his future in the force, especially when he had enemies at senior rank who would thwart him at every opportunity. Jimmy asked Cobble where the force was going to get a full-time DCI when neither of the two successful candidates for promotion to chief inspector had any CID experience. Was it not the case that whoever was appointed DCI would have to be carried by Jimmy himself? Cobble said nothing, but just shook his head.

Frustrated, he abruptly left Cobble's room after thanking him for all his support.

He remained on a downer that week and had lost his enthusiasm for crime fighting. In fact he had thought of typing his resignation and personally going to Scott's office and ramming it down his throat. While dwelling on this, he happened to stumble across an advert in a police publication where detective chief inspectors or suitably qualified inspectors with CID experience were required by a northern English force.

Jimmy tore out the advert and took it home, where he discussed it with Doris. He realised then that if he applied for the position he was admitting defeat. The old advice from his family about staying true to your ethics and not allowing so called superiors to bring you down thundered in his ears, and he knew he couldn't live with himself if he took such a job.

This left Jimmy with just one choice. He had to stay put meantime. This would at least give him an opportunity to plan the downfall of Scott, who had a few skeletons in his cupboard. Jimmy had already gathered some tit-bits about him and was well aware that Scott himself had been the orchestrator of the failed attempt to trap Jimmy when he was stationed at Stratshall.

However, for his plan to succeed he would, like most horse racing trainers, have to utilise some of his stable to the best effect. This would include some internal charges within the police who also had a huge dislike of Scott. He was sure that, with their help, and with some others on a very tight rein, 'Devious Scott' as he had now named him, would be pulled up permanently.